I0647154

Secrets Lie Still

Secrets Lie Still

A Michael Moreland Story

Brad Lussier

RESOURCE *Publications* · Eugene, Oregon

SECRETS LIE STILL
A Michael Moreland Story

Resource Publications
An Imprint of Wipf and Stock Publishers
199 W. 8th Ave., Suite 3
Eugene, OR 97401

www.wipfandstock.com

PAPERBACK ISBN: 979-8-3852-2044-1
HARDCOVER ISBN: 979-8-3852-2045-8
EBOOK ISBN: 979-8-3852-2046-5

VERSION NUMBER 04/30/24

To Ron Minor, a mentor, a fast friend, and the first reader and critic of the Michael Moreland series.

Secrets Lie Still is a work of fiction, and any resemblance to actual events or persons, living or dead, is entirely coincidental. While the author enjoyed making some events and locations in the story historically accurate, he made up a lot of things too. For example, prohibition on Prince Edward Island was in effect from 1901 until 1948. In this book, however, it ended sometime before 1937.

Chapter 1

Michael awoke shortly after the sun crept over the horizon on Wednesday morning, September 6, 1939. His second-floor west-wing bedroom at Highfield had enjoyed a few last minutes of darkness as the sun began its circuit in the sky, eventually sending its rays under the south-facing blinds at the front of the house. He sat up and swung his legs out of bed. His feet would have found the floor were it not for the two pillows he had sent there last night. He had to smile, for he still struggled to understand why a double bed with two occupants needed more than two pillows, much less the six Susan arranged at the headboard every morning. His surplus pair usually found a place in his chair when he got into bed each night, but he also reserved an overnight berth for them on the floor. Susan's generally stayed with her, though they sometimes migrated to his side, leaving him to toss those overboard, too. Still smiling and shaking his head, he rose and padded silently in his bare feet to the chair in the corner, where lay the shirt, slacks, and shoes he had placed there last night. He sat a moment, looking back toward the bed as the first rays of sunlight lit Susan's profile where she lay, sleeping the sleep of the just.

He smiled. "My Susan," he whispered, careful not to wake her. He spoke her name because, for so long, he had only been able to dream of the day when he would wake beside her. At one time, she was Susan Moncrieff, the daughter of Lady and Sir Richard Moncrieff of Suffolk, England, but four months ago, she became his wife, Susan Moreland, of Suffolk, Prince Edward Island. Susan was why he wasn't already up and out at work over an hour ago. She was also why he regularly found himself in bed earlier than ever each night as their first summer together turned toward fall at Highfield. Michael had never known such confidence nor peace of heart as they faced their future together. With Susan beside him, his life was complete.

Turning his eyes from her face for an instant, he found his attaché on the floor beside his chair and reached inside. With his eyes on her once again, he trusted his fingers to extract a notebook and pencil from the leather case, losing sight of her only long enough to find an empty page. As each new sunbeam wrought its magic, the room grew brighter, unveiling the perfection of Susan's sleeping profile. Words spilled from Michael's pencil onto the page, recording the scene that opened before him, a gift for his eyes that he recorded only for hers. Line after line flew from his pencil, though he stopped now and again to erase, correct, and look at her once more as the scene came to life on his page. As the waxing tide of light poured through the blinds and threatened to wake her, Michael left his chair and crossed to Susan's writing desk. He found her fountain pen and a piece of stationery suitable to his task and committed his lines to ink. Once finished, he lifted the paper from the desk, pursed his lips, and let his breath serve as his blotter. Silently, he crept to her night table to leave the page, hoping she would find it before he returned from Charlottetown.

Michael dressed quietly and, with a whisper, summoned their Springer Spaniel from his bed on the floor beside the bureau. After Simon yawned and stretched his legs, the pair made their way downstairs to the kitchen. The rooster in the henyard was already crowing, and Michael knew that Highfield would soon be awake. Venturing outdoors through the kitchen door, he could already see Philippe Henault and Luc Boucher at the barn, leading the Holsteins to pasture after finishing the milking. Michael waved as he started the Ford flatbed truck and idled quietly down the half-mile driveway to Suffolk Road for the fifteen-minute drive to Charlottetown.

Once on the road, Michael sped up, anxious to be among the first at the newsstand downtown. News from Sir Richard at his Secret Intelligence Service office in London had arrived by radio at the communication station in Highfield's attic late last night. There was urgency in his father-in-law's communique, an urgency that Michael, himself an SIS operative, did not find unexpected. For over three years, news from the continent had brought increasing threats to European peace from the Nazi regime in Germany. However, war with Germany was no longer imminent; the war had begun. Michael wanted to read the headlines in today's newspapers before he carried them home to share at Highfield. Knowing the reports from London would prove alarming, Michael was determined to reassure his wife, her mother, and the Highfield family, providing as much hope for the future as he could.

Michael wasn't first at the newsstand but was early enough to collect copies of the two Canadian and two American newspapers he sought. Prince Edward Island was never the first to get the news because island ferries didn't travel as fast as trains and trucks on the mainland. Nonetheless, Michael managed to find what he needed to satisfy his mind and, he hoped, those of the family at home. As he expected, the headlines reported that war had erupted in Europe when Adolf Hitler's Wehrmacht invaded Poland, forcing Britain to respond to Germany's blatant aggression. The front pages of each newspaper echoed the same story.

In the pre-dawn hours of September 1, Germany had invaded Poland with artillery bombardments, Luftwaffe air raids, and infantry attacks, followed by a Kriegsmarine attack at Danzig Bay. As fighting continued through September 2, Britain issued a deadline of eleven a.m. on September 3 for Germany to withdraw its troops, or a state of war would exist between Britain and Germany. At eleven fifteen on the morning of September 3, Prime Minister Neville Chamberlain broadcast on BBC radio that Britain and Germany were at war. Later that day, Germany ignored a similar deadline issued by France. As a result, France declared war shortly after five o'clock that afternoon.

Of particular concern to Michael was news concerning the sinking of a Canada-bound British passenger ship, the SS Athenia, by a Nazi U-boat on September 3. Within hours of the British declaration of war, Hitler's U-boats grew bold enough to target a civilian ship carrying over 1,100 passengers. Besides the British passengers aboard, there were over 500 Jewish refugees, almost 470 Canadians, and over 300 Americans. Hitler's Nazi war machine had begun its attack on British citizens on the first day of the war by sinking a civilian ship, a flagrant war crime.

The SS Athenia had regularly sailed between Britain and Canada's east coast since her launch in 1923. Often bound for the port of Halifax, just two hundred miles from Prince Edward Island, she made an easy target for a German U-boat. Susan's brothers, Nigel and Boyd, both Royal Navy officers serving on ships in the North Atlantic, had also become prime German targets at sea overnight.

For Susan and her mother, no news was more threatening than news of war with Germany, not only for Nigel and Boyd but also for Sir Richard, who lived in peril of German bombing raids in London. Closer to home, the women were also aware that during the Great War in 1918,

German U-boats had found their way close to Prince Edward Island. Although the current war had not yet come to Canada, no one dared to underestimate the enemy's reach.

Other front-page stories mentioned the United States' neutrality policy, reported continued violence against Jews in Germany, and told of other atrocities committed against targeted groups among both German and Polish civilians. There was nothing in any of the newspapers to offer any hope. The times were dark, and Michael knew the news he brought home would provide no comfort.

Chapter 2

Susan winced when she opened her eyes, letting the sun's morning rays close them again and forcing her face into her pillows. Mumbling, she reached one hand behind her for Michael but found only the cold sheets he had abandoned more than a half hour ago. Resigned, she retrieved her robe from the chair beside the bed, found her slippers, and shuffled her way to the bathroom with her eyes still half-closed.

A wet facecloth helped to wash most of the sleep from her eyes, enough for her to notice a note on her night table when she turned back toward her bed. "Michael," she said aloud, expecting he had left her a message to tell her where he had gone and why he had left her so early. But when she picked up the page and felt the texture of the linen stationery, she also recognized the familiar shape of fourteen lines. Michael had written another sonnet for her! With eyes wide open now and a smile leaning toward a giggle, she climbed back into bed with the page in hand, propped up her pillows, and pulled up the covers. Then, collecting herself, she read aloud,

Colors All Appropriate

This morning I rose early as I'm wont
And took my place in corner as I do
And waited for the dawn to bring his font
Of colors all appropriate to you.
And he arrived with palette and with brush
And sleepy-eyed crawled over window sill
And on your cheek prepared to paint his blush
But stopped, withdrew his hand, and stood stock-still.
All rapt, he stared a moment, sighed, then bowed
And turned to make his exit as you slept,

But thought the better, and himself allowed
Just one last look 'fore o'er the sill he crept.
Who once beholds your beauty e'er repines,
To linger long nigh charms no art refines.

Once again, she was overwhelmed. Hardly his first offering, today's tribute was only Michael's most recent among many others. Once, she could only dream that a man could love her this way, but not just any man would do. No, it had to be her Michael. They had survived the puppy love of childhood when they grew up together, but later, both believed that they could never become a couple. It was secrets that kept them apart. Michael's secret told him he was unworthy of her and that her father would never approve of Susan's marriage to a man lacking wealth and family heritage. Susan's secret was her fear that she would someday succumb to the epilepsy her mother endured, a burden she felt she could not bring to a marriage. Thankfully, her mother's wisdom prevailed, helping both to abandon their secrets, and, in one brief moment, their union became possible. The insight her mother shared with Susan's father when Susan and Michael were children proved true. Susan and Michael had been called to become one since childhood.

Michael's work managing Highfield while maintaining essential Secret Intelligence Service communications with her father in London kept him nearby most of the time. Susan stayed busy attending her mother and teaching at Highfield's new schoolhouse. As a result, she and Michael were always busy but never far apart. She remembered now that he had mentioned making an early morning trip to Charlottetown, but the pout that began to form on her face gave way to a smile when she heard the familiar sound of his truck engine in the driveway. She heard Simon bounding up the back stairs a moment later, with Michael's regular footfall not far behind. She ran for her toothbrush and returned from their bathroom just as Michael opened the bedroom door. With his sonnet in her hand, she rushed into his arms and melted into his kiss, adding another and another of her own.

Finally, with her cheek resting against his chest she chided, "You'll spoil me with any more of these, you know, Michael Moreland. You'll have me expecting them every day. What am I going to do with you?" she asked.

"Do with me?" Michael asked. "Well," he whispered, glancing toward the half-closed door and then back into her eyes, "I just walked past a silent dining room downstairs because it seems no one in this house has found a way out of bed this morning." Reaching back to close the door and squeezing her just a little tighter, he whispered, "No one will miss us at the table for some time, Darling, so if you need to know what to do with me," he said, glancing over her shoulder toward her pillows, "I've got one."

Susan's eyes followed Michael's to the bed and hesitated there a moment before she turned to look at him again. As their eyes locked, she uttered a deep sigh and let her hands fall from where they lay around his neck to reach for his at her waist. With his hands captive in hers, she led him toward her side of the bed, her eyes never leaving his. Michael's smile told her he was sure they'd be the last to arrive at the breakfast table this morning until she suddenly loosed his fingers, handed him two pillows, nodded toward her chair, and began to strip the bed. Wednesday was laundry day, and with Michael's help, Susan knew she'd have the bed stripped and fitted with fresh linens in no time. Perhaps, most importantly, all the pillows would return to their proper places.

Though momentarily disappointed, Michael had to smile. He had no reason to doubt that Susan would welcome his attentions and offer her own soon enough.

Chapter 3

When Susan and Michael entered the dining room with Lady Moncrieff, Michael placed the four morning newspapers on the serving table. After seating the ladies, he took his place next to Lady Moncrieff, sitting with her at the head of the table in Sir Richard's absence. All was quiet when Lady Moncrieff rose to speak.

"Nurse Emily, Doris, Alida, Philippe, Jacques, and children," she began, "Michael has returned from Charlottetown this morning with some grave news." Pointing toward the newspapers, she continued, "I have requested that he summarize the headlines for us this morning as we sit together as a family." Lady Moncrieff paused to look at each face around the table. She continued, "We are embarking on some very somber days, potentially many months or even years when we will need to care not only for one another but also for others who will require our help. Michael will be able to give you details which will help you understand the gravity of the times we are facing together."

Michael stood and took a moment to look from face to face, skipping no one before he began.

"Just a few days ago, the nation of Germany under the leadership of Adolf Hitler, their Führer, invaded Poland by land, air, and sea. Poland is an ally, a friend of the United Kingdom and the British Commonwealth, of which Canada is a member. As an ally, we have promised to protect Poland should she be attacked. When Germany failed to cease its invasion after the British Prime Minister's warning, Britain had no choice but to declare war on Germany. Another Polish ally, France, did the same a day later. Hostilities between Germany, Britain, and France have begun."

The room remained silent as Michael continued. "We all know something of the Great War that lasted from 1914 to 1918, mostly from our studies in history, although Lady Moncrieff remembers that war from personal experience," Michael said as all eyes turned to her. He continued, "I was very young when my father was called from England to fight the German army in Belgium and France. I was a most fortunate fellow because my father returned from the war but not without injuries that plagued him for the remainder of his days. As you know, that war also began with Germany as the aggressor. Sadly, it appears that history is repeating itself." The adults nodded knowingly toward one another as the children's eyes stayed riveted on Michael.

"Many other nations will enter this war within the next few days, for Great Britain has other allies who will join her in defending Poland. Several newspapers report that Australia, New Zealand, and India have already joined her. Another newspaper is sure that Parliament here in Canada will declare war on Germany in the next few days," Michael added.

"Children," Michael began, "I expect you will find this news frightening." He continued, "Were we not frightened, we would be foolish. But being frightened and being fearful are two very different things. When we are frightened, we become aware of danger and seek to care for ourselves and others. When fearful, however, we risk abandoning ourselves and others to hopelessness and defeat. I want you to know we have every reason to hope because our cause is just. Great Britain will not abandon the Polish people or any of her allies. The evil we face from Germany will not prevail over that which is good, righteous, and holy. We may be frightened from time to time, but we do not have to live in fear. We must keep these words ready to fall off our tongues, 'The Lord is my shepherd. . . . '" Michael began. All at the table finished the verse with him, "I shall not want."

"We are safe here at Highfield, an ocean away from the war," he said, "but we must redouble our prayers for those fighting on land, on the sea, and in the air. We must remember Sir Richard in London and Nigel and Boyd Moncrieff at sea. Each day, while the war persists, Lady Moncrieff has requested that we join at breakfast and offer our prayers to our good and loving God. Each morning, I will share the latest news we receive from abroad. Our prayers will be our strongest weapons during this war. Now," Michael finished, "Let us give God our thanks for this morning's meal."

After breakfast, when the children had cleared the table, Michael shared more details from the newspapers with Lady Moncrieff, Emily, and the rest of Highfield's staff. Of particular concern to all was the U-boat sinking of the SS Athenia only hours after the war had begun. There was a chance that neighbors or acquaintances from Prince Edward Island were among the nearly five hundred Canadians aboard when the torpedoes struck. "The children may need our help when the names of those who perished come to light," he said.

As the remaining staff left the table, Michael and Susan walked to the library to talk further with Lady Moncrieff. When Lady Moncrieff retired to her chambers a few minutes later, Michael and Susan closed the library doors.

"Michael," Susan said, "my father spent a great deal of time teaching my brothers and me about the German U-boat campaign in the Atlantic during the Great War. I can't forget that U-boats sank nearly four thousand Allied ships, many in Canadian and American waters."

"Yes, Susan," Michael answered, "and there is no doubt that Hitler's Kriegsmarine is better equipped, better armed, and even more determined this time. We will not be unaffected on our side of the Atlantic. Furthermore, because the Germans have already proven they aren't concerned about sinking civilian ships, all the ships sailing between Quebec, Halifax, and England remain potential targets. The RCN is neither adequately equipped nor manned to handle this threat. To my mind, our one hope is that the US will join Britain as an ally."

"I saw the story concerning US neutrality in the New York paper, Michael," Susan said. Britain would have fared far differently without the US as an ally during the Great War. I pray that Roosevelt and the United States will soon come to our aid."

"So do I, Susan," Michael agreed, "so do I."

Chapter 4

"Perhaps they believe it now," Rear Admiral Sir Richard Moncrieff had said to the mahogany-paneled walls of his SIS office on the morning of September 3, 1939. Standing alone in front of his desk, he repeated in a tired voice devoid of victory but filled with angst, "Perhaps they believe it now." Sitting in the leather chair at his desk, he reached for the newly arrived sheaf of reports from his SIS operatives in the field.

Two days earlier, the Polish armed forces had met the unprovoked German attack with only meager resistance. They were no match for the long-readied, highly-trained, war-hungry Wehrmacht prepared to over-whelm them. The advance force launched by the Nazi Führer included an estimated two thousand tanks, nearly nine hundred bombers, and four hundred fighter planes. Sixty divisions of soldiers, almost one and a half million men, followed with a singular goal: surround Warsaw. The Poles fought bravely, and though there were reports that they had inflicted se-vere casualties on their attackers in some skirmishes, they were neither equipped nor trained to meet the Blitzkrieg tactics of their enemy.

Though both Britain and France had declared war on Germany, the Admiral knew that neither was poised to help the Polish people defend themselves. Neither France nor Britain, having committed themselves to politics of appeasement for so long, had anticipated the stunning im-mediacy of the war they had worked so diligently to avoid. In the end, Hitler had had his way. Now, his armies enjoyed the luxury of fighting eastward nearly unopposed, with time to prepare for any eventual attack from France and Britain at Germany's western borders.

The Admiral could not help but return to the chess board in his mind, where he first learned tactical warfare from his father decades ago. Defensive strategies were as necessary as offensive strategies in war, and the Admiral's mind was looking west. The Allied forces of the Great

War had successfully defeated Germany only because the United States had fought side-by-side with them. The Admiral was sure that Britain's survival depended once more on help from the United States. President Roosevelt had so far bowed to his country's desire to remain neutral. However, the sinking of the SS Athenia would remind the US that none of their merchant or passenger ships would sail again free from the constant peril of U-boat attacks.

The Admiral also knew that Britain needed to prepare for the day when the US decided to supply weapons and other raw materials required to wage war against Germany. That meant gold would change hands between the UK and the US, gold that had to find its way across the North Atlantic despite the U-boat threat—gold that Britain needed to prepare to ship *now*.

With the history of a successful test mission last spring when a convoy sailed to Canada at the behest of the King, the Admiral felt it was time to prepare to launch another convoy. This time, Britain's ships would carry a cargo that would ensure she could negotiate with the US in good faith.

The Admiral reached for his telephone. Perhaps the Prime Minister, who was so unwilling to take advice in the past, would be ready to take a call today.

Chapter 5

Luc Boucher was busy with Abe and Billie in the paddock outside the stable as Michael headed for the barn. Luc was a quiet boy approaching manhood now at nearly seventeen. He looked up as Michael arrived and rose to walk toward him.

"Mr. Moreland," he said, "would you have a few minutes to talk, sir?"

"Of course, Luc," Michael answered. "Let's sit down in the tack room, all right?"

"Yes, sir," Luc answered with a smile. "Yes, sir."

Once indoors, Michael noticed that Luc had been spending spare moments cleaning Abe's and Billie's bridles and reins, so he joined him by saddle-soaping some of the tack as Luc began.

"Mr. Moreland, I remember you told us that your father fought the Germans in the Great War, and I understand that Sir Richard fought them at sea, too," Luc said.

"That is correct," Michael answered.

"Mom told me my grandfather, her father, sailed from home here on Prince Edward Island to fight in France in the Great War. He came home, but my mother told me one of his friends did not," Luc said.

"Many men from Canada fought bravely, Luc," Michael said, "hundreds of thousands, and, yes, not all came home."

"My mother told me that there were young men who were eager to join in the fight then, some not much older than me," Luc said. "Others, though, men who didn't want to volunteer at the beginning of the war, were gathered up and sent over later near the end."

"That is correct, Luc," Michael said. "Are you worried you might be sent to fight in this war?"

"No, Mr. Moreland," he answered. "I'm worried I might be too young to volunteer before the war ends. Do you know how old I need to be?"

"I believe the minimum age to enlist is eighteen, Luc, but with a parent's permission, it could be younger," Michael answered.

"I want to be ready to join when I'm old enough, Mr. Moreland," Luc said, "but I don't know anything about soldiering, guns, or fighting. My father was going to teach me to hunt before he . . . " Luc hesitated.

"Died?" Michael asked.

"Yes, died," Luc answered quietly.

"I'm sure a lot changed, then, Luc," Michael said, "and none of it has been easy."

Luc nodded and said, "Still, Mr. Moreland, I need to learn some things my father wanted to teach me. We had two guns at home before the fire, a .22 rifle and a shotgun, but he didn't want me to touch them. They're gone now since the fire. But Highfield has a gun cabinet in the study," Luc asked, "right?"

"That's right, Luc. It does," Michael answered. "Would you like me to teach you to shoot?"

"Yes, please," Luc said with a smile. "I would."

"Well," Michael answered, "let's talk with your mother and Jacques first. If they agree, we could schedule some lessons. What do you think about Joseph joining us, too? You two are the same age, and I'm sure he didn't learn to shoot at the orphanage in England."

"That would be great, Mr. Moreland," Luc answered.

"All right, Luc, but there's a lot to learn about firearms, and safety is first and foremost. While we're at it, we could add some hand-to-hand combat training. Self-defense is an important skill for any man. Would that be all right?" Michael asked.

Luc's smile was never so big. "That would be great, Mr. Moreland. When can we talk about it at home?"

"I'll speak to your mother and Jacques in my travels sometime to-day," Michael said. "I'm sure they'll let you know."

"Great," Luc said as he finished polishing the bridle in his hands. "Great."

"There's just one thing about serving in the armed forces, Luc," Michael said.

"Yes?" Luc answered.

"If the time comes for you to decide about serving, you must know you're supposed to be a soldier, Luc. You'll have to be sure you're sup-posed to go to war. Those are questions you will face when you are a little older. Thankfully, you have some time because you're probably not ready to answer them yet," Michael said.

Luc nodded as Michael continued, "Some men are not called to the battlefield overseas. Instead, they are called to stay at home. If the enemy brings the fight to us at home, we will need them here, ready to fight to defend our homeland. That's one of my jobs here at Highfield," Michael said. "And all of us are called to make sure there's a home ready and waiting for our soldiers when they return from battle, whether they served in Europe or at home. One is just as important as the other, Luc. But neither is something you need to decide right now, OK?"

Luc heard the seriousness in Michael's voice and saw the care in his eyes. Michael had listened to him before he spoke. He asked good questions and offered good answers, but one thing he didn't do. Michael didn't try to convince him of anything. Luc knew the decisions were his to make. He also knew he could trust Michael.

When he stood, Luc offered his hand and said, "Thank you, Mr. Moreland."

Michael shook Luc's hand and, looking him in the eyes, said, "Let's talk again soon, Luc."

Luc's grip remained tight as he answered, "I hope so, sir. Thank you."

Michael wasn't surprised by Luc's questions about the Great War, enlistment, or conscription. Since the war began just a few days ago, everyone on Prince Edward Island seemed to wonder when and how their lives would be affected. Luc was becoming a man. Fighting to protect his home and family would be one of the first things on any young man's mind.

There was a soft place in Michael's heart for Luc. Michael knew what it was like to lose a father, and Luc's father had left suddenly and tragically when Luc was only eleven. Michael knew Luc to be a hardworking, responsible, and honest young man. In the face of his father's death, he had proved a willing support to his mother, even while dealing with his own aching heart. Michael knew Luc would need more time and space to let all his heartaches heal, but today, he had started. Jacques also had a role in Luc's journey to become a man. Michael was confident that he and Jacques could help Luc find himself. The Moncrieffs and Clifton Manor had done so for Michael. It was time for Highfield and its family to care for their own, and Luc was one of them.

Chapter 6

When Nurse Emily Langdon traveled to Highfield from England a year and a half ago, full-time care for Lady Moncrieff was her primary duty. She had joined the family in England when Lady Moncrieff's epilepsy episodes had become particularly persistent and severe. However, during the first six months after arriving on Prince Edward Island, Lady Moncrieff's symptoms had diminished remarkably. The reason was unknown, for her medications had not changed, nor had she substantially altered her diet, daily exercise, or sleeping habits. Whatever the reason, Lady Moncrieff now had little need for a round-the-clock attendant. As a result, Nurse Emily was free to consider other ways to spend her time.

Emily had enjoyed a superior level of education before beginning her nursing training in London. Following several years of comprehensive in-service hospital experience, she joined the private practice that eventually brought her to Lady Moncrieff at Clifton Manor. After visiting the local hospital in Charlottetown and meeting the Chief of Staff, she discovered that her professional skills and training were in great demand.

"Dr. Andrew MacMillan has invited me to apply for a position at the hospital as Chief of Nursing Education," she reported to Lady Moncrieff, Susan, and Michael upon her return from her tour of the hospital.

"Oh, my, Emily," Lady Moncrieff remarked. "What a remarkable opportunity after your first visit to the hospital. Your dossier must have impressed the Chief of Staff."

"I was surprised as well," Emily admitted, "until I observed first-hand the meager level of training the current staff enjoys. There are many with willing spirits but few with a modicum of professional education. It is apparent that those who possess the degree of skills common to most nurses in London are extremely rare here," Emily explained.

"So, under those conditions, Dr. MacMillan will ask for your full-time services at the hospital?" Susan asked.

"He would like that, yes," Emily began, "but when I explained my commitment to Highfield, he was willing to offer a reduced schedule with more limited responsibilities."

"Was he able to be specific?" Michael asked.

"Oh, yes," Emily said. "My title would be Chief of Nursing Education. My responsibilities would begin with an individual evaluation of each nurse's current qualifications, followed by a comprehensive assessment of current training needs. With that assessment completed, curriculum development and subsequent classroom training would follow. Then, leaving the classroom behind for appropriate periods, I would conduct on-site hospital/patient reviews with my students. Then, of course, we would repeat the process after post-testing and re-evaluating the entire program of study. They anticipate a class of twelve to fourteen young women of varying professional experience. Dr. MacMillan has made the schedule mine to generate, but I asked that it be limited to no more than twenty-four hours a week during regular daytime hours."

"That sounds like a very reasonable commitment, Emily," Lady Moncrieff said, "and a wonderful contribution you can offer to meet a very serious need at the hospital. Do you feel that it is a commitment you could make?"

"I am overwhelmed by the confidence Dr. MacMillan has in my ability," Emily explained, "and the opportunity he is offering after such a brief meeting and tour of their facilities is remarkable. During my tour, I confirmed the serious short-staffing problem they are facing. I believe I could help train new nurses to fill many serious gaps in their staff. Of course, this would be a new experience, and I find it a bit overwhelming. However," she said with a quiver of excitement, "I would love an opportunity to make a difference."

"What is the next step, Emily?" Susan asked.

"Dr. MacMillan has asked me to return for a second visit in two days. He has to be away for a day with his family in Quebec tomorrow," Emily explained.

"His family?" Lady Moncrieff asked.

"Yes," Emily said, "his mother and his younger sister, Irene. His father passed away many years ago, so I understand he regularly looks in on his mother."

"And his wife?" Susan asked.

"Oh, he's not married," Emily explained. "After finishing medical school and beginning his internship in New York, he became a resident at a hospital in Quebec, where he worked for several years before taking the position here."

"So, he's a relatively young man, Emily?" Michael asked.

"Thirty-six in November," Emily said. "When we had lunch, he mentioned his sister is my age," she added.

"Thirty-one?" Lady Moncrieff asked. "His sister is thirty-one?"

"Yes, ma'am," Emily answered, "thirty-one."

"And your meeting in two days," Michael asked, "is at the hospital again?"

"Yes," Emily said, "but not in the classrooms or the wards this time. He asked me to meet with him over lunch at his office."

Lady Moncrieff, Michael, and Susan dared not look at each other as they shared the same thoughts. Still, their eyes met surreptitiously, and all were quietly excited for Emily's professional opportunity at the hospital and perhaps a personal opportunity on another front. They could hardly wait to hear the results of her second meeting with young Dr. MacMillan.

Chapter 7

On the way to downtown Charlottetown this morning, Michael stopped at Freeman Ford. The Model T power plant for the sawmill needed a new set of spark plugs and an oil change. Michael left the flatbed idling outside the main service door as he stepped inside to enter the parts department. Bill Stewart looked up from his place at the counter as Michael came through the door.

"Michael Moreland," Bill said as he stepped from behind the counter to shake Michael's hand. "It's been some time since I've seen you here. All your vehicles have been running fine, I take it?" he asked.

"No problems that regular maintenance can't prevent," Michael answered. "I don't wait until they quit, Bill. I'd rather attend to their service schedules so they don't quit," he laughed.

"A man after my own heart," Bill agreed. "So, what brings you in today? How can I help you?"

"I need some spark plugs for the Model T engine that powers the sawmill and a case of oil. I like to keep oil on hand for that engine and our other vehicles," Michael answered.

"Those parts are always in stock here, Michael," Bill said, "but while I gather them, tell me what's new on your patent application for the cooling shroud."

About a year ago, Michael had encountered an overheating problem with the Ford flatbed, a problem common to many Ford flathead V-8 engines. Finding no solution from the service department at Freeman Ford, Michael had fabricated a cooling shroud, a sheet metal enclosure attached to the radiator that allowed the engine's fan to pull cool air through the radiator more efficiently. It worked so well that Freeman Ford considered copying Michael's design to satisfy their other customers. Bill Stewart had suggested that Michael apply for a patent for his invention.

"You know, Bill, I haven't heard anything since I had all the draw-ings prepared, and my lawyer sent in the patent application about a year ago. I should probably inquire," Michael said.

"Well, I could hear your truck idling outside when you came in, knowing you weren't worried about it overheating. Most other folks have to shut theirs off to keep them cool," Bill laughed. "Let me get that case of oil from the storeroom in the garage."

Michael smiled as he remembered the day he had shown Steve Freeman, the owner of Freeman Ford, and Andy McNeil, the service manager, the radiator shroud he had installed on the flatbed. Unknown to Michael, Bill had bet Andy twenty dollars that the radiator shroud would work—even before Michael had finished fabricating it. Bill's faith in Michael won the bet and earned him nearly a half week's pay that day. For Michael, though, Bill's confidence in his ingenuity and craftsmanship was worth a great deal more.

After Michael left Freeman Ford and stopped at the newsstand and the post office, he and Simon headed back to Highfield. As was his practice, Michael took the mail to the study before opening it. As he sat at the desk and sorted through the stack of envelopes, he was surprised to find one posted from the office of Thurston Leighton, Esq., his patent attorney in Quebec. He quickly tore the envelope open, leaving the rest of the mail behind.

Michael found two pages and a smaller envelope inside. He recog-nized the first page as a summary of hours and fees for Atty. Leighton's services. He had seen those statements in the past. Michael was always surprised at the cost of legal work, but he knew the costs were custom-ary and necessary. Putting that page aside, he read the second page, a cover letter explaining that the enclosed envelope contained a cashier's check for fees collected from two firms manufacturing the Moreland Radiator Cooling Shroud.

Reading no further, Michael tore the second envelope open to find a bank draft for \$3,120.73. He sat wide-eyed, staring at the check in his hands, deaf to the sound of steps coming down the hall and Susan's approaching voice calling, "Are you there, Michael? I saw your truck in the yard, but . . . " her voice going silent as she entered the study. She was surprised to see Michael sitting at the desk, transfixed by the piece of paper in his hand.

Taken aback when he didn't move or speak to acknowledge her, Susan stepped behind his chair and gently put her hands on his shoulders. She bent low and spoke softly into his right ear, "Michael?"

She felt his shoulders relax under her hands as he turned his head to her voice.

"Susan," he said, "look at this!"

Never having seen a cashier's check before and lacking any experience with banking, Susan asked, "What is it, Michael?"

"It's a bank draft, Susan, sent by Atty. Leighton, our lawyer in Quebec. It's the proceeds from licensing fees paid by two manufacturers producing the Moreland Radiator Cooling Shroud."

Susan read, "Three-thousand one hundred twenty dollars and seventy-three cents." Then she asked, "Is that a lot of money, Michael? I'm afraid I can't freely translate Canadian dollars to British pounds."

"Yes, Susan," Michael said, "it's a lot of money."

"Is it enough to buy another car, Michael?" she asked. "I came to ask you to drive me to Charlottetown because Philippe is still away on errands, and I need to shop for Mother."

"Yes, Susan," Michael said, still looking at the check. "It's enough to buy several cars. Nice ones."

"Several, Michael?" she asked. "I can't believe it! What else does Atty. Leighton have to say?"

Michael realized he hadn't finished reading the cover letter. Going back to it now, he found another surprise.

"Susan, this is hard to believe, but three additional firms have applied for permission to manufacture the shrouds. There is no telling how much money this could mean," he said, still stunned by the contents of the attorney's letter.

Silently, Michael gathered the pages, returned them to the envelope, and placed them back in his attaché. Then he stood, pushed the chair under the desk, and turned toward Susan. As their eyes met, his came alive in celebration, and he scooped her up in his arms like a baby and spun her around until both were laughing and dizzy. Once again on her feet and in his arms, her cheek against his heart, she said, "I always believed you would surprise yourself someday."

"Surprise myself?" he asked.

"Yes, Michael. You have always sold yourself short as if you were somehow lacking. You know that, don't you?" she asked.

After a moment, he answered, "I suppose I do, Susan."

"So, can we be done with that now, Mr. Moreland? A successful inventor like you doesn't need to apologize to the world for anything. Agreed?" she asked.

"Agreed," he answered.

"Good. Then I believe we need to celebrate," Susan said. "Could we start with lunch uptown and then maybe a stop on the way home at Freeman Ford to look at a new cabriolet?" she asked.

Michael leaned back with his hands still on her waist as she looked up at him.

Ignoring the twinkle in her eye, he began, "Actually, I think we need to stop at the bank first, do your mother's shopping second, and then consider lunch. How does that sound?"

Susan wrinkled her nose, clearly disappointed, but Michael wasn't finished.

"Then," he said to her surprise, "we'll have to stop at St. Onge's before we go to Freeman Ford."

"What do we need at St. Onge's?" she asked.

"I was thinking about a new pair of driving gloves," he answered. "If my wife will be driving a new red cabriolet, I think she'll need matching red gloves, too, don't you?"

"Of course," she laughed as she hugged him. Then, looking back into his eyes, she said, "But about lunch?"

"Yes?" Michael answered.

"Let's make it a quick one," she said as she stroked his neck and looked into his eyes. "I think we need to save some time for dessert when we get home," she smiled.

Michael was too busy kissing her to disagree.

Chapter 8

L t Nigel Moncrieff, an airman serving the Fleet Air Arm of the Royal Navy aboard the HMS Furious, was pacing the deck as the carrier steamed north on the east coast of Scotland. It had been just over two weeks since Germany invaded Poland, and the Furious had been training and performing anti-submarine sweeps in these waters ever since. Tensions were high aboard the Furious this morning, and with good reason. The crew had just learned that a German U-boat had sunk the HMS Courageous the previous day.

The Courageous, another aircraft carrier with two dozen Fairey Swordfish torpedo-bombers aboard, had been part of a hunter-killer group traveling in convoy with four destroyers patrolling for U-boats on the west coast of Ireland. After two of her destroyer escorts were called away to rescue a merchant ship under attack, the Courageous found herself stalked by a U-boat. The captain ordered evasive maneuvers, continuing to hunt for the U-boat that was hunting her. After two hours, the Courageous turned into the wind to launch her Swordfish. However, before the torpedo-bombers could find the air, the U-boat launched three torpedoes, two striking the Courageous amidships. She capsized and sank in less than twenty minutes, taking more than five hundred men with her, including her captain.

Nigel's pacing, first aimless, became a parade march on deck as his angst sought order, direction, and a cadence that would help him navigate the maelstrom of feelings spinning in his head. His soul craved the safety of logic and the security of straight lines, military turns, and the left-right-left that endured in the sinews of his muscle memory, anchors ready to rescue him from the ache that threatened the fragile remnants of his faith.

Eventually, he slowed his pace while he sought a word to identify even one feeling among the swirl of emotions he sought to contain. *Anger* came to him first. He knew he was angry with the U-boat captain, crew, and the Führer who had sent them. He was furious that two Royal Navy destroyers had been called to abandon the convoy to save a merchant ship. He was angry that the captain of the Courageous chose the wrong moment to turn the ship into the wind, presenting a broadside target that the U-boat couldn't miss. Nigel knew his anger wasn't logical, and it wasn't righteous. It just was.

Frustration came to him next. Nigel knew he was frustrated that the Courageous and the Furious were among the hunted. He was frustrated that there was no enemy to face, only one who hid below the surface and seemed to wear a smirk as he attacked from his advantage. Even as the ship under his feet steamed north on the surface, Nigel knew the enemy could be stalking from below, unseen, undetected, constantly attacking from a blind side. No warrior could fight an enemy he couldn't see.

Then, there was *fear*. Nigel hated to admit fear, even to himself. But fear was the partner of frustration that clung to a man who felt vulnerable and constantly susceptible to attack. Fear came from helplessness, and Nigel felt defenseless aboard the Furious until he was in the air. In the cockpit, he had weapons. In the cockpit, he could defend. In the cockpit, he could attack. However, he had only hours in the cockpit, but day after day at sea.

Finally, there was *grief*. The Fleet Air Arm was small, and every man wearing its wings was a brother. Nigel knew airmen aboard the Courageous. He had studied with some at Dartmouth, sailed with others, and trained with many at airfields in the UK and on the other side of the world in India. He knew their stories, their families, their faces, their smiles. How many of his friends were gone now? Did any of their aircraft find the air to attack the enemy? Were they able to land safely ashore? Face after face of his comrades passed in his mind's eye. He never thought he could miss these men this way, but today, he was grieving. Tomorrow, though, he knew he might be the one to be missed next.

Nigel looked out to sea, felt the crisp breeze on his face, and looked up at the sky. He felt no threat from anything he could see, but when he looked over the water, he cursed at what he couldn't see below the surface. In another moment, though, his reveries ended. He heard nothing but the ship's klaxon and the announcement, *"Action stations, action stations. Set condition one throughout the ship. This is not a drill."*

Nigel's moments of introspection were over. He ran to the flight deck.

Chapter 9

I n his office at the Royal Air Force base in Charlottetown, Flt Lt Grayson Royce had finished his classroom instruction for the day and was completing his daily flight log. An RAF combat pilot and flight instructor, Grayson had arrived at Prince Edward Island nine months ago, excited to be part of the British Commonwealth Air Training Plan. His initial assignment required him to design a training program and prepare facilities for a class of prospective RCAF pilots. With the curriculum design complete, the student pilots were his for six months of classroom and cockpit training. After successful training in Charlottetown, each man would be ready for further combat training as an RCAF fighter or bomber pilot. As excited as he had been to begin the program some months ago, Flt Lt Royce couldn't help feeling frustrated on this Friday afternoon in the fourth week of September, 1939.

Shortly after his arrival in Charlottetown, he had been called back to the UK on a special training mission, which returned him to Prince Edward Island ten weeks later. Although the mission abroad had delayed training the young RCAF pilots sorely needed on this shore, it also provided Flt Lt Royce with flight time and combat experience invaluable to the Commonwealth, especially now that war with Germany had begun. Nonetheless, he was frustrated that his students were far behind the original curriculum schedule he had worked so hard to develop last spring.

Of course, it was no one's fault. No instructors with his experience and skills were available for his students during his absence abroad with the RAF. With no qualified replacement, the training program had lain fallow. Nonetheless, no critical eyes had been focused on him, nor could he fault any of the recruits in the RAF's training program. No, he wasn't frustrated with the program, the students, or himself. People weren't the problem. It was the war.

The growing Nazi threat of war had required him to leave his students and return to the UK, and he could make peace with that. Now, however, he was privy to much of the current RAF battle intelligence from the UK, and he found some of it troubling. Flt Lt Royce had learned about the friendly fire incident at Barking Creek in England one week ago, when two incoming RAF fighters had been mistakenly shot down by their comrades, killing one pilot. More recently, he had also received reports that the Royal Navy submarine Triton had sunk the Royal Navy submarine Oxley, mistaking it for a U-boat. Fifty-three lives were lost. Mistakes like those were troubling, but most upsetting was news of the U-boat sinking of the aircraft carrier HMS Courageous with most of her men aboard. Flt Lt Royce had trained several Fairey Swordfish pilots serving on the Courageous only months ago. Their names and faces marched across his memory daily since their ship went down.

But, there was another target of his frustration, and though personal, the war was still the major factor. Thirty years old when he arrived in Canada, Flt Lt Royce had one year left in his enlistment. His father, an RAF pilot during the Great War, had died serving in Europe. Grayson was happy to follow his father into the RAF, serving now for more than six years, but he had planned to return to Derbyshire at the end of his enlistment. He had met a girl in Charlottetown who had turned his head and captured his heart as no other had before. He wanted to take her home next spring, but the war had changed everything. He wouldn't be going home until the war ended, and he feared that wouldn't be anytime soon.

But it was Friday night, and Michelle was waiting for him. Then again, she waited for him almost every night he was free, and nothing made him happier. His frustrations and worries were no match for just one of her smiles. They had plans for dinner and a movie at the Prince Edward Theatre tonight. Michelle wanted to see Ginger Rogers in *Fifth Avenue Girl*. Truth to tell, Grayson had no interest in seeing Ginger Rogers on the big screen. Only one girl was on his mind, and she would be sitting beside him.

While Grayson was at his desk thinking about Michelle, she was working at the counter of Verrier's Hardware, her father's business, where she lived with her parents in the apartment upstairs. A life-long resident of Charlottetown, Michelle had always longed to find her Prince Charming and leave town with him forever. Finally, she had met him and hoped to return to Derbyshire as his wife. But now, the war had intervened.

Michelle's father, Armand, had served the British Secret Intelligence Service for over twenty years, providing secure communications across the Atlantic by radio. Michelle had also been recruited by SIS four years ago when she was only twenty-one. Of course, Grayson was not privy to this information, but time, and perhaps a wedding ring, would change that.

Tonight, though, Michelle and Grayson would leave thoughts of the war behind, at least until the newsreels ran before the feature movie. Until then, it was their conversation and the energy of the Bosun's Berth, their favorite pub, that they craved. Grayson was already driving his staff car in Michelle's direction as she straightened the seams on her stockings and checked her lipstick one last time.

Chapter 10

Michael met with Luc and Joseph, both sixteen, in the study at Highfield early on Sunday afternoon. Both young men were eager to get their hands on one of the rifles or shotguns locked in the gun cabinet in the corner. Luc, who had grown up on Prince Edward Island, had seen firearms before but had no hands-on experience. Joseph, an orphan from Ipswich, England, had never seen a gun. His charm with guns was primarily related to the energy that Luc brought to the subject.

The guns remained in the cabinet when Michael led the young men to the study. Michael had several things to teach them before he was ready to place a firearm in either of their hands.

"Safety first," Michael began. "Those two words are the most important words you need to remember from the time we open that gun cabinet until we lock it again."

Luc and Joseph nodded attentively and repeated, "Safety first."

"The first gun you will fire will be a single shot .22 rifle," Michael said, "and when you squeeze the trigger, the bullet will leave the barrel traveling over one thousand feet per second."

Both young men's eyes opened a little wider, and they smiled as they looked at each other before turning back to Michael.

"What's more," Michael continued, "the bullet can travel more than a mile before it hits the ground."

"A mile?" Luc asked, incredulous.

"Yes," Michael said, nodding, "a mile. So, gentlemen, when you fire the rifle, you must know where the bullet is going. You can't take a bullet back, and you can't stop it once the rifle is fired. With one squeeze of the trigger, it is gone forever, and you are responsible for everything in its path."

Luc looked at Michael and sat back in his chair. Joseph, however, leaned forward and said, "Mr. Moreland, I'm not sure I want to do any shooting."

"Why is that, Joseph?" Michael asked.

Joseph began, "Because if I miss my target and the bullet keeps going, it could hurt someone a long way off. I don't want to hurt anyone just because I miss."

"Joseph, that's a concern I respect, and it makes me feel that I can trust you with a firearm," Michael said.

Joseph smiled as Michael continued, "You can't take a bullet back, so you must know your target with every shot. You must also know what is in front of it, what is behind it, what is to the left, and what is to the right. You must never point a firearm at anything you are not willing to destroy."

Joseph and Luc nodded, looking intently at Michael as he went to the gun case, unlocked it, and returned with a .22 bolt action rifle and a 20-bore double barrel shotgun. Careful to point neither at anything but the floor, Michael laid them on the desk before the young men.

"Which one is loaded?" Michael asked.

The young men looked at Michael, the guns, and each other.

Finally, Joseph said, "We don't know."

Michael asked, "So, both could be loaded and ready to fire?"

Both young men nodded.

Michael said, "But you don't know, so . . . "

Luc interrupted, "You should treat them as if they are loaded, just in case."

Michael smiled. "That's right, Luc. Treat every gun as if it's loaded and ready to fire."

Again, the young men nodded their agreement.

"Always know your target, what's in front of it . . . " Michael paused as Luc and Joseph joined him.

"What's behind it, what's to the left, and what's to the right," they finished together.

"Correct, gentlemen," Michael said, "because once you squeeze the trigger, you can't . . . "

"Take a bullet back, and you can't stop it," they said in chorus.

"And the two most important words to remember before you unlock the gun cabinet?" Michael asked.

He was pleased to hear a final chorus, "Safety first."

"Gentlemen," Michael said with a smile, "you have just passed your first test in firearm safety. Now join me on this side of the desk so we can get your hands on this rifle and this shotgun."

The young men beamed, and with their newly acquired respect for the firearms they were handling, Michael schooled them in the differences between a rifle and a shotgun, their practical uses, how to load and unload them, and how the safety worked on each. Then they cleaned each before returning them to the gun cabinet and safely locking them within. When they had finished, Michael had one last word.

"Meet me after lunch tomorrow afternoon at the flatbed," he said, "and we'll take two .22 rifles out to the sawmill and set up our shooting range."

Two smiling young men followed Michael to the kitchen for lemonade.

Chapter 11

T wo days after Michael and Susan took delivery of Susan's new red 1938 Ford Deluxe Club Cabriolet from Freeman Ford, Susan drove Nurse Emily Langdon to her appointment with Dr. MacMillan at his office in Charlottetown. Susan waited in the car while Emily went inside to be sure no emergency had called the doctor away. When she returned to the car, Emily fairly quivered with excitement.

"Dr. MacMillan requested that I accompany him on his afternoon rounds following our meeting at lunch. He would like some time for us to confer on his thoughts concerning improved patient care," she said. "He suggested that he drive me back to Highfield after our evaluation."

"How do you feel about that, Emily?" Susan asked.

Emily began, "I'm not sure how I feel, Susan. I find myself at sea here in a professional setting compared to the familiarity of Highfield. In London, nurses and doctors hardly spoke except when caring for patients, and they kept to a narrow protocol. Never did a doctor ask a nurse for a professional opinion." Emily paused before saying, "I'm confident that Dr. MacMillan is an honorable man, but I don't want to impose on Lady Moncrieff or you by bringing someone to Highfield without consulting you first." She thought for another moment and reasoned, "The additional evaluations Dr. MacMillan is suggesting today are certainly consistent with the goals we discussed for my proposed work. Therefore, Susan, with your consent, I'd like to affirm his request."

Emily's nervous ramble made Susan smile. She could tell Emily was flattered on more than one front but didn't know how to negotiate either. Susan was sure time would settle her, so she didn't hesitate to respond, "Then we will see you later today upon your return to Highfield, Emily. You have Highfield's telephone number if you need to call, correct? Don't be afraid to use it."

"Of course, Susan. Thank you," Emily said as she smoothed her hair, took a deep breath, and returned to Dr. MacMillan's office.

Susan waited until Emily was safely indoors before she started the convertible to drive downtown. She thought briefly about lowering the top, but after recalling Steve Freeman's demonstration at Freeman Ford, she had second thoughts. Two could better accomplish the process, and she was sure Michael would help her when she needed him. Instead, she drove straight to Verrier's Hardware for her lunch date with Michelle.

When she arrived, she wasn't surprised to find Michael's flatbed parked outside. She remembered that earlier in the week, he had mentioned he had business with Armand today, which left her free to spend time with Michelle. As she walked toward the store, she saw Armand and Michael looking out to admire her car. Together, they met her at the door.

"Good morning, Mrs. Moreland," Armand began with an informal bow and a smile. "I was just admiring your taste in automobiles."

"Why, thank you, Mr. Verrier," Susan said, matching his formality. Looking back toward the curb as Michael joined her, she said, "I like it very much myself."

"I was hoping to show it off to Armand, Susan," Michael said. "Would you spare us a few minutes before you and Michelle drive away?"

"Of course," she answered, handing Michael the keys, "just so long as I can't find a single scratch when I return."

Michael snapped to attention with a smile and saluted. "Yes, m'lady, as you wish, m'lady. We'll keep it safe and untouched here at the curb," he said as Armand laughed.

Michelle appeared at the door just then, and Susan entered the store while the men walked to the curb.

"It was the last of the 1938 models Freeman had," Michael told Armand. "I had seen it in the showroom when I stopped at the parts department last week. As I understand, the man who ordered it originally couldn't complete the deal, so Steve Freeman was glad to sell it at a substantial discount."

"That red combined with the tan top makes it stand out from anything else parked on the street this morning," Armand said. "Let's have a look under the hood."

As he raised the hood, Michael said, "As you would expect, it has the 85 horsepower flathead V-8 and," Michael pointed out, "the first of the Moreland radiator cooling shrouds."

Looking at the radiator just ahead of the cooling fan, Armand couldn't miss Michael's invention.

"They are standard equipment on some 1939 models, so I had Steve Freeman install one before we took delivery. I won't be worrying about this car overheating while Susan is on the road," Michael smiled.

Armand shook his head. "You've done it again, Michael, but those two gals would look even better driving this around town with the top down today." Looking up at the clear sky, he added, "What do you say?"

Michael smiled, too, and when Susan and Michelle arrived, the bright red cabriolet looked its best, top-down and ready to go. Playing the parking attendant at the curb, Michael handed Susan the keys as he opened her door. Armand opened Michelle's passenger door at the same time. It was a perfect magazine photo opportunity with two stunning young women in a new red car with the top down on a clear, sunny day.

Leaning in to kiss her cheek, Michael whispered to Susan, "Vermillion red."

Puzzled, she turned to him and repeated, "Vermillion red?"

"Yes," he answered, "that's the factory color of the car, Susan. It matches your lipstick perfectly." Then, looking across to Michelle, he added, "I'm counting on you two to behave today. There are lots of sailors on the streets this weekend, all looking for pretty young ladies. I'm counting on you two to ignore them all."

Michelle laughed, saying, "I can ignore all the sailors, but one airman always catches my eye. I might have to wink at him if I see him."

"Then I'll count on Susan to give me a full report at the end of the day," Michael laughed. "Carry on, ladies," he said with a salute. "Take no prisoners."

Looking at each other and shaking their heads, Susan and Michelle eased away from the curb, smiling and waving past the rumble seat.

"We're lucky men, you and I," Armand said as he waved back.

"I'll say," Michael agreed. "We need to treasure these days, Armand. The newspapers on the seat of my truck bear no good news. When darker days come, let's remember days like this when the sun is shining, the breezes are warm, and those we love are safe at home with us."

A block away now with the top down, Susan and Michelle enjoyed the sunshine and the air.

"The Cask and Cork?" Susan asked Michelle as they rounded the corner toward downtown.

"That's fine with me, Susan," Michelle answered, but let's find a corner table if we can."

"Let's," Susan agreed as she found parking on the street. The perfect September day must have kept people on the street or in the stores because the pub was nearly empty when they arrived. The waitress ushered them to a corner table and brought them two chilled glasses of pinot grigio.

After they ordered, Michelle began, "Grayson took me to the movies last night to see Ginger Rogers in *Fifth Avenue Girl*. I was hoping for a welcome distraction from his work and mine, but I lost him during the newsreels."

"How so?" Susan asked.

"Well, the newsreels were all about the war, and all day, every day, he's busy preparing RCAF pilots to go to war," Michelle said. "But there's more than that," she added.

"Tell me," Susan asked.

"Well, you know his enlistment is up less than a year from now, and he wasn't planning to re-enlist," Michelle said. "He's been looking forward to going home, but ... "

"Now, the RAF probably won't let him go as long as the hostilities continue?" Susan asked.

"Right," Michelle said.

"And that affects more than just Grayson, doesn't it, Michelle?" Susan asked.

"Of course," Michelle began. "I was a wreck when he left for the UK unexpectedly last spring, and then he came home injured from the crash on the flight deck of the aircraft carrier. I'm not ready for him to go to war."

"And?" Susan prompted.

"And?" Michelle asked.

"And you were hoping to find yourself in Derbyshire to meet his family as a couple," Susan answered.

Michelle nodded, "Uh-huh."

"A married couple," Susan added.

A tear rolled down Michelle's cheek as she said, "Yes."

"From what Michael has told me," Susan said, "Grayson has had a similar schedule and goal in his mind. So, you two have only one question to answer."

"What's that?" Michelle asked.

"Are you going to let a war stop you from something that's supposed to be, Michelle?"

"You make it sound simple," Michelle answered. "but it's not."

"Why not?" Susan asked.

"We talked last night. We talked for a long time," Michelle said. "You know Grayson has a sad history. His father died in his cockpit in the Great War and left a widow with children. Grayson was proud to follow his father into the RAF, but he's afraid he'll repeat that history."

"And you, Michelle?" Susan asked. "What's holding you back?"

"You just asked me if I was going to let a war stop me from something that's supposed to be," Michelle said. "Well, I don't trust myself to know what's supposed to be."

"Why not?" Susan asked.

"Because I've been pretty sure about some things before, and I was wrong," she answered.

"Like what?" Susan asked.

"Michael, for one," Michelle said. "I was sure he was the one. I've told you the story, so you know. But he wasn't the one. I lie to myself, Susan. When I was finally ready to give up on Michael, I told him what I had discovered about myself. 'A girl's heart tells her what she wants to hear until she won't bear with its lies anymore.' I can't lie to myself anymore," she said.

"But Grayson is not Michael, Michelle. Michael couldn't give his heart to you. He had reserved it for me years before. You saw it in a single tear when he sang a French song about a lost love," Susan said. "Remember?"

"Yes," Michelle said.

Susan continued, "I asked you if you were going to let a war stop you from something that's supposed to be, right?"

"Yes," Michelle answered.

"You once looked into Michael's eyes and found the truth, right? A tear gave him away. You knew he could never give his heart to you, right?" Susan asked.

"Yes," Michelle said.

"Then tell me, Michelle," she asked, "what do you see when you look into Grayson's eyes?"

"Oh, Susan," Michelle said as the tears came, and she reached for the tissues in her purse.

Susan sipped her wine until Michelle could speak again.

"The man's in love, Susan, almost as much as I am," she said.

"So, Michelle," Susan said, "I'll ask again. Are you going to let a war stop you from something that's supposed to be?"

Susan didn't have to wait for an answer. Tears and hugs relaxed into another glass of wine, followed by a luncheon feast featuring grilled lobster rolls and New York cheesecake. With their lunch date complete, two beautiful women drove away in a handsome red convertible.

Chapter 12

When Grayson learned that Armand Verrier had served in the RCN in England under Rear Admiral Moncrieff following the Great War, he was intrigued and wanted to know more. After all, Grayson's father and Sir Richard had been close friends at university.

Grayson had met Michelle's parents, Anna and Armand, several times informally, but they hadn't spoken for more than a few minutes. Ever since he returned from his last flight assignment in the North Atlantic when his biplane crashed on the flight deck of the HMS Furious, he had felt he should find an opportunity to know them better. Furthermore, with the start of the war in Europe, he was convinced it was time to share his intentions regarding his relationship with Michelle. He had served abroad long enough to understand the concerns parents of young women have when their daughters are seeing servicemen. He knew they trusted Michelle, but Grayson wanted them to know they could trust him, too. He especially respected her father's military service, and during wartime, he felt Armand would understand an RAF officer's viewpoint better than many men could.

When Grayson first spoke with Michelle about meeting with her parents, she didn't warm to his idea at first, primarily because of her mother's continuing recovery from her twenty-year captivity following the Great War. However, after talking with her mother, Michelle arranged dinner for the four of them at home. Meanwhile, Grayson was content to postpone an introduction to Michelle's brother, Steve, until the RCN granted him leave from his post in Halifax.

Though not a practiced cook, Michelle teamed with her mother and father, and they prepared some delicious swordfish steaks, new potatoes, and some fresh greens, the last of the season. Their conversation over dinner was cordial and candid but touched on nothing serious. After dinner, though, when they retired to the parlor for coffee and dessert, the tone of their conversation changed.

Grayson began, "Mrs. Verrier, Mr. Verrier . . . " but Armand stopped him with a smile.

"Please, Grayson, let us be Anna and Armand," he said. "Otherwise, we begin to feel very old," he laughed. Anna nodded, and the last of the ice was broken.

"Of course, Anna and Armand," Grayson laughed. "I'm just a bit nervous, I suppose. On my best behavior, if you will," he said. They laughed together again as he continued.

"I'm sure Michelle has told you that my home is in Derbyshire in England. My family, on both sides, have lived there for many generations. It's only my mother and my sister, Nancy, since my father died in the Great War," Grayson said. "I followed in my father's footsteps through university and eventually into the RAF. I have a small album that travels with me when I am away from home."

He reached into his breast pocket and produced a leather-bound photo album with pictures of his mother and sister and their family home, Fletcher Hall, in New Mills. Other photos of the surrounding area included some beautiful scenes of the Peak District. Michelle had seen the pictures before and was able to point out some things she knew her parents would enjoy as they gathered around the coffee table to share the album. Armand smiled when Michelle showed him the sign "Ironmonger" over one shop door, the British term for someone who deals in hardware. The pictures of the Royce home and the village scenes where the homes, shops, and mill buildings, all constructed of brick and stone, offered a sense of history, substance, and permanence. They also offered a sense of security that Grayson hoped the Verriers would appreciate.

As they returned to their seats, Grayson spoke again.

"I'm not a young man among many of my fellow airmen anymore, so it fits that I serve as an instructor more often than a combat pilot. Now, when I had intended to conclude my service in the spring, I believe my king and country will need my service more than ever. Of course, I will serve in whatever capacity is required."

Anna and Armand nodded as Grayson continued.

"Looking back over my thirty-one years, I consider myself a most fortunate man. I have seen a good part of the world, enjoyed my travels, and met many fascinating people. Now, however, I find myself yearning for the old and the familiar, that is, home. Travel offers no further fascination for me. I am ready to leave it behind and settle down."

Changing the subject, Grayson said, "Throughout those same years I spent studying at university, flying with the RAF, or in other pursuits, I have met many young women. Most remained mere acquaintances, while others became friends. None, however, has captured my heart until now." As he paused, Armand interrupted.

"Thank you, Grayson, for speaking so candidly. Anna and I have observed your care and respect for our daughter, which speaks to your character. We have had no reason to doubt your intentions or sincerity," he said.

Grayson nodded and said, "Thank you."

Armand continued, "You have been generous tonight in sharing your family history, photos of your home and family, and your hopes for your future." Armand paused before saying, "We know we are still strangers to you in many ways. Before you open your heart further tonight, please allow us to share some of the history of our life here on this small island."

"I would appreciate hearing whatever you wish to share," Grayson said.

Armand began, "Anna and I were born here. Both of our families go back many generations on Prince Edward Island. We married shortly before the Great War when my service to the RCN began. My military service did not end in 1918, however. As I mentioned earlier, with nearly a year left in my enlistment, the RCN required my radio skills in England, where I served under Admiral Moncrieff."

Anna spoke next. "Grayson, you may not know that this island housed hundreds of war prisoners during the Great War. While Armand was away in England, I was among many local men and women who tended to the needs of those prisoners. One evening, a few weeks after the war had ended, several prisoners escaped the camp, taking one of the local women with them. One among the number of those escapees held that woman captive for the next twenty years. Only six months ago did she escape and find her way home to Charlottetown to be reunited with her family."

Anna paused, but Grayson's eyes never left her face. Softly he said, "Please go on, Anna."

Summoning her breath, Anna said, "I am that woman. Though beaten, tortured, and held captive for twenty years, I was finally able to escape.

When I was kidnapped, my son was four years old, and Michelle was only two. In fear for my life and constantly looking over my shoulder for my pursuer, I began a twelve-hundred-mile trek home, where my daughter, husband, and son received me with love. Many in our town believed that I had left with a prisoner voluntarily, and my family bore the burden of that fallacy, enduring many years of gossip that was hard for them to bear. Please understand, Grayson, that we are still healing together," she said, looking at Armand and Michelle. "We are determined to take back those twenty years now that we are together again."

Grayson, overwhelmed by her story, stood, approached Anna, and bent to one knee. Then, taking her hand, he lifted it to his lips. Looking into her eyes, he said, "You, Madam, will ever remain a hero of the Great War, a woman to be revered. You will ever have my respect and gratitude for your sacrifice."

A tear trickled from Anna's eye as she reached out her hand to touch Grayson's cheek.

As Grayson returned to his seat, Armand said, "As Anna has told you, we are a family who is still healing. Michelle is healing with us. Our reunion has been a complete joy," he said, looking at Anna and Michelle who nodded their agreement, "but our wounds are still fresh, and our healing is not yet complete."

Grayson nodded, saying, "I understand, Armand."

They sat together in silence for a moment before Grayson raised his eyes to look from face to face. He spoke once more.

"I would like all of you to know," he began, "that when I first met Michelle, I discovered a woman of confidence, a woman with a sense of stability and a strength of character that have foundations whose sources I now recognize," he said, looking at Anna and Armand. "I cannot adequately express the respect I have for you, for your sacrifice and your survival while bearing a horrific burden that none should have to bear."

Turning to face Michelle, then back to include Anna and Armand, Grayson said, "In these difficult days, not unlike those of the Great War, time is a most insecure commodity. We lack the luxury that peacetime affords." He continued, "I am a man under authority. Orders for combat duty may appear at any moment, and our enemies are fierce and, I fear, better prepared for battle than are we. Nonetheless," he continued, "I choose to look forward to victory and peace and a life in the country that I love."

Michelle and Armand nodded with Anna as she said, "And we all join you in that hope, Grayson."

He responded, "Lacking time's luxury, perhaps God offers us a greater gift. I believe we can live fully and celebrate the moments we have now, not waiting for a future that is not assured to us and remains out of our grasp."

Grayson stood, faced Michelle, and said, "With your permission, Michelle, I wish to address your parents for one moment."

Not knowing what to expect, Michelle offered a halting, "All right."

Turning to face Anna and Armand, Grayson began, "In these tenuous times, I have little to offer you. All the same, I choose to hope that I may spend the remainder of my life with your daughter and, someday, bring sons and daughters home to you for your blessing. With your permission, I would like to ask Michelle if she will have me as her husband."

Surprised and overwhelmed at Grayson's request, all Anna and Armand could do was look at each other, speaking only with their eyes. Then they turned to Grayson and nodded.

Unsure of their response, Grayson asked, "Make I take that as your 'yes,' then?"

Finally able to speak, Armand said, "Yes, Grayson."

Grayson reached into his pocket and said, "Anna and Armand, I promise to be a faithful husband to Michelle and a faithful son to you."

Michelle sat speechless in her chair as Grayson turned to her and knelt.

In his hand was a gold ring set with a shining diamond solitaire. With her left hand in his, Grayson looked into her eyes and said, "Michelle, such as I am, and with all that I have, I love you. I beg you, please, Michelle, will you be my wife?"

Her simple "yes" was all Grayson needed to hear. He slipped the diamond on her finger and stood with her hands in his as they sealed their betrothal with a kiss.

Chapter 13

A t his desk at SIS headquarters on Broadway in London on Sunday night, September 24, 1939, Rear Admiral Sir Richard Moncrieff sat back in his leather chair, about to prop his feet on his mahogany desk as he prepared to open the three thick folders before him. Thinking again, he leaned to his right to open his bottom drawer and retrieve a bottle of Dewars and a glass. After pouring three fingers and returning the bottle to its station, he took a sip and opened the first of the three folders. Leaning back again, he prepared to review and summarize the reports he had received over the last twenty-four hours. Aware that his superiors wanted only the short version, he regularly prepared notes citing only the essential details. He hoped the remaining two folders, newly arrived from his aide, might offer something encouraging. With another sip and with his pen in hand, he began to rehearse the events described within.

On Sunday last, the Soviet Union invaded Poland from the east while the German Wehrmacht continued its invasion from the west. Although the Poles lacked artillery, ammunition, and numbers to match their invaders, they continued to fight bravely. A week earlier, the Polish political leadership had evacuated to Rumania. Sadly, the British Expeditionary Force that had landed in France during the first week of September remained at the Belgian-French border, unavailable to assist the war-weary Polish army.

Again, one week earlier, SIS intelligence operatives in Dublin had radioed that the aircraft carrier, HMS Courageous, had been sunk off the coast of Ireland, losing almost all of her crew, including her captain, one of Sir Richard's personal friends. At last report, the HMS Furious and the HMS Revenge, each with one of Sir Richard's sons aboard, were sailing in waters to the east and north, all thickly populated with dreaded German U-boats. Sir Richard paused to offer a silent prayer for their safety.

Returning to his work, he found more recent reports with more troubling news. SIS operatives in Poland reported that Germany's Luftwaffe had begun indiscriminate bombings of Warsaw, attacking not only military targets but civilian targets as well. They made no exceptions for neighborhoods, schools, and hospitals. No target, however defenseless, was free from the terror of their bombs. Sir Richard could not fathom how Hitler could order such atrocities or how his airmen could obey orders to inflict them. The helpless Polish population continued to endure unspeakable horrors.

Sir Richard found only one positive report in the binder. The Polish submarine, Orzel, though damaged by German minesweepers after escaping its port in Poland, had steamed to the Baltic Sea three weeks earlier and proceeded to Tallinn, a port in neutral Estonia. Though sabotaged there by Estonian military officials who confiscated her charts and navigation aids, the Orzel managed to escape the harbor. Over the next several weeks, while lacking wireless radio to identify herself, the Orzel suffered attacks by German and British ships who mistook her for the enemy. Forty days after leaving Poland, she found her way to the east coast of Scotland, where she was escorted to port by a Royal Navy destroyer. Sir Richard had to marvel at the tenacity of the Orzel's crew, the same determination the Poles displayed on all their battlefields.

With his notes complete on the first folder in his cache, Sir Richard enjoyed one more sip from his glass before turning his attention to the remaining two folders. He opened the first, spread out several pages, and began reading. A brief moment later, his eyebrows rose as he found himself looking to the future with reasons for hope.

In the spring, he had been privileged to accompany a top-secret convoy that sailed from the UK to Halifax, Nova Scotia. That mission was a test for several future missions, all of which would involve shipping cargoes of gold bullion to Canada. The evacuation of those funds from the UK would serve a dual purpose. First, the British treasury would be secure in Canada if London fell to Germany. Second, a portion of the bullion was required to purchase arms and other wartime necessities from the United States.

Sir Richard was pleased to learn that the success of the spring mission had made a current critical mission possible. The bulletin in his hand indicated that a second convoy, loaded not with crates of concrete blocks but with gold bullion, was scheduled to leave Britain within a fortnight. Rear Admiral Lancelot Holland, another personal friend, had been charged with overseeing the mission.

The second folder gave a further reason for hope. It contained a communique with a specific request from the United States Office of Strategic Services, the US equivalent of the UK's SIS. OSS, far from Europe and lacking the hard-earned surveillance experience that SIS had garnered during and since the Great War, had written to request assistance from SIS in training its operatives destined for foreign fields.

Sir Richard smiled, but not at the thought that OSS had found its resources inferior to those of SIS and needed her help. No, he smiled because this request was evidence that the United States had come to a welcome conclusion: though officially neutral, the United States was ready to ally once more with the UK.

A moment later, Sir Richard discovered the third folder offered a further reason to hope that help was coming. The final folder contained a copy of President Roosevelt's address to Congress three days earlier. The President had requested an amendment to the US Neutrality Acts, allowing nations at war with Germany to purchase arms from the US.

With the text of Roosevelt's request to Congress and a copy of orders for a gold-laden British convoy to Canada in his hands, Sir Richard didn't need to read tea leaves to draw his conclusion. The US was ready to supply the UK's wartime needs. The gold required to purchase those sorely needed goods would soon be sailing across the North Atlantic.

Sir Richard raised his glass and eyes to toast an unseen guest above. Thankful that the UK's most necessary ally had not abandoned her, he could do but one thing more; he offered a prayer of protection for the Royal Navy fleet at sea.

Chapter 14

On a Sunday morning in late September, the sun brought a clearing sky to Highfield after a light overnight rain. Michael and Susan were driving on Suffolk Road toward St. Peter's Cathedral in Charlottetown. However, this Sunday differed from every other Sunday they had attended mass at St. Peter's. Today, they were arriving in a new vermillion red Ford cabriolet. Susan, ever generous, had suggested that Michael drive her new car.

"Careful, darling," she said as they drove down the red gravel driveway. "Let's not splash through all the puddles and soil the paint," she said past her knit brow.

Michael had to smile. "Of course," he said, "though if it's too much of a mess when we return, we can always wash it."

"Oh, that's a good idea," she said, "because some of these puddles may still be here when we get back."

"Yes," he agreed, "and we'll have to be careful with any mud on our shoes and clean the floor mats."

"That's right," Susan said, looking down to inspect her feet. "I hadn't thought of that."

"Then there are the whitewall tires to consider," Michael added. "They'll need a little extra attention to look presentable."

"They will?" Susan asked. "They won't simply rinse clean?"

"Oh, no," he answered. "But don't worry. I bought some whitewall tire cleaning solution at Freeman Ford. You'll find it in the garage. There's a brush and a bucket just for the tires. There are instructions on the container. Rinse, apply, wait, scrub, rinse, and repeat. I'm sure you'll have all four tires done in under an hour," he said, hiding his smile.

Susan's face dropped as she considered the tasks awaiting her when they returned from St. Peter's, but a glance in Michael's direction caught his smile, and she reached over to slap his arm.

"Michael Moreland," she began, "you are a merciless tease!"

"And you, my dear wife," he laughed, "are an easy target. I know you love your new car and want to keep it looking new, and I'll be happy to help you. Even though the red mud will be with us forever, it will wash away every time. Let's give the mud its day, though, and limit the washes to once or twice a week, OK?" he asked.

"OK," Susan said. "But, just as long as you know, Michael, that I love Carmine, and I'm very grateful you bought her for me."

"Carmine?" Michael asked. "Have you named the car, too?"

"Well, yes, Michael," Susan said. "You wouldn't let me name the piglets or the calves, but when I got up yesterday morning and looked outside, the sky had a red line at the horizon the same color as Carmine. So, that's her name."

"Well," he said, "then Carmine it is. However, it's hard for the poet in me to ignore the obvious that 'Carmine' and 'car *mine*' offer a hint of double meaning that piques my attention."

"Oh, Michael," she said, "Don't worry. I let you drive her today, didn't I?" she asked, feigning innocence. "Now, let's find a parking place where no one can hit her."

Powerless but to smile, Michael parked on the curb in front of St. Peter's and opened Susan's door, looking up just in time to see Michelle and Grayson crossing the street to join them. Something about them was different today, though. In his RAF uniform, Grayson carried himself with a relaxed assurance, a settled confidence that neither Susan nor Michael had seen before. Michelle, too, wore an air of surety and peace, but her eyes, ever her giveaway, were smiling and afire. Looking away from Grayson and Michelle and back to each other, both nodded, knowing they had seen something they could neither deny nor name. As the couples met on the sidewalk, Susan was the first to speak.

"Ordinarily," she began, "I'd say, 'Good morning,' but looking at both of you, it seems nothing about this morning could get any better. Please don't make us beg. Tell us!"

Michelle looked at Grayson, who waved his outstretched hand as if to say, "After you." Then, looking back at him again, Michelle smiled, reached for her wrist, removed the white glove from her left hand, and held it out for Susan and Michael to see.

The eruption of joy on the sidewalk drew every eye on the block as Michelle and Susan embraced, laughed, cried, and laughed some more. Michael's handshake with Grayson became an embrace, followed by a second handshake. Once the women were willing to stand still, Michael hugged Michelle as Grayson and Susan shared their own hug. Eventually, they quieted enough to enter the church, but their smiles were a giveaway to a congregation that couldn't help watching the couples as they found their seats.

A fine, warm day in harvest season meant the congregation would probably be smaller than usual. Many parishioners had to stretch the hours of every day to keep their farms in order and felt they couldn't afford to lose an hour on a Sunday. For those who had left their work to worship, Fr. Hunt kept his homily short. Following the story of the wedding at Cana from John's gospel, he chose to illumine Mary's words, "Whatever he says to you, do it." Susan and Michelle were still discussing the homily as they left the narthex.

"You challenged me," Susan. You asked me, "Are you going to let a war stop you from something that's supposed to be?"

"That's right, Michelle, I did," Susan agreed.

"But, as sure as I was at that moment, I wasn't sure an hour later. So, Susan, I actually prayed, which you know isn't my first stop," Michelle laughed, "and suddenly, I knew. I just knew it was supposed to be, and it would happen when He," Michelle said, pointing to the sky, "wanted it to. And that night, out of the blue, Grayson spoke with my parents, produced a ring, and here we are."

"And then this morning in church, we hear, 'Whatever he says to you, do it,'" Susan laughed. "I don't think that's an accident, Michelle."

"Right," Michelle said. "Maybe it's a way to think about the future, too."

"Maybe?" Susan asked as she raised her teacher's eyebrows and laughed.

As Michael and Grayson approached, Michael said, "Folks, we know they ran out of wine at Cana, and were it not for a miracle, the guests would have gone home thirsty. Grayson and I have concluded that we need to hurry to the Cask and Cork for lunch before they run out of wine, too. After all, a couple of toasts are in order today. Care to squeeze into Carmine with us for the ride?" Michael asked.

"Carmine?" Michelle said, looking from face to face.

Michael grinned and looked at Susan, who rolled her eyes and shook her head as she began to explain. Both couples had to laugh again as they walked to the curb.

Chapter 15

It was a cool Saturday afternoon in late September, and Michael was in the woodshop at a bench with three rifles, still in their cases, while he waited for two young men to arrive. Luc and Joseph had finished their firearm safety training two weeks ago, and Michael had worked with them to lay out a shooting range not far from the sawmill. The target area was set against an earthen bank to ensure safety, and both boys were gaining better accuracy after each lesson. So far, they had been shooting a Remington Model 33 single-shot rifle, an inexpensive and accurate gun found in many farmers' homes across Prince Edward Island. By their third lesson, both Luc and Joseph were showing promise at a range of fifty yards. Michael had helped them become comfortable shooting from various positions, and they were almost ready to shoot away from the range. Live targets were their goal, but there was just a little more work to finish before Michael would be ready to set them free in the woods and fields.

Highfield had planted four acres of corn in the spring in part of the east pasture that lay slightly lower than the surrounding ground. Part of the pasture drained toward the cornfield, providing enough water to produce two fine crops of corn, one variety for the table and another for the livestock. With the corn harvest over and the cornstalks cut, Canada geese had already found a favorite feeding ground. The field, set low as it was, made good ground for Luc and Joseph to try their skills. By adding some decoys, Michael hoped to attract even more geese.

Michael had cut two old tires into three pieces each and set each piece on the floor with the arch up. Near one end of each arch, he had cut a two-inch hole at the top of the tire where he could force a white pine stake through the tire and into the ground. He had shaped the upper end of each four-foot-long stake to resemble a goose's head.

When the young men arrived at the wood shop, Michael had several cans of paint and brushes available. He had already painted the top third of the wooden stakes black and added detailed colors to make the heads look more authentic. As Luc and Joseph came closer, their eyes lit up with anticipation.

"That's right," Michael began, "we're almost ready to do some hunting. First, however, we have some work to do to get these decoys ready. Why don't you get some brushes out and start on the next two heads."

The boys went to work immediately, and six decoys were ready for the field before long. Though the paint wasn't entirely dry, they put a tarp on the back of the flatbed, loaded the decoys, and drove out to the cornfield. Even as they arrived, several geese flew away, honking their disapproval as they found the air.

Luc and Joseph located the pieces of tire throughout the field, digging each one into the soft soil to make it secure. Then, forcing the stakes through the holes in the tires, they drove them in with a two-pound sledge hammer, leaving just enough length to keep the neck and head in proportion. With all six in place, Michael's touch-up brush finished the job. The boys marveled at how realistic the decoys looked as they rode back to the shop with Michael.

When the paint brushes were clean, Luc and Joseph didn't hesitate to use some turpentine to clean their hands. Then, they put the rifles on the truck and climbed onto the flatbed for the ride back to the pasture. When they arrived, Michael took some time to discuss the safest place for a hunter to position himself so that any errant shots would hit the higher ground, keeping anyone downrange safe. That decided, Michael paced off fifty yards from the decoys and asked Luc and Joseph to ready their rifles.

"We're not shooting geese today," Michael said. "Your work will be easier today than when you're hunting live game. Today, we're shooting decoys. They stand still, don't get frightened at your every movement, and can't fly away. This is the easiest hunting you'll ever do. Of course," Michael added, "decoys don't taste quite as good as real geese, either."

While Luc and Joseph grinned, Michael continued. "You may have noticed that each decoy's head is about the same size as your fifty-yard bullseye at the shooting range. Let's see what you can do in a field from fifty yards. Remember, your target is the head, nowhere else."

Over the next few minutes, both boys took several shots at each of the six decoys. They varied their shooting positions but stayed low in the high grass, knowing that live targets were easily frightened and ready to fly away. When both made their last shot, they checked the decoys. They found that they had hit each target at least once. Michael was obviously pleased.

"That is fine shooting for your first outing," he said, "fine shooting. I am pleased with your progress. Now, let's go back and shoot another round."

The boys all smiled as they followed Michael back to their starting point, but then he kept walking farther away, pacing out an additional fifty yards. Luc and Joseph followed, confused but willing. At the hundred-yard point, Michael stopped and said, "Let's set up here."

The boys gave it their best, but they could hardly see their targets at a hundred yards. Each shot his six rounds, but upon inspection, no decoy showed a hit.

Michael wasn't the least surprised.

"Gentlemen," he said, "don't be discouraged. I believe your skills are fine. There was only one problem. I didn't give you the right tool for the job. Follow me. I have something to show you."

Returning to the hundred-yard location, Michael opened a third gun case and brought out a Remington Model 24 semi-automatic rifle equipped with a Lyman scope. Luc and Joseph watched in awe as Michael loaded not one but ten bullets through a port in the stock. Then Michael pointed toward the decoy farthest away on the right-hand side of the cornfield.

"Let's see what happens, gentlemen," he said. Michael took a sitting position, shouldered the rifle, aimed, and squeezed off a shot. Standing again, he said, "Let's take a look."

When they arrived at the decoy, they found three bullet holes. Since Luc and Joseph had made two from fifty yards, the third had to be Michael's.

Michael winked at both young men and said, "Let's see what you can do now!"

There were smiles all around when Luc and Joseph prepared for their next shots. First, though, Michael unloaded the rifle so the boys could familiarize themselves with it. They learned to load and unload it, practiced sighting through the scope, and were finally ready to do some shooting.

They could hardly have been more pleased. When they left the pasture that afternoon, there were no live decoys in the cornfield. With the help of the scope, each shot found its mark. Back at the shop, Michael gave the boys six more stakes to paint, but these were made of oak and not intended for target practice. Before they left the shop, however, Michael added one last task.

"Tomorrow after lunch," he began, I'll meet you here with the Model 24 and ten bullets. By three o'clock, Doris will expect you back with geese for supper. Now, get out to the field early, and remember to stay low and quiet. If it will help, gather some brush to make a blind. Then, wait until the geese fly in and settle, and patiently choose your best shot. They might fly away at the gun's report, but often, they'll stay put while you harvest a second and a third. Take no more than three, understood?" Michael asked.

Nothing could discourage the smiles on the young men's faces, not even when Michael reminded them that Doris would be expecting the geese to arrive butchered and ready for the oven.

Chapter 16

On the morning of October 3, 1939, Lt Boyd Moncrieff, a senior communications officer on the battleship HMS Revenge, had just left the radio room after an overnight shift. Though in sore need of sleep, his mind would not allow him that luxury. Just yesterday, the Revenge received new orders that sent her steaming north from her convoy duty in the South Atlantic. Bound for a port as yet unnamed in the UK, the Revenge would soon be crossing the Atlantic to join the North Atlantic Escort Force, based in Halifax, Nova Scotia. Boyd had sailed from Portsmouth to Halifax not four months earlier on a Royal Navy exercise. His father and brother had also sailed in that convoy, a test for a future mission vital to Britain's national security.

Boyd welcomed orders to abandon convoy escort duty in the South Atlantic to sail north. Whether their course took them up the Channel or to the west of England, he knew the Revenge would be more likely to engage the enemy in those heavily patrolled waters. German U-boats had sunk over fifty ships since the war began, most of them British merchant and passenger ships sailing in northern waters. Nonetheless, it was the sinking of the HMS Courageous off the coast of Ireland a few weeks earlier that gave every British sailor a heightened reason for concern. So, as the Revenge steamed north today, every sailor aboard, including Lt Moncrieff, faced a renewed challenge to pit his resolve against his fear.

Boyd remembered his last visit to Canada and his family's time together at Highfield. Highfield seemed like a dream now, a storybook estate and a safe haven in a faraway country, a child of his father's forethought. He savored his memories of four days of freedom and contentment, an oasis at the end of a pressure-filled mission. He remembered his mother and how well she looked, his sister and her joy at her wedding, and Michael, Susan's new husband and Boyd's friend since childhood.

Boyd was glad they were all safe on Prince Edward Island, an ocean away from the danger in Europe. Though he would be in Halifax again soon, he doubted he would see Highfield again until the war ended. He would have to preserve his memories of that brief visit until then.

Eventually, Boyd dozed, but only for an hour or so. When he awoke, his father and brother, Nigel, came to mind. According to the latest reports, the German Wehrmacht remained singularly occupied with the war in Poland. Thankfully, Germany had not targeted the UK's military bases, manufacturing centers, or the city of London as many feared she would. Still, no one could say how much longer his father would be safe at SIS headquarters in London. Not privy to the locations of other ships, Boyd could only presume that Nigel was somewhere not far from the UK, probably in the North Sea. Then Boyd remembered another serviceman, a family friend with whom he and his brother had recently served, RAF Flt Lt Grayson Royce. Far from European hostilities, Grayson was training pilots on Prince Edward Island.

Boyd's thoughts turned to Halifax, his destination port in Canada. Grayson had met Michelle Verrier in Canada and seemed quite taken with her. Boyd remembered that Michelle had a brother, Steve, stationed in Halifax with the RCN. Boyd toyed with the thought of finding Steve in Halifax, but finding an RCN officer at port in Canada was improbable under the best circumstances. During wartime, it would be nearly impossible. Though Boyd knew he was yearning for some kind of contact, even the thought of having a beer with someone he'd never met served to warm him for a moment.

Shaking his head, Boyd couldn't help taking stock of his life. He was alone with a thousand other men on a ship in the Atlantic Ocean. A few were friends, but he could characterize no relationship closer than cordial. He was jealous of those who were always writing to wives or sweethearts, showing off photos, and starving for news from those waiting for them at home. Boyd's home was at Clifton Manor in Suffolk, but no one there was waiting for him.

So far, Boyd had spent his life following his father's example, never daring to ask what he wanted for himself, and here he was, alone. He was the second son who always tried harder but never won the prize. Rationalizing, he thought, "Nigel's alone, too," but he knew that wasn't true. After all, Nigel was with Nigel. He was the first son, a little larger than life and able to approve of himself with every breath. Nigel oozed confidence, always said the right thing, and saw things coming long before they arrived. Nigel acted. Boyd reacted.

No, Boyd knew his family would never fill the hole in his heart. He needed someone else. Michael had found Susan, and Grayson had found Michelle. Wartime was no time to think about finding the right woman, but Boyd wasn't willing to give up on that possibility today.

"Who knows?" he said as he sat up in his bunk and turned his feet to the floor. "Maybe I'll have leave in Halifax. Maybe I could get to Highfield, tour Charlottetown, and see who's available there."

Standing beside his bunk, he turned toward the mirror on the door. As he looked in the mirror, he paused and shook his head.

"You and your ideas, Moncrieff," he said to the man looking back. "Put them away, old man. You're thousands of miles from Halifax or Highfield. Today, only one thing matters. We have a war to win."

With that, Boyd became Lt Moncrieff again. After straightening his bunk, he headed back to the radio room.

Chapter 17

"According to Grayson, something big is about to happen at the airfield in Charlottetown," Michelle said to Susan and Michael, "and Grayson's role seems essential at the start."

Michelle was sitting in the back seat of Susan's car while the trio drove to an address on Brighton Road near Victoria Park in Charlottetown.

"Grayson dropped the keys off at the store this afternoon," Michelle said. "He's tied up for another hour in a meeting, but he'll join us at the Port O' Call as soon as he can."

"So Grayson's quarters at the base won't be available any longer?" Michael asked.

"No," Michelle began, "because two more instructors are arriving, and the number of trainees will more than double. As the senior officer here, the RCAF has found him a house away from the airfield."

"So the keys you have are for a house in Charlottetown?" Susan asked.

"Yes," Michelle answered, "in Brighton. It's the vacation home of a retired RCAF officer, an Air Commodore from Ottawa. The house has been in his family for generations. He's been called back to help organize the training in Ottawa, so the house will be available for at least the next year, possibly longer. Grayson has already seen it, but he hasn't told me very much. He wants me to draw my own conclusions."

Michael looked again at the address label attached to the keys Michelle had given him. "It's only a short drive from the airfield," he said, "and Brighton is a very posh neighborhood. I'll wager the house will be lovely."

When they turned into the driveway, Michael had to smile. His prediction was correct. The house, a handsome two-story white clapboard home, boasted three second-floor dormers and a slate roof. Four red brick chimneys told them they could expect to find several fireplaces within. Michael estimated the lot covered almost an acre, all fenced and landscaped with several gardens. At the end of the brick driveway stood a two-car garage.

"Oh, my," Michelle gasped. "This *is* lovely."

After leaving the car and walking the brick path to the front door, Michelle tried the key and entered with Susan right behind. A moment later, Michael joined them at the entrance, where they were all suitably impressed. The quality they admired on the interior was entirely consistent with what they had observed on the exterior. The first floor boasted high ceilings and a generous and comfortable sense of space. Mahogany floors, paneled walls, and open staircases led to room after lovely room. There were four bedrooms, three bathrooms, a kitchen, a dining room, a parlor, and a study. As Michael surmised, they found four fireplaces, all with sculpted mantles and raised stone hearths.

The house was also fully furnished and in move-in condition. After twenty minutes of wandering through every room and inspecting every closet, Michelle and Susan extracted Michael from the basement, where he had finished inspecting the utilities. They gathered in the front entry.

"Michelle," Susan said, "this house lacks nothing, but Grayson will wander around in echoes here."

"You're right," Michelle said. I don't like to think about him driving home, turning into the driveway at the end of the day, and unlocking this door by himself."

"Maybe he won't be alone that long," Michael suggested, hiding his smile while examining the wall paneling in the entry and avoiding eye contact with the ladies.

"That's not really ours to discuss, though, is it, Michael?" Susan said, glancing his way.

"Of course not," Michael agreed, "only a passing thought, not a conclusion, but . . . " Michael said as Susan interrupted.

"But, we'd best be on our way," Susan said, looking at Michael, "or we'll be keeping Grayson waiting alone at the restaurant."

Just then, the telephone on the table at Michelle's elbow rang. Not expecting anyone to call and uncomfortable answering a telephone in another's house, Michelle let it ring a second time. As the three looked at each other, all eyes told Michelle to pick up the receiver. Finally, she did and offered a tenuous "Hello?"

"Michelle, darling, it's me," Grayson said.

"Oh, good, Grayson," Michelle said, nodding toward Susan and Michael.

"I'm just driving away from the . . . " Grayson said as Michelle interrupted.

"Driving away?" Michelle asked, still looking at Susan and Michael, "Then we'll leave now, too."

"But wait," Grayson said. "Tell me. What did you think of the house?"

"We all love it," Michelle said, "but we're all wondering if you'll be comfortable here. Anyway, we'll talk at the Port O' Call, all right?"

"Fine," Grayson said, "and I'll tell you all about my last meeting today then, too?" he asked.

"OK," Michelle said, "see you in just a little while."

Michelle hung up the telephone, and they took their last look at the house before closing and locking the door. Back in the car again, Michael drove toward Summerside.

"So, Michelle," Susan asked, "has Grayson heard from his mother or his sister since your engagement?"

"Yes," Michelle said. "After he wired them on Monday, he heard from both by telegram on Wednesday. They sounded surprised, of course, but happy. His mother said something about his age and that it was about time he made her a grandmother."

"That sounds encouraging," Susan said. "As much as his proposal surprised your parents and you, it's nice that it didn't shock his family in England."

"Yes," Michelle said. "We took some photos, and we'll send those over as soon as we get them developed."

At the Port O' Call, they waited in the car for a few minutes before going in to get their table. Grayson arrived as the waiter was taking orders for drinks.

"Make mine a dry martini, please," Grayson said, "Hendricks if you have it, thank you."

"Of course," the waiter replied and was on his way to the bar.

Before he sat, Grayson took Michelle's hand and kissed it. Once in his seat, they couldn't help sharing another kiss, raising a blush on Michelle's cheeks and a smile from others at a neighboring table. Michael and Susan could not have been more delighted with friends who made such a happy couple.

After they had ordered dinner and were enjoying their drinks, Grayson asked Michelle about her impressions of the house in Charlottetown.

"So, Michelle," he asked, what did you think?"

"It's beautiful, every detail, but . . . " Michelle began.

"But, what?" Grayson asked.

"I just tried to picture you driving home from the airfield every day to a big lonely house, that's all," Michelle said.

"Well," Grayson began, "I don't have to move there for two more weeks. I'll still be in my quarters at the airfield until then."

"But after that?" Michelle asked.

"That's what I wanted to tell you on the telephone," Grayson said, "about my last meeting of the day."

"What else can the RCAF have to do with an empty house in Brighton?" Michelle asked.

"Well," Grayson said. "That's what the meeting was about. Now, I don't have to be alone in the house if you don't want me to."

Confused, Michelle asked, "If I don't want you to? What have I got to do with it?"

"Everything," Grayson said. "You see, my last meeting of the day wasn't at the airfield. It was with Fr. Hunt at St. Peter's. He has reserved the church for us on July 1, ten days from now. If you will have me, we can marry and move into the house in Brighton together."

"Oh, you!" she laughed as she threw her arms around his neck and hugged him. "Of course, I'll have you!"

Susan immediately looked to Michael with the question in her eyes, "Did you know about this?"

They didn't need words because Michael's face told her he was also amazed. Grayson had called him this morning before morning prayer, and Michael had done no more than meet him at St. Peter's and introduce him to Fr. Hunt at the end of the service. Michael left them to their conversation while he finished his errands in town. Although Michael knew Fr. Hunt was always happy to welcome another newlywed couple to the parish, he, like Susan, was surprised by a wedding date only ten days away. However, the schedule did not dampen the joy at the table. It followed both couples to their cars when they drove away from the restaurant.

Alone for the first time today, Michael and Susan kept a leisurely pace as they drove home to Highfield.

"I am so happy for them," Susan said. "Grayson is such a gentleman and so much more of a man than Michelle ever expected for herself."

"There's no question they're in love," Michael said, "and it hardly matters that they come from different continents. This match was made in heaven."

"Well," Susan said, "we know a little something about matches of that sort, don't we."

It wasn't a question, and Michael knew Susan didn't need an answer. One look into her eyes confirmed what he already knew. She rested her head on his shoulder for the remainder of the ride home.

Chapter 18

D r. Andrew MacMillan, Chief of Staff at Charlottetown Hospital, had attended medical school and completed his New York City internship at New York Hospital. There, he enjoyed exposure to many of the latest developments in medical science. After returning to Canada to complete his residency in Quebec, he longed to bring all that he had learned to Charlottetown Hospital. Before he could do so, however, he believed that many basic standards in patient care at the hospital needed to rise. He decided to begin with nursing education.

Recruited by Dr. MacMillan, Nurse Emily Langdon had been working at the Charlottetown Hospital under his direction for eight weeks now. Although her primary responsibilities involved the assessment of training needs, curriculum development, and classroom training for the nursing staff, Dr. MacMillan frequently called her away from the classroom when he required her nursing expertise in emergencies. The sad truth was that he could depend on no other nurse, not because the nursing staff was unwilling, but because they lacked Nurse Langdon's education and the experience she had gained at the College of Nursing in London. Especially when treating traumatic injuries and facing other life-threatening emergencies, Dr. MacMillan found her skills among the hospital's most valuable assets.

In eight short weeks, Nurse Langdon had become his right hand on the nursing staff. She seemed to have an innate ability to think his thoughts with him, anticipate his orders, and act when seconds counted and lives were at stake. Her gifts had already made a difference in the level of care that Charlottetown Hospital was able to provide its patients.

Beyond her professional skills, however, he had observed her interactions with her students. He recognized the sensitivity she exercised with them and her quiet ability to challenge her students without discouraging them, even when they failed to meet the high standards she required. He appreciated the urgent encouragement she exercised from her care, a care that kept her criticism always constructive. He watched as she found ways to engage even the most reticent learners, a gift that brought them back to their next shift, eager to do a better job. The positivity she instilled helped her students care for their patients as ardently as she did.

She was also consistently professional with her patients, always willing to listen and spend the extra time they sometimes required, once again providing an example for her students. After only eight weeks, the nursing staff was turning a corner, and Charlottetown Hospital was able to offer a markedly improved level of care.

Beyond his professional relationship with Nurse Langdon, though, Dr. MacMillan found himself looking forward to seeing her each day. He longed to know her, not only as a fellow professional who shared his passion for the healing profession, but also as another person who cared for people. Perhaps, someday, he mused, they could care for each other. The sound of her voice could already draw him out of his office to look for her in the hospital corridor. Her smile always encouraged his, and although he longed to look into her eyes, he feared he might get lost there. Only several years separated them, and if he dared abandon himself to his thoughts, he knew he could visualize her not as a colleague but as much more.

"Cease, desist, MacMillan," he said aloud. His conscience required that he remain ever professional in his relationships with hospital employees, but this one was unlike any other.

On an afternoon shift during her eighth week of service at the hospital, Dr. MacMillan sent an orderly to rush Nurse Langdon to the Accident Room to help him care for a patient. Leaving her class of nurses behind, she hurried to find Dr. MacMillan attending a young man covered in blood. Two other nurses stood by as Dr. MacMillan struggled to stop the bleeding coming from a severe wound on the man's right forearm, several inches below his elbow. Nurse Langdon didn't bother to gown. Instead, she hurried to the doctor who begged, "Tourniquet, right arm above the elbow, hurry!" Immediately, she retrieved and applied the tourniquet while Dr. MacMillan continued to apply pressure to the gaping wound from which the young man's lifeblood was flowing. Pale and unconscious now, their patient was barely breathing. With the bleeding controlled by the tourniquet, Dr. MacMillan investigated the wound.

Not a clean cut, the wound was a laceration caused by a farm implement, leaving the patient still in his work shirt soaked in blood to his shoes. While Nurse Langdon monitored and reported the patient's vital signs, Dr. MacMillan directed the remaining staff.

"Oxygen," he ordered, sending another nurse and an orderly to retrieve the equipment.

With the bleeding controlled, Dr. MacMillan sought to close the wound. Lacking another surgeon or an anesthesiologist, he proceeded with Nurse Langdon attending. With oxygen administered and Nurse Langdon's help, Dr. MacMillan sutured the affected artery and closed the wound. The unconscious young man, in shock and weakened by the loss of blood, was fighting for his life. His heart rate continued to fall, and his blood pressure was dangerously low,

"He needs blood," Dr. MacMillan said. "Prepare for transfusion."

Nurse Langdon was at a loss. There was no donor prepared to supply the required transfusion.

She said, "Dr. MacMillan, sir, we have no donor. Is there a family member hereabouts or is someone else available, someone with the correct blood type?"

Removing his surgical gown, Dr. MacMillan answered, "We have no matched donor. My blood is Type O. I can donate. Prepare a gurney," he said to the orderly standing by.

As he lay on the gurney and rolled up his sleeve, Dr. MacMillan instructed Nurse Langdon, "Direct the transfusion to the uninjured arm. Monitor vitals continually. When his blood pressure rises and approaches a normal range, discontinue the transfusion."

Nurse Langdon was in uncharted territory. Never had she seen an injury so serious. Never had she participated in such a transfusion. Never had an attending physician supplied a transfusion while treating an injured patient. It was now left to her not only to administer the transfusion but also to determine when to end it. The life and safety of both the patient and Dr. Macmillan were in her hands.

She said, "Dr. MacMillan, are you sure, sir? Without you, sir, no other doctor will arrive here in time to save either this patient or you. Again, Dr. MacMillan, are you sure," she begged.

Looking into her eyes, he answered, "Nurse Langdon, I know this procedure defies our protocol and challenges your experience, but this young man will die if we do not give him this chance. It is our only hope to save his life. We must do it. We will depend on God's grace to strengthen me to attend to him following the transfusion if necessary, but he must have blood now, or death is certain. Please, Nurse Langdon, proceed."

Nurse Langdon followed his orders. Some twenty minutes later, she discontinued the transfusion. The patient's heart rate and blood pressure had risen above a point of danger. Dr. MacMillan, still conscious, rested while continuing to monitor his patient's progress. Although the doctor's vital signs reflected the stress and blood loss he was enduring, he left the gurney, quickly inspected the wound he had sutured, and, with the help of an orderly, found his way to his office.

Thirty minutes later, Nurse Langdon arrived at Dr. MacMillan's office, where he sat in his chair, reclining and resting but awake.

She knocked and called from the door, "Dr. MacMillan?"

Raising his head, he answered, "Yes."

As she entered the office, she said, "Doctor, the patient has stabilized. Dr. Curtis arrived from Summerside and is attending him now."

Dr. MacMillan nodded as Nurse Langdon continued, "We believe you may have supplied as much as one and a half pints of blood, Doctor, more than is recommended or safe, sir. I've come to check your vital signs."

"Thank you," the doctor said, "But tell me. Have the patient's relatives been notified? They need to know that he will survive."

"Yes, sir," she answered. "They arrived shortly after the transfusion was completed. I spoke with them myself."

"Thank you," he said as he rose to his feet and stepped toward her. Suddenly, however, his knees buckled, his eyes began to close, and he fell into her arms, still struggling to stay on his feet. Her embrace was strong, and her cheek rested against his as his chin fell to her shoulder. She lowered him back into his chair as one of her knees found the floor, leaving them face-to-face.

His eyes, though closed at first, opened slowly to see her face. "Emily," he smiled, the first time he had uttered her first name.

"Yes, Dr. MacMillan?" she answered as she returned to her feet.

"I must apologize for my ineptitude. I find myself a bit weakened, though I am sure the condition is temporary," he said.

"Dr. MacMillan . . . " she began.

"Andrew," he said quietly, with eyes half closed. "In my office, Emily, from now on, I am Andrew to you, please."

Blushing, Nurse Langdon struggled to say, "Andrew, I must check your respirations, heart rate, and blood pressure now."

Recovering from his moment of weakness, he said, "Check them if you will, Emily," as a trace of a smile appeared on his face, "but I'll wager you will find a somewhat elevated heart rate."

"Elevated, sir?" she asked.

"Elevated, *Andrew*," he corrected.

Blushing again, she obeyed, "Elevated, Andrew?"

"Yes," he answered. "I would expect we could consider that reaction normal for a man who has just found himself in the arms of a beautiful young woman," he said quietly.

"Dr., I mean, Sir, no, I mean Andrew," Emily stumbled, "I'll take a moment to check and see."

Although his blood pressure remained low, his heart rate was indeed elevated. His respirations remained rapid, as well.

"As I predicted, Emily?" he asked.

"Yes," she answered, shaking her head and looking down to suppress her smile.

"Then may I expect you to return regularly to check them for me?" he asked.

"Yes, you may," she smiled. "Every half hour, Andrew," she said, struggling a little less this time.

"I'll depend on that," he said. "Actually," he added with another smile, "I'll look forward to it."

Nurse Langdon smiled as well, although she felt much less like Nurse Langdon and much more like a beautiful young woman at that moment.

Chapter 19

The days grew shorter at Highfield as autumn arrived, bringing its fall palette of colors to the trees. The next frost would begin sending the leaves to the ground, but until then, the colors remained a feast for the eyes. The harvest was over now, the root cellar was well stocked, and the larder shelves were filled with canned vegetables for the winter.

Michael and Jacques had arranged for the Lady M to spend the winter in the barn, away from the elements she would face outdoors at the boatyard. Under Jacques' supervision, Luc and Joseph had cleaned the barnacles and painted the bottom. With her plumbing and engine winterization complete, she was ready for a long winter's nap.

Geese continued to find the flock of decoys in the cornfield, though earlier flocks had already devoured the last of the corn. The boys were always ready to hunt, though, and Highfield enjoyed goose for dinner regularly. So did the neighbors, for Michael was quick to send the boys out to share the bounty. At the moment, though, Highfield faced another type of hunting chore. A fox had found his way into the henhouse over the weekend, killing several chickens. Michael knew the fox would be back to do more damage, but he also knew that the boys would love another reason to get their hands on a gun. They were meeting him at the woodshop in a few minutes.

When the boys arrived, Michael had two 20-bore double-barrel shotguns on the bench. Although he had shown them the difference between a shotgun and a rifle during their earlier safety lessons, neither had yet shouldered a shotgun. Today was the day.

Michael loved the enthusiasm that Luc and Joseph brought. They seemed eager to learn no matter what Michael had to share with them. Of course, shooting would probably always be their favorite, but woodworking and auto maintenance also offered solid appeal.

"We're dealing with a fox, gentlemen," Michael began, "and foxes hunt like cats, often at night. So your hunting will be a lot different from goose hunting."

The boys nodded as Michael continued.

"Sometimes you will see a fox at a distance where a rifle would be your best choice of weapon. However, a shotgun is better when closer to the house or the outbuildings. Do you remember why?" Michael asked.

Luc answered first, "The shotgun shoots a lot of smaller pellets in a pattern, so it's easier to hit a moving target," he said.

Joseph added, "And a shotgun doesn't shoot as far as a rifle, making it safer when shooting at birds overhead or game close by."

Michael was pleased with their memories, saying, "That's right, boys, on both counts. Still, the most important rule is to know your target, as well as . . . "

The boys joined Michael to finish, "what's in front of it, what's behind it, what's to the left, and what's to the right."

Michael smiled again. "All right, gentlemen. We're using 20-bore double-barrel shotguns. The barrels are different; one is intended for a closer target, and the other is intended for one farther away. You have two triggers. The front trigger is for a closer target, and the rear trigger is for a target farther away. Does that make sense to you?"

The boys were all nods and grins. After another few minutes of instruction, Michael and the boys were all in the flatbed, heading out to the cornfield for some practice. Once the boys had the basics of loading and unloading, how the safety worked, and the difference in the shotgun beads and the rifle sights, they shot a half dozen shells each.

"Now, I've noticed that a fox can develop some habits, like hunting at the same place at the same time each day," Michael said, "so keep track of any sighting you make for future reference. Also, remember, they're a lot more like cats than dogs. They can climb, too, and can sometimes be found in trees."

"What if Joseph and I set up a schedule for the next week so that one of us is ready in the early mornings and one later toward night? Would that work?" Luc asked.

"Let's find out, Luc. In the meantime, we'll lock the shotguns and shells in the woodshed. You know where to find the key, right?" Michael asked as the boys answered with a nod.

By the end of the week, Highfield was safe from at least one red fox. An overnight rain on Wednesday left the ground around the henhouse muddy enough to yield a set of tracks the boys couldn't miss. On their Thursday morning and evening shifts, the boys locked their eyes on the trail they had discovered. After supper on Friday night, a single shotgun blast yielded one dead varmint who wouldn't be hunting chickens at Highfield any longer. Keeping the tail as a trophy, Luc and Joseph buried the carcass in the cornfield. Michael had to smile. Once again, the boys had done their job.

Chapter 20

Lt Nigel Moncrieff, sailing aboard the HMS Furious north of Scapa Flow, found himself pacing the flight deck once again, trying to tame his anger and settle his mind. With Scotland far behind and the North Sea waters pounding the bow tonight, danger was all around. He had struggled with a like frame of mind less than a month ago, the day he learned that a U-boat had sunk the HMS Courageous off the west coast of Ireland. A number of those who perished that day were brothers-in-arms from the Fleet Air Arm. At that time, he thought no greater loss to a Royal Navy ship and her crew was possible. He had just learned that he was wrong.

Two nights ago, the Furious had been anchored in the harbor at Scapa Flow, berthed adjacent to the HMS Royal Oak. Last night, a U-boat managed to penetrate the aging blockships and anti-submarine nets at Scapa Flow and hit the Royal Oak with three torpedoes. Sinking in only a few minutes, the Royal Oak went to the bottom, taking over eight hundred men with her.

Every Royal Navy officer knew the history of Scapa Flow during the Great War. The Germans had scuttled more than fifty-two ships there during the last days of the war. Forty-five of those were later raised and salvaged, but now the Royal Oak, with eight hundred of her crew, was on the bottom among the remaining German shipwrecks.

Consumed with anger and frustration once again, Nigel found himself in a battle within. He, with so many others, felt powerless against an invisible enemy who too often struck with impunity. Although the Royal Navy had sunk two U-boats in waters west of the Hebrides last month, all eighty-two men aboard those submarines had survived, rescued by the Royal Navy, and were now confined as prisoners.

"Anger, frustration, fear, and grief," he repeated to himself. "Anger, frustration, fear, and grief," he said aloud. A month ago, he had identified these four enemies within, enemies he determined that he had to subdue. Ruled by any of the four, he knew he could fail to meet his call to battle. He had a charge to keep; he couldn't be faithful if he indulged in their distractions.

"A charge to keep I have," he said to himself. A lyric from a hymn long buried in his memory suddenly came to his aid. "Wesley, I think it was, but maybe not," he said. "No matter, still true, nonetheless. Perhaps the Chaplain will know."

Lt Moncrieff left the deck and found his way below to his cabin. Though he often prayed for protection and peace before retiring, he added prayers tonight for all those who perished on the Royal Oak, for all those aboard the Furious, his brother aboard the Revenge, his father in London, and his mother, sister, and brother-in-law in Canada. He took time to name his anger, frustration, fear, and grief and finished, saying, "A charge to keep I have, Father. Enable me to keep it faithfully, I pray, for King and Country."

Chapter 21

Most engaged young women have the luxury of months to plan their weddings. Michelle, however, had less than ten days to settle every detail of hers. She had marveled at Susan's gift for planning parties, and after remembering how she arranged every detail of her own wedding, Michelle thought of no one but Susan to help plan hers. First thing on Thursday morning, she reached for the telephone to call Susan, but the telephone rang before she could pick up the receiver. It was Susan calling.

"Michelle," Susan said, "with only nine days before your wedding, you have much to do. I woke up early this morning and started making a list. You probably already have your own, but if I can help, then I'm all yours."

Michelle had to laugh. "Susan," she said, "I was reaching for the telephone when it rang, and there you were. I'm so glad you called. I need all the help you can give. May I come out to Highfield so we can start?"

"Absolutely," Susan said. "I've got the study laid out with a few to-do lists, and I'll find some nourishment for us in the kitchen. Tea or coffee this morning?" she asked.

"Coffee, please," Michelle answered, "and I'll be with you in fifteen minutes with scones from Tea for Two!"

"See you then," Susan said.

Michael and Jacques were busy felling some red oaks at the edge of the pasture near the North Path this morning, a job that would take the rest of the day. Luc, Joseph, and Phillipe were on hand to remove the brush and cut the smaller boughs into firewood. They planned to begin cutting the trunks into fireplace lengths, ready for splitting. Already, they were working to supply winter fuel for next year.

When Michelle arrived, Susan had a proposed schedule for the next eight days completed, noting everything from Michelle's wedding dress fittings to bridal bouquets and boutonnieres for the best man and the groom. She included a rehearsal dinner menu, a reception luncheon menu, and all the remaining fittings for the maid of honor and the bride's attendants. Michelle found she had little to add.

Susan said, "We just have to determine a location for the reception. Where did you have in mind, Michelle?"

Michelle answered, "Fr. Hunt offered St. Peter's fellowship room," but Susan could tell Michelle wasn't entirely excited about that possibility.

"You don't sound convinced," Susan remarked.

"I'm not," Michelle said. "It's a lovely room but not at all like a home. I'm used to a family inviting guests to their home."

"Were you thinking of your home?" Susan asked.

"Oh, no," Michelle laughed, "it's not big enough."

"Grayson's new home?" Susan offered.

"I considered that," Michelle answered, "but Grayson has hardly moved in, and we have so much to do to prepare it for both of us."

"Then how about Highfield?" Susan said, "Would you feel at home here?"

"Of course," Michelle answered, "but, Susan, that is so much for us to ask. Are you sure your mother would approve?"

"Approve, Michelle?" Susan laughed. "Please! She considers you family, so I'm sure she'll be delighted. You know how much she admires your parents, don't you? She'll be over the moon! Now, let me see your guest list."

Within half an hour, Michelle and Susan had finished preparing menus for the bridal luncheon, the rehearsal dinner, and the wedding reception and were on their way to Charlottetown to look for a wedding dress. Michael would soon find out that he was in charge of the groom's schedule, because Susan had some suggestions for those details, too. By late afternoon, Susan was home, pleased that Michelle had found a perfect wedding dress at St. Onge's. With only minor alterations required, her dress would be ready by mid-week. Michelle was going to be a beautiful bride!

An hour later, Susan and Doris had finalized the menus for all the meals and refreshments at Highfield. Soon after, Susan completed her list of floral arrangements and sent the florist the final order. Of course, other details would always present themselves, but Susan was confident that the essentials were in place.

With an afternoon cup of tea, Susan sat back in the settee in the west sunroom, her feet on the hassock. As the sun faded behind the trees, she heard one of the horses neigh and looked out at Abe and Billie in the paddock. Just then, Emily approached and tapped at the open door.

"Yes?" Susan answered. Then, turning, she saw Emily and said, "Emily, please come in. I was just enjoying my tea. Would you like a cup?"

"No, thank you, Susan," she replied. "I was hoping you might have a moment to talk."

"Of course," Susan said. "Always. Come, sit down with me and tell me what is on your mind."

Still in her nurse's uniform, stained with blood, Emily sat on the edge of her seat next to Susan. Clearly troubled, she apologized, saying, "I'm so sorry that I present so poorly, Susan. There was a rather desperate emergency at the hospital today, but we were able to save a young man's life."

Emily described the horribly injured young man and the severe wound to his arm. She also rehearsed the emergency surgery and the blood transfusion that Dr. MacMillan had accomplished with her help, saving the young man's life. As she finished, she was sobbing into her handkerchief.

"Emily," Susan said, "you helped to save a man's life under desperate conditions. I'm sure you are overwrought under such stress."

"Perhaps," Emily agreed, "perhaps, but let me relate the remainder of my story," she asked.

Emily explained the moments following the transfusion when the patient's vital signs stabilized and the time she spent alone with Dr. MacMillan in his office. Emily blushed to tell Susan how Dr. MacMillan had asked her to call him Andrew while he addressed her as Emily.

"He stood when I entered his office to record his vital signs after the transfusion, but he grew unsteady on his feet and fell into my arms. I'm afraid we found ourselves in a rather compromised, cheek-to-cheek position when he could finally sit. That was when he said those things," Emily said, looking away.

"What things?" Susan asked.

"He told me I was a beautiful young woman and that he expected I would find his heart rate elevated after he'd fallen into my arms." Emily hesitated a moment before going on. "He also said he looked forward to me attending him as he recovered after the transfusion." Pausing again, Emily said, "Andrew, I mean Dr. MacMillan, was in a state of physical and emotional weakness," Susan, "and I know, as Nurse Langdon, I would like to excuse everything he said during those moments of weakness, all of those words that made me feel valued, and beautiful, and even," she hesitated, "loved. But . . . "

"But what," Susan asked.

"But, Susan," Emily began, "I never felt more alive or more one with another human being than when Andrew and I were saving that man's life. And afterward, when Dr. MacMillan approached me, not as a doctor speaking to a nurse, but as a man who needed my help—no, *wanted* my help—and wanted not just my help, but wanted *me*," she said, "I never felt more alive in my life."

"Yes," Susan said, "please, go on."

"I am afraid, on the one hand, that all of his words and all that I felt were a product of one moment when we strove together to save a life. On the other hand, however, I feel something far deeper. He appreciated me then, but I sensed he had for some time. I believe he hopes to know me more fully. I believe," she hesitated, "dare I say this? I believe that he may be infatuated with me."

"And?" Susan asked, tempting Emily to take the next step.

"And," Emily said quietly, "I feel the same for him." With that, Emily folded her hands in her lap and looked toward the floor.

"Emily?" Susan said, but Emily did not look up.

"Emily?" she said again, to no response.

"*Emily*," Susan said, loud enough to pierce her distraction.

"I'm sorry, Susan," she said, raising her eyes from the floor.

"Why would it be wrong for you to be in love with Dr. MacMillan?"

"Oh, Susan," she said, "I'm sure you know."

"I'm sorry, but I don't," Susan said. "Tell me, please."

"Because love will lead either to marriage or to sin, Susan. A nurse gives her life to her calling, not to a man. Nurses don't marry, nor do they fall to vice," she said.

"Where did you learn that, Emily?" Susan asked.

"Why, in London, while a student there," Emily answered. "We all knew it. Nurses in London never marry."

"But are there no married nurses in Charlottetown?" Susan asked.

"Well, one or two," Emily allowed, "but they were married before they became nurses."

"And you learned this standard in London, correct?" Susan asked.

"Yes," Emily answered.

"And how many years ago was that, Emily?" Susan asked.

"It was more than twenty years ago," she said, "when I first dreamed of being a nurse as a young girl," Emily answered.

"Well," Susan began, "I am happy to tell you that times have changed. You have believed a lie, not an intentional lie or a vicious type of lie. It's the same type of lie that Michael once believed. Because he did not come from money or high society, he considered a union with me impossible," Susan said. "At the same time, I believed my migraine headaches would lead to epilepsy as it seemed my mother's had, making me ineligible for marriage. We both believed lies that threatened to prevent us from marrying."

Emily nodded as Susan continued.

"And now, Emily, you are placing an outdated standard on yourself. Nurses *do* marry today, and sometimes they marry doctors, which is all the better. After all, who could better understand the high calling of a doctor than a nurse?" Susan asked.

Emily sat silent and amazed.

"If you are supposed to be married to Dr. MacMillan," Susan said, "everything in you will tell you so. If he is supposed to be married to you, he will damn every historical or professional restriction and pursue you until you can no longer refuse him." Susan said.

They sat silently for a moment until Emily began to sob. Susan reached over to hold her in her arms. Eventually, Emily calmed down and received the handkerchief that Susan offered.

Drying her eyes, Emily said, "Susan, I have never felt more worthy. I have never felt more loved. However, I am afraid it was merely his physical weakness and the intimacy of those moments that caused Dr. MacMillan . . . "

Susan interrupted, "Andrew," she said. "He asked you to call him Andrew, Emily."

"Andrew," Emily said. "I'm afraid it was the stress of those moments and his weakness following the transfusion that suddenly made me seem desirable to him."

"Then, Emily," Susan said, "let's see what happens tomorrow. Do you expect he will have recovered and be at the hospital tomorrow?"

"Yes, Susan," Emily answered, "I do."

"And will you see him then?" Susan asked.

"Yes, because we have a meeting tomorrow to review goals for the upcoming week," Emily said.

"Well, when you return from the hospital, would you come to see me tomorrow? Then, perhaps you can tell me what we need to know. Agreed?" Susan asked.

"Agreed," Emily answered, "agreed, Susan," she said with a hint of anticipation in her eyes. "Thank you."

Emily left, and Susan, looking forward to tomorrow's conversation, smiled as she finished her tea.

Chapter 22

Sir Richard Moncrieff drank alone again tonight in his office at SIS headquarters in London. The bottle of Dewars and the glass he kept in his bottom drawer regularly found their way to his desktop at the end of the day. Tonight, however, was different. As he raised his glass in a silent toast, he felt the presence of a friend. Yesterday, he had learned that the Royal Oak had been sunk at Scapa Flow with the loss of more than eight hundred fine men. In a later report today, however, he also learned that among them was a personal friend, Rear Admiral Henry Blagrove, with whom he had served during the Battle of Jutland in the Great War.

Sir Richard was long-practiced in holding his feelings at arm's length. His years as an officer in the Royal Navy and as a senior strategist at SIS had taught him to let nothing an enemy could do become personal. Tonight, however, he struggled to maintain his standard.

His sons were sailing in the same waters, hunted by the same enemy that had taken both the HMS Courageous and the HMS Royal Oak in less than a month. Since the war began, U-boats had attacked or sunk more than sixty-five other vessels, including merchant and passenger ships. Sir Richard took comfort in only one piece of intelligence to which he was privy. The HMS Furious and the HMS Revenge, with his sons aboard, would soon be sailing in convoy away from the killing fields of the North Sea, heading west across the Atlantic. Although Nigel and Boyd would still be at risk there, Sir Richard knew that, as a rule, convoys provided greater safety than ships sailing alone.

Once transferred to Halifax, the Furious was scheduled to become the hunter, searching with other Royal Navy ships for Kriegsmarine attackers seeking merchant vessels bound for the UK. At the same time, the Revenge was on its own mission to Halifax with cargo bound for

Quebec and Montreal. Sir Richard knew his sons were safer in waters across the Atlantic than in the North Sea.

Reports from the continent remained bleak. German and Russian forces in Poland continued to ravage the defeated Poles. Reports of atrocities against Jews, including the establishment of ghettos and forced labor camps, arrived daily. Though Hitler had sent offers of peace to Britain and France, he included no proposal to abandon the territories in Poland and Czechoslovakia he had attacked. Even Britain's Prime Minister remained unconvinced that Nazi aggression would cease at any time soon.

After Sir Richard returned his glass and bottle to their place in the bottom drawer, he opened his top drawer to retrieve some stationery and his pen. He had sent a radio message to Highfield earlier in the day, knowing Michael would share it with Angela and Susan. Now, however, he began to pen a letter to Angela. Nothing soothed her angst better than his letters. Somehow, writing to her soothed his as well.

When he finished writing a half hour later, he sealed his letter and left it for his aide to post in the morning. Retrieving his Walther PPK from his desk, Sir Richard secured it in his shoulder holster, reached for his topcoat and attaché, and headed for the elevator. He had one destination in mind tonight—his flat and his bed.

Chapter 23

After breakfast this morning, Doris asked to talk with Susan for a few minutes.

"It's my girls," Doris said. "I'm afraid they're becoming young women in a world I don't recognize. It's different than when I was young, Miss Susan."

Susan interrupted, "I'm just Susan, Doris. The children aren't in earshot, so it's just us," she smiled.

"Of course, Susan," Doris answered. "It's Ingrid I worry about most. At fourteen, she's become a young woman when I wasn't looking. I'd worry less if she wasn't so pretty. Perhaps it's good she doesn't know it," she said.

"But young women her age never think they're pretty, remember?" Susan asked. "Unfortunately, we usually took our cues from the boys, didn't we? We all knew the girls the boys couldn't resist!"

"Well, that's part of the problem," Doris said. "We have Joseph at home with us, and Francis and some other boys are at school. I don't know if you've noticed, but Ingrid is blooming, if you see what the boys see," she said, rolling her eyes, "and they're noticing. I want her to remember who she is and care for herself properly."

"Of course you do, Doris," Susan agreed. "Is there anything I can do to help?"

"I was hoping you would ask," Doris said. "It's like this, Susan. To my girls, you're a princess. When Michael showed them your family photos before you arrived at Highfield, they thought you were royalty. Now they know the facts, but they still want to grow up to be like you."

Susan had to laugh, but she understood. "I think I know the photo you mean, Doris, but it's probably my father's sword that tips the balance," she said. "But I understand your predicament. Here's an idea.

What if I offered some lessons in deportment, social skills, and some values, especially the self-respect every young woman needs to own? Without it, she won't demand respect from others, especially the boys. What do you think?" Susan asked.

"I think you've read my mind, Susan," Doris smiled. "They look up to you and will hang on your every word, I'm sure. If I may say so, you are the example of a woman I want my girls to become one day. Thank you for caring for them," Doris said, taking Susan's hand.

Susan offered her other hand as well. "Doris," she said, "there were people who cared for me in the same way. Now it's my turn, but," she added, "it is also my pleasure." Susan laughed, "I can't wait to get started. Let me put pen to paper and make some plans, and we'll begin on Saturday morning when they finish their breakfast chores. Will that work for you?"

Doris pulled Susan's hands into a hug, and the women fairly beamed with expectation. Saturday promised to be a special day for Ingrid and Patrice.

Susan recalled her childhood and the social demands family life required at Clifton Manor in England. There was always an upcoming formal tea, a party, or another social event requiring petticoats, white gloves, and tightly curled hair. She hated those formal occasions, but she also learned from them. Life had few formalities here on Prince Edward Island, but good manners and well-defined social skills were always in order. Perhaps they could spare the extra petticoats and stiff curls, but the girls would be young ladies when she finished. Most important, though, was that they would know and respect themselves and require that respect from others, especially the young men.

"Let's make some ladies out of these beautiful young women," she said with a smile as another idea began to form in her mind. "Let's get Michael to take on a similar challenge for the young men." With another knowing smile, she said, "Yes, let's."

Of course, when Susan cornered Michael in the garage a half hour later, he wished his teachers at Clifton Manor had offered a class entitled "How to say 'no' to a woman." It's not that he disagreed with the need for the class Susan suggested for the boys. The only problem, he explained, was that his schedule was already full. Of course, within a few minutes, Susan found a hole or two in his schedule, providing all the time he would need to help the boys. Defeated once again but smiling as he shook his head, he swept her to a corner behind her convertible, where she soothed his remaining reticence with a deposit of kisses, which he managed to pay back with some of his own. Fortunately, neither kept a ledger, so they knew they'd have to meet again soon to settle accounts.

Chapter 24

Michelle sat with her mother in their parlor, still marveling at Grayson's enthusiasm and the energy he brought to planning their wedding. The wedding was only a week away, but she found herself without a long list of tasks to accomplish, able to sit and enjoy a moment at home. She hadn't expected a chance to relax this close to the wedding, but she had to admit she loved it.

"Mom," Michelle said, "You have to see the house. It will be like our own little palace. Of course, we'll have to make it ours, but that will be fun."

"I'm sure you'll enjoy making your nest, Michelle," Anna said, "but let's get you married first. Now, what remains among the details?"

"That's just it," Michelle said, "Grayson has already taken care of the church and reviewed the reception details with Susan. He has scheduled a photographer for the rehearsal, the bridal party, family photos here at home, the groom and the groomsmen at the church, and the wedding and the reception. His mother and sister will be able to see everything in photos as soon as we can mail an album to England."

Before Anna could say a word, Michelle said, "And he has hired cars to drive all of us to the church and then to Highfield after the wedding. And because the RAF won't let him travel very far for a honeymoon right now, he has a suite reserved for us at the Hotel Charlottetown and some other plans that are still a surprise for me," Michelle said, "I feel like a princess. I've never imagined a man caring for me like this."

"It appears, my dear," Anna said, "that you have waited for the right one."

"That's just it, Mom. I thought it was Michael for months, and when that plan crashed, I was shattered. I know now that I was fooling myself when I thought I was in control. I think I'm learning to trust as you did while you were away for so long. When my hopes were crushed, I actually learned to pray, and, since then, I know a little bit more about listening."

"Miracles have sustained us this year, Michelle," Anna said. "For twenty years, I prayed that I would someday be able to put a tortoiseshell barrette in your hand, and I will never forget the night my prayers were answered. And now, I'm here to enjoy your wedding. My heart is full, Michelle," Anna said, taking Michelle's hands, "and all the more to find that such an honorable man loves you. I can only say that God is good."

Michelle and Anna paused to savor their moment together before Michelle began again. "I haven't told you about the people in the wedding party yet, Mom."

"Tell me now, then," Anna said.

"Well," Michelle began, "Susan will be my matron-of-honor, of course, and you remember Ingrid and Patrice from Susan's wedding?" she asked.

"Yes," Anna said, "one was a bridesmaid, and the younger was the flower girl, as I remember."

"That's right," Michelle said, and they'll play those roles again. I wanted to ask you about someone else, though."

"Who would that be?" Anna asked.

"Another bridesmaid, Mom," Michelle answered, "but a little older. Emily Langdon."

"Nurse Langdon?" Anna asked. "Oh, my, Michelle, she was such a help to me when I came home. I think that's a wonderful idea."

"I was planning to ask her this afternoon," Michelle said. "Lady Moncrieff has been doing so well that Emily has been free to work at Charlottetown Hospital for several hours daily. I think I'll be able to see her later today when she returns from work."

"I hope you can, Michelle. Now, back to the wedding party. The best man is Michael?" Anna asked.

"Yes, Mom," Michelle said, laughing. "I forgot the men. Michael is the best man, Steve is a groomsman, and Luc and Joseph Boucher will be ushers."

"I'm glad your brother could get leave, even if it is only for seventy-two hours," Anna said. "After all, you'll only be getting married once. He can't miss it."

Armand appeared at the top of the stairs, signaling Michelle that her afternoon shift had begun at the store. It would be a short shift today, leaving her time to drive to Highfield to speak with Emily.

As was her habit, Susan was taking her afternoon tea in the west sunroom at Highfield. She could hardly believe that just yesterday Emily had returned from the hospital after helping Dr. MacMillan save an injured man's life. But just then, Emily tapped at the open door.

"Susan?" she said.

Susan turned to look over her shoulder toward the door. Twenty-four hours had wrought an amazing change in the woman Susan greeted. There was new life in Emily's eyes, and Susan couldn't wait to find out why.

"Come in, Emily," she began. "I watched the car come up the drive, and I took the liberty of pouring you some tea. Please sit down."

Emily sat across from Susan, a tea table between them. She raised the cup to her lips for one sip before setting the cup and saucer back on the table.

"I must tell you, Susan," she said, "I must tell you," she said again, almost breathless with excitement.

"I hope you will," Susan laughed, "please do."

Emily began eagerly, "It is as I suspected."

"Which is?" Susan asked.

"Why, Dr. MacMillan," Emily said before correcting herself. "I mean, Andrew," she said, savoring his name as it fell from her lips. "Andrew does have feelings for me."

"Yes?" Susan asked, nodding for Emily to go on.

"Yes. I told you yesterday all the things he had said, how he asked me to call him Andrew, and how he said he was sure his heart rate would increase when I was near. Do you remember? I was taking his vital signs."

"Yes," Emily," Susan interrupted, "please go on."

"Well, I was afraid that all his feelings resulted from the excitement in the Accident Room or the transfusion he had just endured. Today, however, he was much recovered," Emily said. "I saw him briefly in the corridor this morning, but there was no time for us to talk. This afternoon, however, our regular meeting to discuss goals for the week was scheduled for two o'clock. We met in his office, and . . . " Emily hesitated.

"And?" Susan asked.

"And," Emily said, "he invited me to sit with him at his worktable. I expected he would sit at his desk, and I would sit opposite him, as usual. Today, however, he had arranged a chair for me beside his. After I sat down and retrieved my planning book, he closed the office door, which he had not done before."

"I see," Susan said. "Please go on."

"Andrew had tea and a plate of raspberry-filled pastries ready at the table. He asked how I took my tea, and I told him. As he poured and added my cream and sugar, he said, 'I must remember this next time, Emily. And raspberry? It was only a guess on my part, he said, 'but I so hoped it might appeal to you.'"

"And then?" Susan asked.

"When I told him that I was rather keen on raspberry, he seemed pleased and plated a pastry for me," Emily said. "We didn't discuss anything about our work for the next twenty minutes or more. He simply wanted to talk. He wanted to know all about me, you know, my birthplace, my family, and my childhood. He sat and digested all I had to say about my time in London during the Great War and while I was in nursing school. When I could say no more, he began to tell me about his life."

"And after that," Susan urged.

"After that, he spoke about how important it was for colleagues to maintain their professionalism on the hospital floor. However, he told me he hoped we could leave our professional demeanor behind when we were away from others and enjoy a more personal rapport. He said he felt we had more to offer each other, something that surpassed the mere professional, the cerebral, something that approached the heart. And then . . . " Emily said.

"And then?" Susan prompted her once more.

"And then he took my hand, Susan, and held it in his, my palm to his palm. With the other hand, he stroked my fingers, then lifted my hand to his lips to kiss it, but not once, Susan. No, not once, but three times, as he said, 'Emily, I must tell you what I have learned about a physician's calling. Ours is a high calling, of course. Each day, we are required to make decisions which may save lives. Though our training and practical skills are vital, our hearts provide an essential addition. To care, to care for souls, is our true calling. Beyond our skills, it is our care that will push us beyond ourselves to serve our patients.'"

Emily paused and looked away for a moment, thinking before continuing.

Looking again at Susan, she said, "Then he said to me, 'Emily, from the day you arrived at this hospital, I observed a nurse with extraordinary skills, not only those in which she was trained and had worked diligently to learn. No, there were more gifts stored in your heart. Some revealed themselves in the way you cared for your students, always encouraging them to care for their patients and one another while exercising their practical skills. I began to call you to the Accident Room knowing that your practiced healing skills, learned in London, and gifts of care, already available in your heart, were ready to be shared, not only with those you train but also with our patients during those times of their greatest need.'"

Emily continued, "He paused for a moment, Susan, before looking into my eyes and saying, 'Emily, I am no longer a young man. I have searched for years while finishing my studies in two hospitals, searching for another who shares my passion for our patients and seeks to lead others to the same dedicated care. I had given up until I met you and watched you inspire a ragged group of nurses, teaching them by your example what it means to fulfill a calling and truly care for those in need. Now, away from New York and Quebec, I find myself overwhelmed to meet one of such rare beauty with such gifts and a heart full of care. Emily, forgive my simplicity. I will confess but this. I am smitten, and, without a hope that someday you could care for me, Emily, I am lost.'"

Emily lifted her face to look at Susan, who asked, "And what happened then, Emily?"

Emily said, "He kissed my hand again."

"And then?" Susan asked.

"Then he stood," Emily added, "saying, 'Forgive me for being so forward, Emily. I don't mean to overwhelm you with the angst that years of dashed hopes have left me. But, now that I have found you, I make but one request. Please consider all I have said, and if in your heart there is room for a man such as I am, I pray that we may speak again whenever you wish.'"

Emily paused again before looking at Susan and saying, "Then I stood, and we looked at each other for a moment. He bent to kiss my cheek, but I didn't let him."

"No?" Susan said, surprised.

"No, Susan. As his lips approached my cheek, I turned to look again into his eyes. Then our lips met, and he wrapped his arms around my shoulders as I reached to embrace him. I'm not sure how long it lasted, Susan. It was a bit clumsy, my first kiss, you know, but really, Susan," Emily said, her eyes aglow, "it was perfect."

Thankfully, both their teacups were on the table when Susan leapt to embrace Emily, whose tears of joy and laughter would not stop.

Just then, Michelle appeared at the sunroom door. Seeing Susan and Emily within, she was already backing away when Susan looked up and called her inside.

"Come in, Michelle," she said, "We've been so busy talking I didn't see your car pass by the window. Emily has been catching me up about her work at the hospital."

When Emily heard Susan say, "her work at the hospital," she couldn't prevent another burst of laughter, which brought Michelle to their side.

"Now I have to know, ladies," Michelle said. "No holding out on something this good."

Emily looked at Susan as if to ask permission, to which Susan replied, "It's your story, Emily, but it's too good to keep to yourself. If you don't tell it, I don't know how I'll be able to restrain myself from doing it for you!"

Emily looked at Michelle and said, "I think you'd best be seated for this, Michelle."

Together, the ladies took their places on the settee with Emily in the center. She rehearsed the whole story for Michelle as the women celebrated each pause with laughter. By the time Emily got to the kiss, they were exhausted. Before the gathering broke up, Susan went to the study and returned with a bottle and three glasses.

"I understand from what we learned today, Emily, that you're rather keen on raspberry," Susan said, "so let us toast the future with a taste of raspberry cordial."

"Oh, dear," Emily said, her face dropping. "I find I need to make a confession."

Surprised, Michelle asked, "A confession?"

Emily began, "Yes. You see, I've never been all that keen on raspberry. However," she smiled, "it became my favorite the moment it fell off Andrew's tongue!"

When their laughter subsided, the ladies sipped and talked, and Michelle took the opportunity to invite Emily to join her wedding party. Overwhelmed, of course, Emily accepted Michelle's invitation, looking forward to the fitting for her dress in Charlottetown the following afternoon.

"I'll pick you up at the hospital tomorrow," Susan said, "and we'll gather Michelle, and we'll go to St. Onge's together if you like."

"That will be lovely," Emily said, "and if Andrew is available, perhaps you two could meet informally."

"I'll hope to meet him then," Susan said, "but for now, ladies," she said, lifting her glass, "here's to love and laughter. Long may they be ours!"

The ladies emptied their glasses and, with hugs all around, left the west sunroom to the last rays of the October sun.

Chapter 25

Sitting at his desk in his airfield office in Charlottetown, Flt Lt Grayson Royce thought back to the weekend. On Friday, he and Michelle were having dinner with Michael and Susan when Grayson announced the subject of his last afternoon meeting. Unknown to Michelle, he had scheduled a meeting with Fr. Hunt at St. Peter's Cathedral to reserve a date for their wedding. Grayson chose a date just ten days away. Michelle, completely surprised, was overwhelmed with laughter and tears, and although he had proposed only weeks ago, she agreed on the wedding date in an instant. In retrospect, however, Grayson felt guilty. He wanted to apologize to Michelle for his impulsivity in setting the date, effectively denying her any part in the decision. It was no way to begin a marriage where they made decisions together. Grayson felt his compulsion to set the date was related to some seminal events from his childhood. It all began during the Great War.

Grayson was seven when his father left home to fly as a reconnaissance pilot with the Royal Flying Corps. He marveled that his father could fly almost three miles in the air with a camera attached to the fuselage of his airplane. At that altitude, sometimes flying above the clouds, he took photos of enemy artillery and troops to help British soldiers direct their forces on the ground. Grayson's mother drew some comfort, knowing that his aircraft would be flying beyond the range of enemy fire.

Soon after reporting for duty, though, Major Royce chose to pursue training as a fighter pilot, flying a Sopwith Camel, a biplane equipped with two machine guns and several twenty-pound Cooper bombs. He flew mission after mission with other equally daring airmen. Though his Sopwith was often hit by enemy fire, he was left unharmed. It was in May of 1917, during the Battle of Arras, while strafing German artillery positions, that he and his Sopwith were shot down by ground fire.

Although he was able to guide the limping bi-plane back behind British lines, the crash and resulting fire took his life.

Ten-year-old Grayson, his mother, and his sister were left with only their memories. The photos of his father smiling in the cockpit of his Bristol Scout and later in his Sopwith Camel remained Grayson's inspiration, leading him to join the RAF six years ago. With his enlistment nearly expired, Britain was again at war, and Grayson knew the RAF would need his continued service.

He sat back in his chair, remembering the last time he saw his father at the railway station in New Mills. There were dozens of families saying goodbyes that rainy day in March. Most soldiers boarding the train wore British Army uniforms, but his father, a Major in the Royal Flying Corps, stood out from the rest. That day, Grayson had charge of his sister, Nancy, and their umbrella. Once at the station, though, he closed the umbrella, and it became his machine gun as he became a gunner shooting at the enemy from his father's airplane.

Grayson remembered his mother clinging to his father at the station. Mother had pressed his uniform the night before, but today, she feared her tears would soil his shoulder as she clung to him. He remembered his father brushing away Mother's tears with the handkerchief he took from her hand, reassuring her that he would be home again soon. Just before he boarded the train, Father had taken Grayson aside to say, "Grayson, you're the man of the house until I get home. Take care of your mother and your sister for me." Grayson nodded as his father took his hand, shook it firmly, and knelt to look into his eyes. "Make me proud, Son," were his final words before pulling Grayson close to embrace him one last time.

When the official RFC notification of his father's death arrived two years later, Grayson fell numb. Despite his father's request, he was unprepared to care for anyone. His family's prayers, every morning, every meal, every night before bed, and every Sunday at church had gone unanswered. He couldn't handle his own grief, much less his mother's and his sister's. Initially, he cried hot, angry tears. Then, not knowing why, he began to eschew his tears as useless, foolish, and unmanly. He did what he could to please his father, though, caring for Mother and Nancy, cooking breakfast when Mother couldn't get up in the morning, getting Nancy ready for school, and even doing the marketing on occasion.

One phrase, once spoken, still lived in Grayson's soul. "Make me proud, Son." He never thought of his father without hearing those four words. That echo was a constant and unrelenting companion, a measure by which he learned to live. Those words directed him in whatever arena he was called to perform, domestic, academic, or as an officer in the RAF.

Grayson's aide knocked at the door to deliver the morning mail, and Grayson returned from his boyhood in New Mills to the reality of October 1939 in Charlottetown. Putting his father's last words aside, he thought once more of Michelle. She had lost her mother when she was but two, and for twenty years, she had lived with an empty place in her heart, only recently and miraculously filled by her mother's return from captivity. How would Michelle cope if his orders sent him to Europe? He'd had those thoughts for two weeks now. At the same time, he remained more firmly convicted than ever that he and Michelle were to be married. Following that conviction, he had sought the earliest opportunity for them to take their vows.

But now, there was even more to consider. As an RAF training officer assigned to prepare Canadian pilots for battle, Grayson had received some recent assessments concerning the current state of the Canadian military. First, the Royal Canadian Army numbered less than 5,000 men, with another 51,000 reservists whose training was meager and incomplete. The RCA's weapons and equipment dated back to the Great War. Second, the RCAF had fewer than twenty combat-worthy aircraft to defend their nation from enemy attacks on the east and west coasts. They desperately needed hundreds of modern aircraft and many more airmen ready to fly them. Third, the RCN's fleet included only six ships, all aged destroyers, the smallest in their class among warships. Clearly, Canada was unprepared and poorly equipped for war.

Of course, Grayson's immediate concern was his training assignment in Charlottetown, which, he discovered, would be expanding immediately. The recent addition of RAF personnel in Charlottetown was only the beginning of a nationwide aircrew training program of incredible proportions originating in the UK. Called the British Commonwealth Air Training Plan, trainees from around the globe, 13,000 in all, were destined for training in Canada as pilots, navigators, gunners, bombers, and radio operators. Construction of new airfields and training facilities was about to begin nationwide.

For Grayson, the sudden expansion of the RCAF's training program offered a chance for some stability. Certainly, his life would be in less peril if the RAF needed him to train new airmen in Canada, compared to flying a fighter in a warzone in Europe. However, the location of his service was not guaranteed, for even if he stayed in Canada, the plan included building airfields and training facilities in dozens of locations across the country. Soon, he could be training pilots as far away as Canada's west coast.

But then, he heard an echo within, "Make me proud, Son."

That echo persisted for four years at Eton, beginning when he was thirteen. While following in his father's footsteps, his mother's refrain remained constant, "Remember, Grayson, what your father said . . . " No matter how well he performed, his achievements rarely satisfied her need to keep his father's memory alive. After another four years of study at Oxford, Grayson considered no other career option than enlistment in the Royal Air Force.

To Grayson, his last chance to make his father proud meant flying as his father flew, risking his life as a fighter pilot in wartime. Today, he heard an almost audible voice whispering, "Why aren't you applying for combat service?"

Shaking his head, Grayson stood to compose his thoughts. His heart's desire was to marry Michelle, stay in Canada, and fulfill his commitment to the RAF as a training officer for as long as they needed him.

"Michelle," he said aloud. "She trusts me but doesn't know the memories that echo within. She needs to know. She deserves to know. Love owes her that."

Chapter 26

With a wedding a week away, Susan and Michael found no better time to begin their deportment classes with Highfield's young women and young men. Of course, it was a busy time at Highfield with a wedding reception upcoming, but the wedding party was small, and all were old friends. Each of the young people had a role to play in preparing and serving from the menus, but they also needed to prepare for their roles in the wedding ceremony. Part of that preparation involved their lessons in deportment.

Because Ingrid and Patrice had spent time with Susan and Michelle over the last year at sleepovers and other celebrations, Susan found the girls eager to spend time with her now, hanging on her every word. But the time they would spend together now wasn't about dressing up and trying out makeup. Susan had carefully prepared lessons for her students in areas of their lives where they were ignorant in the kindest sense of the word. The girls met her in her dressing room, where Susan invited them to sit on her settee.

"So, ladies, Susan said, we have a limited time to cover everything I have planned for you, so we'll begin with deportment. Can either of you tell me what 'deportment' means?" she asked.

Patrice looked at Ingrid, who shrugged before turning back to Susan. Ingrid shook her head and said, "We don't know, Miss Susan."

"Then we're starting at the right place," Susan said. "How you behave and present yourself, whether in private or public, determines the quality of your deportment. Please notice that I said '*your* deportment,'" she continued, "for each of us is responsible for our own. If you are polite when you speak, dress appropriately, and remain respectfully soft-spoken, the world will recognize your excellent deportment."

Ingrid and Patrice nodded as Susan continued.

"Wherever we travel in our public lives, we will be judged by how we present ourselves. Often, we have but one opportunity to present ourselves well, for the world is quick to judge and often long to remember. So, with only one opportunity to make a good first impression," Susan said, "we must make sure that we present ourselves well."

Susan held their attention as she continued, "Polite people who smile and enjoy being helpful encourage others to do the same. If we are grumpy and rude and use coarse language, the world will find us objectionable, judging our poor deportment. Those who make others uncomfortable by their poor behavior are neither remembered well nor soon forgotten. We must carry ourselves and present ourselves every day in the way we wish to be remembered. Does that make sense to you, ladies?" Susan asked.

"Yes," the girls echoed.

"Now," Susan said, "tell me about a time you remember when someone's deportment either frightened you or made you feel uncomfortable."

The girls had no problem recounting instances where they were offended, whether by having their feelings hurt, feeling judged, or feeling unsafe. Sometimes, their hurt feelings had come from feeling poor in town among wealthy people who ignored or avoided them on the sidewalk. At other times, older girls at their previous school had treated them poorly. Then there were the boys who seemed to be able to make any girl uncomfortable by staring or pointing while talking to the other boys.

"So, adults, other girls, and boys can all affect us by their deportment, correct?" Susan asked.

"Yes," Ingrid said as Patrice nodded.

"And what can you do when that happens?" Susan asked.

"Mom says to ignore them," Patrice said, "but that's not always easy."

"No, it's not," Susan agreed. "Sometimes we can avoid them, and other times we may have the freedom to leave a room or go elsewhere, but it is always up to us to remain polite. Often, that isn't easy."

The girls were quick to agree.

"I have one more question, ladies," Susan said. "I want you to think hard and be honest with me. Have you ever been somewhere when someone made you feel unsafe, you know, when something felt . . . " Susan paused as she searched for a word.

"Creepy?" Ingrid asked.

"Yes, that's a good word for it," Susan agreed.

"Yes," Patrice said. "There's a man who sits on the porch at the feed store who always looks at me."

"And there are two boys there, too, who whisper to each other and walk around me, looking," Ingrid said.

"Excellent, ladies," Susan said happily. "When you get that feeling, listen to it, use your feet, and find a safe place with adults, if possible. That is very important. I'm proud of you for telling me about it."

The girls all smiled as Susan said, "We'll discuss more at our next meeting, but now we're going to spend some time on a young lady's posture. So, let's stand and walk out to the staircase. Here is a book for each of you to wear."

"To wear?" Patrice asked.

"Yes, Patrice, on top of your head, like this," Susan said as she placed a book on her head. "Now, follow me up and down the stairs with your book in place."

With a little practice, the books spent less time on the stairs, but it was clear that the girls needed more practice before mastering their tasks.

Meanwhile, Michael was meeting with Luc and Joseph in the study. Keeping their attention off the gun cabinet was Michael's first job, but once the boys understood that requirement, Michael offered them the lesson in deportment that Susan had crafted so well. Half an hour later, when they finished that portion of their class, Michael asked an additional question of his own.

"Gentlemen, I have a question for you," he said as he handed them a sheet of paper and a pencil. "I don't want you to answer right away. This is a time for thoughtful consideration before you respond. I want you to write your thoughts on your paper, but I won't be collecting them. They'll be yours to keep. I'll let you know when I need a verbal response," Michael said, "OK?"

The boys nodded.

Michael began, "My first question is this. When does a boy become a man?"

The boys looked at Michael and then at each other. Eventually, each made notes on his paper before Michael's second question.

"All right," Michael said, "turn your papers over for your second question." As they did, Michael asked, "When does a girl become a young woman?"

A sudden awkwardness filled the room. The boys didn't seem comfortable looking at each other or Michael, and as time passed, neither had written more than a few words on his paper.

"All right," Michael said, "you can put your pencils down and turn your papers over to the first side."

Michael began as the boys turned their papers, "I'm sure you had some good answers, but we're not here to gather facts. You see, every boy will mature in his body eventually and go through the physical changes that will make him a man. However, there is a time given to both of you, Luc and Joseph, that does not involve changes in your bodies. The changes that make you young men will happen in your attitudes about yourself and others."

The boys looked at Michael, but nothing in their faces showed they understood him.

"Being a man is not about your age, your size, or how much work you can do," Michael said. "Being a man is about your heart. It's about who you are." He continued, "Being a man is about how you treat others, especially women, young or old, whom you are to respect, protect, and serve. Being a man is about caring for others in need, whoever they are."

Michael continued, "Some boys never become men, even though they live into old age. They live small, uncaring lives. Others, like a shepherd boy named David, take on giants because they know who they are and who they serve. If you, Luc, and you, Joseph, want to be men, then your eyes will always be open to the needs of others, especially the needs of women and all others we can help. That's what makes a man."

The boys nodded, catching the vision Michael shared with them, perhaps thinking back to a time when a man somewhere had once cared for them.

"You are growing up with young women, Luc and Joseph. I need to be able to count on you as men to show them the honor that is due to them because we, as men, are their protectors. Can I count on you for that, men?" he asked.

"Yes, Mr. Moreland," they answered.

"Thank you, Luc. Thank you, Joseph. Thank you, young men," Michael emphasized. "I will rely on you in the future to remember our call."

As the young men rose to leave, Michael added, "By the way, someday you'll need some skills to help you protect those in your care. Your classes in hand-to-hand combat begin after school tomorrow.

Two big smiles shone back at Michael's as the boys left the study together.

Chapter 27

Grayson and Michelle returned from breakfast at Tea For Two after attending morning prayer at St. Peter's. They talked in Grayson's staff car on the curb in front of Verrier's Hardware for almost an hour.

Before he finished, Grayson shared the story that had kept him awake most of the previous night after he and Michelle left Michael and Susan at the Port O' Call. He left no stone unturned, especially concerning his relationship with his parents and all the years he had spent trying to please them. He rehearsed how he had worked harder in every arena of his life, always trying to make his father proud but never sure he had succeeded. When he began to consider applying for combat duty during the last several weeks, a final attempt to please his father, he knew he had to make a bigger decision that embraced the future, freeing him from the past. That choice was Michelle, and Grayson was committed to abandoning anything that might come between them. He needed to apologize to Michelle for allowing his old demons to threaten the new life he craved with her.

When he finished, Michelle was grateful to understand much more about the man she was about to marry. Nothing he had told her made her love or respect him less. If anything, she loved him more. He bore wounds from his childhood, as everyone does. He had given himself orders and made himself promises, as everyone does. He had failed to meet his parents' expectations, as everyone does. But then Grayson did something that not everyone else does. Grayson had trusted her, unafraid to reveal his wounded heart, injured pride, and fears of failure. He was a man like every other man, but now more than ever, a man Michelle knew she could trust. Grayson finished where he had begun their conversation, apologizing for hurting the woman he loved.

"So, please forgive me, Michelle, for leaving you out of a decision we should have made together. Even after abandoning my thoughts of combat service, I pushed ahead, anxious to be in control, speaking with Fr. Hunt without you. I presumed on you and gave you no choice but to accept a wedding date I had chosen. We should have chosen it together, Michelle. Would you please forgive me?" he begged.

He could not have asked a safer question. Michelle reached to embrace him, and he melted into her arms. His wounded heart was safe next to hers, for her forgiveness was immediate.

"Yes, Grayson," Michelle whispered into his ear. "Now and always, for on Saturday, two wounded hearts will become one, until death us do part. I'm glad we don't have to wait one extra day to start our journey together."

Grayson and Michelle walked hand-in-hand to her door. They felt a quiet exhaustion that many couples feel a few days from marriage. But their weariness wasn't the result of the burdens that wedding plans often bring. No, their tiredness was different. It came from the quiet relief of putting old burdens down.

Chapter 28

On Tuesday afternoon, when Susan arrived at Charlottetown Hospital in her cabriolet, Emily stood waiting inside, looking out the window from the office lobby. Excited to be on her way to a fitting for the bridesmaid's dress she would wear at Michelle's wedding, she hurried to the car as soon as Susan drew up to the curb.

"Oh, Susan," she said as she closed the car door, "I've never been a bridesmaid before. In truth, your wedding was the first I've attended."

"With your nursing career in London, where nurses didn't marry, I'm not surprised," Susan said.

"Tell me about my responsibilities, if you will, Susan," Emily said. "I so want to do well."

Susan explained that the wedding rehearsal on Friday evening would settle all the details for Emily's duties during the wedding service. "Mostly," Susan explained, "your responsibility is to help me make sure that Michelle needs to do nothing but walk down the aisle and look serene. There are times when I will have to hold the bouquet she carries," Susan said, "so I will hand you mine. You'll have one, too, so it's a simple matter of holding both and handing mine back when my hands are free again."

"I think I can handle that," Emily said. "Is there anything else?"

"Often bridesmaids are paired with groomsmen who serve as their escorts, but Michelle's wedding party is rather sparse. I'm paired with Michael, of course. During the wedding ceremony, you'll be paired with Michelle's brother, Steve."

"Oh, yes," Emily said, "I met Steve at the Verrier home when I was attending Anna."

"Of course," Susan said, "when we process down the aisle ahead of Michelle, we will assemble on the left, the bride's side, while the men will assemble on the right with Grayson."

"I see," Emily said, trying to visualize the wedding party in the church.

"As I understand it," Susan began, "Michelle has invited Steve's girl-friend to the wedding. I'm sure she and Steve will sit together for the luncheon and reception afterward."

"So, I'll be alone then?" Emily asked.

"Yes," Susan said, "unless you were to ask Michelle if she might invite a guest of your choice. Does anyone come to mind?" Susan asked, smiling.

"That would be somewhat forward of me, wouldn't it, Susan? Why, neither Michelle nor Grayson nor anyone at Highfield has met Andrew," Emily said.

"Perhaps," Susan allowed, "but the guest list is very short, so numbers aren't a problem. Michelle would need to meet Andrew and offer the invitation, though," Susan continued, "so, if Andrew were able to drive you home to Highfield tomorrow afternoon while Michelle and I are decorating . . . " Susan said, casting a knowing eye Emily's way.

"Then I could invite him in and introduce him to you and Michelle?" Emily asked.

"What a wonderful idea, Emily! I wish I'd thought of it!" Susan said, laughing. "Andrew might also enjoy meeting Lady Moncrieff, a longtime supporter of St. Luke's Hospital in Lowestoft."

"Susan," Emily said, "are you sure Michelle and your mother want to meet Andrew? Would I be presuming on them?"

"I'm sure Michelle will be fine," Susan said, "and I know my mother has been hoping to visit the hospital for some time. You'd be helping her to be received there in the future. Besides, if you agree, leave Michelle and Mother to me. I'll let you know in the morning."

In another moment, Susan slowed the car as they approached St. Onge's. She saw Michelle on the sidewalk near the front door as they approached the curb.

"Oh, there's Michelle now," Emily said. "Remind me to tell both of you about my morning meeting with Andrew today, will you, Susan?"

"Another meeting with Andrew?" Susan asked. "Of course, I'll remind you," she said. Suddenly intrigued, Susan knew that once Emily's fitting was finished, the ladies would have something interesting to discuss. She could hardly wait.

Michelle had chosen fall colors for her attendants' dresses, an orange, leaning toward apricot. Having never been fitted for a dress before, Emily took a little longer than usual, changing out of her uniform in the dressing room. To everyone's surprise, Emily resembled a Hollywood movie star when she entered the fitting room. Standing almost three inches taller than either Susan or Michelle, in a dress clinging to her figure, she could hardly believe her reflection in the mirror.

"Oh, my," she said, "can that be me?"

Isabel, the seamstress from St. Onge's who was fitting the dress, said, "Oh, yes, Miss. It is you, but I must apologize. We'll have to do a little better for you. Let's see," she said, backing away for a better look. "We'll need to take the waistline in here," she said, adding some pins at the waist, "and we'll give you a little more breathing room up above where you are filling out the bodice so amply," she added, looking at Susan and Michelle who could do nothing but nod. Giving Emily an approving look, Isabel added, "I'm afraid our standard in-house measurements don't account for women with starlet figures like yours, Miss." Then, as Emily blushed, Isabel added, "But, then again, with eyes that blue, Miss, there'll be many who'll hardly notice a dress this fine."

Susan and Michelle looked on in complete surprise. They were accustomed to seeing Emily in her nurse's uniform or dressed modestly, always in several conservative layers. Today, they were discovering an Emily they'd never known before.

Still blushing at the compliments that salted Isabel's comments, Emily looked out again at Susan and Michelle, who beamed back at her. Isabel added a few more pins, and after adjusting the hem, Emily was ready to return to the dressing room. Three thoroughly delighted women left St. Onge's for lunch a short time later.

With Emily still tittering excitedly in the car, Susan looked in the rearview mirror toward the back seat to catch her attention.

"So, Emily, you said you had another meeting with Andrew today?"

"Yes, I did," she said. "It was an unscheduled meeting, though. Fortunately, I had taken my tea earlier, and I'd already planned on taking lunch with you after the fitting at St. Onge's, so our meeting ended just before you arrived at the hospital, Susan."

As Susan pulled up to the curb at the Cask and Cork, Emily said, "I can tell you more inside."

After the ladies had ordered lunch, Susan caught Michelle's eye before turning to Emily to ask, "So, Emily, you had a meeting with Andrew earlier?"

"Yes," Emily began, "But it wasn't really a meeting. Andrew had no business to discuss today."

"What do you mean?" Michelle asked.

"Well, Andrew had hardly closed the door when," Emily paused, "we seemed to find ourselves back where our last meeting ended."

"But that meeting ended with a kiss, if I remember correctly," Susan said.

"Yes, you are correct," Emily agreed. "Today, Andrew and I entered his office, and he invited me to sit on his settee. As I took my place, Andrew walked to his desk and removed his stethoscope. When he returned and sat beside me, he surprised me as he reached up, gently unpinned my cap, and placed it on the table next to us. Then he reached for my hands, one at a time, lifted them to his lips, and kissed each gently. Then he moved even closer, looked into my eyes, and we began again where we had left off the last time we were alone."

Leaning toward Emily, Michelle asked quietly, "He kissed you?"

"Oh, yes," Emily said, nodding, her eyes wide. "He looked deeply into my eyes, leaned forward, and without saying a word, embraced me, holding me close as my hands found their way toward each other at the back of his neck. Then, gently but firmly, he kissed me. This kiss was very different from our last," Emily said, breathing deeply.

"Different?" Susan asked.

"Well, you may remember that our first kiss was a surprise for both of us, actually, and quite clumsy," Emily said, "but not this one."

"So, it wasn't a surprise, or it wasn't clumsy, Emily. Which?" Michelle asked.

"Both," Emily answered. "I expected it might happen again when he closed the door, and we were alone. But, last time, the kiss was just, well," she thought, "a kiss. This time, there were several, and they were not at all like our first," Emily said, shaking her head.

Leaning forward, Susan asked, "How so?"

Emily leaned closer for privacy before saying, "Our first kiss was the type a mother or grandmother might offer, perfunctory, you know; more like a debt than a delight, rather dry and dispassionate." Then, as her eyes widened, she continued, "Today, I assure you, Andrew's kisses were certainly not dry. Neither were they dispassionate!"

"I see," Susan said as her eyes widened, and Michelle mouthed a knowing, "Oh-h-h."

"If I had to describe them in a single word," Emily said, looking toward the ceiling and pondering, "I would have to say his kisses were hungry, perhaps even ravenous." Then, with her eyes smiling, she added, "And, I would also have to say that they made me feel, well," she sighed, "delicious."

Michelle and Susan looked at each other and then back at Emily before Susan said, "And did you respond to his kisses in kind, Emily?"

Emily shook her head. "No, I didn't," she said, "at least not at first. I was a bit overwhelmed by his energy at the beginning. But by our second and third kisses," she said, nodding, "I did respond, having learned so much from *his* kisses. And," she said meekly, but with a hint of a smile, "he seemed to enjoy that very much."

"Why do you say that, Emily?" Michelle asked.

"Well, he didn't use words, of course," Emily said, "but do you know the sound one makes when the peach jam on one's morning scone is just perfect? Mmm-m-m? That was the sound he made, a sort of inner sigh of delight that he repeated again and again during each kiss."

Unknown to Emily, Susan and Michelle were captive to her every word. Finally, Susan asked, "And then, Emily?"

"Well, a few seconds later, he turned his attention to my neck and kissed a path to my left earlobe, nibbling at it when he arrived. I lifted my ear toward him just a little to make his task easier, you know. He seemed to enjoy my earlobe and my neck, where he placed his kisses just under my ear," she said, pointing, "but I'm afraid my starched collar provided an unwelcome obstacle. He had just begun to whisper something in my ear when there was a knock at the door, and he was called away."

"And that was all, then?" Michelle asked.

"Yes, that was all. It was a rather abrupt ending, but I must confess my heart rate remained elevated for some time afterward. Talking about it now is still exciting," Emily said, blushing.

The women took a moment to catch their breath before Susan broke the silence.

"If I may offer some advice, Emily?" Susan asked.

"Of course," Emily answered, "please do, Susan."

"You must always remember that it is up to us as women to maintain our feminine decorum when alone with a man. We must not begin to enjoy the moment so thoroughly that we fail to remain in charge. You do understand what I mean, don't you?" Susan asked.

"I believe so, Susan," Emily said, "and thank you. I am traveling on uncharted ground. I've never imagined that a man could take an interest in me like this. As you know, I've eschewed relationships with men because of my profession. Now, though, everything has changed, and I so appreciate both of you," she said, looking at Susan and again at Michelle, "for caring for me. If that is not an imposition, I hope we can talk like this often."

Susan and Michelle had to laugh as Susan said, "Don't worry, Emily. We thrive on girl talk. Call on us, anytime!"

Chapter 29

While the French failed to advance on the western front and the British Expedition Force waited in Belgium, SIS headquarters in London continued to receive distressing reports of German and Russian atrocities in Poland. Sir Richard stood amazed at the inhuman behavior that SIS sources continued to recount.

Indiscriminate Luftwaffe bombings on civilian targets and residential districts in the first days of the war had killed tens of thousands of Poles. Even worse, reports of the initial attacks by the Wehrmacht's ground forces included episode after episode of indiscriminate shootings of prisoners of war and civilians. Though the horror of many such events had been recognized and documented by Hiler's SS, Hitler issued a blanket pardon for all German personnel involved. The same troops burned more than five hundred towns and villages and collaborated in hundreds more mass shootings over the next several weeks.

The Russian army was no less cruel. Although they invaded Poland sixteen days after Germany's initial attack, in the first weeks of the war, SIS estimated that Russia took more than 300,000 Polish prisoners. Many were killed in mass executions, while others were deported to Russia to serve in labor camps.

Meanwhile, reports of other horrors perpetrated against civilians in Germany and Poland, especially Jews, came in daily. As far away as Vienna, thousands of Jews had been deported to Lublin in Poland, where many others had already been gathered and imprisoned. Polish university professors, business executives, bankers, churchmen, and other noteworthy community leaders among the populace frequently disappeared overnight or were killed trying to escape. Sir Richard concluded that Hitler was not interested in dealing with the best Poland had to offer. His goal was to strip a nation of its leaders to create a nation of slaves that he could control by terror.

With winter approaching, civilians remaining in Poland were facing starvation along with all the suffering that the winter cold would bring. At the same time, the occupying German and Russian troops grew no less cruel, with new rumors daily of atrocities involving women and children, often committed while helpless fathers and sons were held at gunpoint and forced to look on.

As he read, Sir Richard could not help but feel guilty for the comforts he knew and the safety his family enjoyed, but more for the inaction of the British and French forces sitting and waiting, aware of the suffering in Poland. The world was watching, too, calling the war the "Bore War" in England or, more recently, the "Phony War," as the US press had dubbed it. The war at sea continued to claim its toll on merchant, passenger, and military targets. In that realm, Sir Richard knew only one comfort: his sons serving in the Royal Navy were far from the dangers the men in bunkers and foxholes in Belgium and France knew. Although U-boats were a constant threat to any British ship at sea, Sir Richard, a man well acquainted with war at sea, remained confident in Britain's naval prowess. That confidence, though, still depended on one more powerful and more able than the Royal Navy.

"God keep them," he prayed, "comfort them with your rod and staff," he begged as he left his office tonight. The damp London air greeted him at the door as he walked toward his flat through the early evening fog. He wondered what the weather was bringing to Highfield tonight. Yes, it was time to send Angela another letter. He would have one ready for the post in the morning.

Chapter 30

D r. Andrew MacMillan, a consummate professional dedicated to fulfilling his call to the healing arts as the Chief of Staff at Charlottetown Hospital, looked into his bathroom mirror as he prepared to shave early on a late October morning. All who knew him in his familiar role as a hospital administrator and a highly skilled surgeon would find it hard to recognize him as the man he faced in his mirror today. A dreamy-eyed, sophomoric, smitten young man looked back at him, belying his nearly thirty-six years. Nowadays, it seemed the most mundane tasks had the power to confuse him, as he had discovered a moment earlier when he realized that the shaving cream he had just squeezed into his hand was, in fact, toothpaste. Once again, the immediate moment was lost to him, for his mind continued to wander an hour into the future when Nurse Emily Langdon would report for her regular shift at the hospital.

This statuesque, dark-haired, blue-eyed woman enthralled him, though she had never made the least effort to attract his attention. On the contrary, it wasn't her appearance but her professionalism that appealed to him initially. However, after working closely with her during a life-saving episode in the Accident Room, the young doctor's life seemed to change forever. Her care for their patient and him during those hours had left an indelible impression on him that eclipsed his rational mind and had since been inscribed on his heart.

During his years at university and later at medical school, he had worked with many young women. Still, those times had remained lonely times out of necessity. His primary objectives were his education and medical training, which required a singular dedication. As an intern, he dared not allow himself the luxury of a romantic relationship, which might jeopardize the concentration required by the demands of his profession. In Charlottetown, however, in the simple setting of this rural hospital, he had discovered a woman who had the power to steal his concentration at a glance. Though he might have once despised her power to distract him, today it held him happily captive. So, this morning, he paid particular attention to shaving closely, applying just the right amount of bay rum, and combing every hair into place. He wanted nothing in his appearance to distract or offend her. He hoped, rather, that he might find a way to attract her, as it seemed he had been able to do the last time they met. He had been bold then, inviting her into his office, holding her, kissing her. But then, when she kissed back, responding to the passion that overcame him, his hope for an answer to his loneliness rejoiced.

He blushed when he remembered his boldness, though he marveled at her response as she followed his lead and entrusted her obvious inexperience to his care. Overwhelmed and surprised by his passion, he was strangely relieved by the interruption of a knock at his door. Given another opportunity, however, he wondered if he might be bold enough to ignore a similar knock in the future.

Today brought a different challenge. Although Emily and he had met professionally only briefly during his rounds yesterday, she had taken that moment to ask a favor. Stopping at the second-floor solarium reserved for family and visitors, she asked, "A moment, Dr. MacMillan?"

"Of course, Nurse Langdon," he responded as they stopped just inside the open door.

"I should like to ask the favor of a ride home to Highfield this afternoon and perhaps a moment or two of your time within upon our arrival," Emily asked.

Thinking a moment, he answered, "I've nothing scheduled then, so barring an emergency that might delay me, I'm sure I can oblige."

Emily smiled as he continued, "But, may I ask what I might expect at Highfield when we arrive there?"

"Of course, Doctor," Emily answered. "Please forgive me," she said, embarrassed by his need to ask. "I would like you to meet Lady Moncrieff, her daughter, Susan, and another friend visiting there. Lady Moncrieff has long supported the medical community in Suffolk, England. Since she is new to Prince Edward Island, I feel certain she would enjoy meeting the Chief of Staff of Charlottetown Hospital."

The words "longtime supporter" captured the doctor's attention.

"Then I shall be all the more delighted to make such a visit," he said, smiling, "and," he began, looking to see if anyone might overhear, "I shall enjoy the moments we share away from the hospital as we drive."

"Thank you, Doctor MacMillan," Emily said. "Shall I await you in the lobby at the end of our shift?" she asked.

"I'll park my car at the curb just outside the lobby, and I will look forward to meeting you there, Nurse Langdon," he said with a smile in his eyes.

It took both a few moments to recover after their conversation. Overjoyed, both worked to regain a posture of professionalism, which required them to relax smiles that rebelled at being suppressed. Andrew wondered if this invitation was tantamount to a first meeting with Emily's family, a step indicating a significant advance in the seriousness of their relationship from her perspective. Unknown to him, though, Emily, not yet fully accustomed to thinking of herself as a marriageable woman, merely hoped to impress Highfield and Michelle and perhaps secure an escort for Michelle's wedding. As the afternoon at the hospital wore on, she found herself somewhat distracted at the thought of being alone with Andrew in his car for the drive to Highfield. One part of her hoped the drive would offer only fifteen minutes of idle conversation, while another hoped for something more exciting. She suspected that Andrew might be suffering from the same distraction this afternoon.

She was correct.

In his office during the last half hour of the day, Andrew dedicated himself to clearing his desk of its wealth of weekly reports and correspondence. When he had restored sufficient order, he spent a moment in his lavatory checking his appearance and exchanging his white lab coat for his gray tweed sports jacket. With his briefcase in hand, he left the hospital to retrieve his car in the parking lot and drove to the sidewalk in front of the lobby entrance. When he arrived at the curb, he could see Emily within. She was already on her way out as he walked to the door.

Still wearing her nurse's cap when Andrew opened the car door, she thanked him and sat down. They smiled but said nothing until they pulled away from the curb.

"I know we both feel somewhat awkward, Emily, afraid that our small hospital community is watching our every movement," Andrew said, "and for a perfectly good reason. They are!" he laughed.

With the ice broken, Emily laughed as well.

"Thankfully, they have become very much like family to me," she said, "so I must believe they are merely curious rather than anything less kind."

"I hope it stays that way, Emily," Andrew said, "because I don't want anyone's opinion to distract us from a professional relationship that I find entirely appropriate."

"Of course, I agree, Andrew," she said. "Entirely appropriate."

They drove in silence for several minutes, both knowing there was so much more to be said.

"Emily," Andrew began again, "May I share my mind with you concerning our relationship?"

"Of course, Andrew," she said, not knowing what to expect.

He began, "Although our call to healing demands the highest professional standards, I believe our humanity, that part within," he said, pointing to his heart, "which gives us the ability to empathize and care for others with whole and healthy hearts, requires a substantial degree of consideration for ourselves as well."

"I would not disagree," Emily said.

"I feel I am being very bold," he continued, "but I find myself helpless to be anything but bold these days. I am a man of faith, and a word from my childhood catechism keeps ringing in my head, a word that failed to impress me in the past. May I share it with you, Emily?" he asked.

"Yes," she answered, "if you feel I am one you can trust with such a confession."

"I do," he said, "and it is this. 'It is not good for man to be alone.'"

"I recognize those words from the book of Genesis," Emily said, "in the garden, just before God made woman."

"Precisely," Andrew answered, pleased that Emily was familiar with the words he shared, "just before God made woman."

Neither said anything for a moment before Andrew spoke again.

"Emily," he said, "I have concluded that I have lived a solitary life too long. I sense that perhaps you have, as well. I fervently hope that you will join me in exploring the possibility of ending our solitary lives and sharing new lives together. I know I am asking a great deal of you, especially since our relationship is in its infancy. However, I would be most grateful if you would be willing to consider such a question."

They drove for another moment before Emily answered.

"Andrew, I have believed too long that my call as a nurse has made a relationship with a man impossible. I am convinced now that such a conclusion has been in error."

"Then," Andrew said, "could I hope we might shed our loneliness together?"

"In many ways, Andrew," she said, "I believe we have already begun."

As Andrew reached his hand across the seat toward Emily, she gave him hers. Their hands remained clasped until he slowed the car to downshift and turn into Highfield's driveway. Then he stopped the car and turned to her.

"There is one thing more, Emily," he said. "I need to ask your forgiveness. I was far too forward during our last moments in my office. I must confess that I find you almost irresistible, but that is no excuse for my lack of self-control. Please know that I shall do better in the future."

"Of course, I forgive you," Emily said, "although I find there is little to forgive. I confess that your kisses are the first I've known, and I am sure my responses have been awkward. Nonetheless, let us rely on each other's conscience in the future. In that way, we will bear the responsibility for each other. It does take two, I am told," she said with a smile.

A moment later, they arrived at Highfield's front entrance. Emily reached to squeeze Andrew's hand and shared another smile before he left the car and opened her door. Together, they walked to Highfield's front door, Emily's hand on Andrew's arm.

Chapter 31

Emily awoke the morning after Andrew's visit at Highfield, thankful for the magical hour they spent with Lady Moncrieff, Susan, and Michelle. Rehearsing the hour moment by moment in her memory, Emily remained convinced that no visit could have been more cordial. During afternoon tea in the west sunroom, Andrew was overjoyed to discover that he and Lady Moncrieff were of one mind concerning the need for an amply funded hospital in Charlottetown. He was thrilled to find a new supporter. Then, after meeting Susan and Michelle and learning of Grayson and Michelle's upcoming nuptials, he was pleased to receive an invitation to the wedding, especially as Emily's escort.

Overnight, however, Emily's mind traveled back to her childhood years in Suffolk and to her time in London with her grandmother. She had made some discoveries that she hoped to discuss with Lady Moncrieff and Susan. She was delighted that they could talk in the study after breakfast.

As Lady Moncrieff and Susan sat together on the settee, Emily began, "Thank you for taking the time to speak with me this morning."

"Of course, Emily," Lady Moncrieff said. "Please tell us what is on your mind."

Emily began earnestly. "I believe I've discovered a principle, a tenet by which I learned to live, even as a child," she said, "but now I believe this precept is not based in truth."

Emily paused as if overcome by the weight of her thoughts, but Lady Moncrieff encouraged her, saying, "Please, Emily, go on."

Beginning again, Emily said, "I was taught that passion in one's life is not a portion allotted to the poor. Rather, I learned that prudence was our portion. Because passion and prudence are such opposites, I learned to eschew the desires and cravings that others feel when they dare to yearn for something that might satisfy their hearts. I believed that feelings like those were the traffic of storybooks, not of real life. I learned not to dream beyond the day. In time, I hardly dared to dream at all. My life grew very small."

As Emily paused, Susan nodded and said, "Please go on, Emily."

Beginning again, Emily said, "In the last few weeks, there has been a change in how I see my lot in the world. The witness of others testifies that they have recognized passion in my work, especially in my care for those in need and those I teach," she explained. "Though I've begun to believe that is true, I also recognize that life is much larger than one's work. I find myself ready to challenge that ruling principle which has prevented me from hoping that someday someone might feel passionate about me, loving me with a love I might dare to requite, making a couple, if you will."

Emily stopped to collect her thoughts, breathed deeply, and said, "And now to cases. If I allow my relationship with Andrew to progress to a logical conclusion, marriage could become a consideration. He has, in fact, intimated as much. However, I also consider my current commitment to you, Lady Moncrieff, to be a precedent for the future. I want you to know that I remain grateful to you and the Moncrieff family and committed to your care. Whatever the future brings, please know that I will allow nothing to interfere with my commitment here and the responsibility I owe to all of you at Highfield."

Almost out of breath and needing a moment to gather herself, Emily looked toward the floor, breathed deeply, and looked up to find Lady Moncrieff's offered hand. Relieved, Emily reached for the outstretched hand and waited to hear what she would say.

"Emily," Lady Moncrieff began, "it seems our family here has been remarkably blessed with a wonderful gift of late. By some divine intervention, it appears that several of us have found freedom from fallacies that have previously ruled our lives. I cannot tell you how delighted I am to learn that you have discovered yours."

Lady Moncrieff continued, "Of course, your portion in this life includes passion, and if that passion includes your love for a good man who will cherish you in like manner, I believe our relationship cannot suffer. On the contrary, Emily, I believe it will thrive," she laughed, "for dear Emily, I don't believe your possible marriage to Dr. MacMillan would leave me bereft of my kind and faithful nurse. Quite the contrary," she continued, "I believe I should instead gain the long-sought care of a doctor!"

With that, she stood to offer her arms in an embrace as Emily rushed to her with a tearful smile of relief. Susan joined both as tears turned to the laughter that only freedom brings. A moment later, they heard Michelle's voice at the front door. Patrice had answered her ring and appeared with a polite knock at the study door.

Summoning her most professional voice, Patrice said, "Excuse me, Lady Moncrieff, but Miss Michelle is here to discuss some details concerning the wedding with Mrs. Moreland."

"Oh, please show her in," Lady Moncrieff said, "we've been expecting her."

With less than twenty-four hours remaining before the service at St. Peter's, Susan sat assured that only the most minor details required attention. The bridal luncheon was set for noon today, while Michael and Steve had plans for Grayson's lunch. The wedding rehearsal was scheduled for five-fifteen, with a rehearsal dinner to follow. The day was full, and all looked forward to the wedding tomorrow at ten o'clock.

"Hello, all," Michelle called as she entered the study. "Mom and Dad are still busy finding some gloves for Mom, and Steve is spending the morning with Brenda, his girlfriend. Grayson has already taken our packed bags for delivery to our honeymoon suite, wherever that is," she laughed. "He hinted at another surprise he has planned for me, but then he ran off to attend to his errands, leaving me guessing. I couldn't stand to be alone another moment at home, so please forgive the intrusion," she said, smiling.

"A bride is permitted any number of intrusions on the eve of her wedding, Michelle," Susan laughed, "but I think your visit hardly qualifies as an intrusion. Please join us."

"Thank you," Michelle began. "I can't think of a detail that needs my worrying, but my nerves won't stop."

"Then we may have to ply you with wine at lunch to help you relax," Susan laughed.

"Or," Lady Moncrieff said, looking toward Emily, "perhaps Nurse Langdon could consult with her gentleman friend, who might provide a suitable sedative for a bride plagued by nerves."

"Oh, Lady Moncrieff," Emily said, her face falling and looking very serious, "I would, but Andrew is in surgery this morning and on call at the hospital for the remainder of the day."

"Emily," Lady Moncrieff laughed as the others joined her, "please don't fret. I intended my suggestion to be humorous." As Emily brightened,

Lady Moncrieff continued, "But, fear not. All of us," she said, as she cast her eyes on the surrounding faces, "will help you learn to laugh with us and at ourselves during Michelle's wedding and well beyond."

"Yes, we will," Susan added, but now, we have only an hour or two before our luncheon with the bride. So, while I whisk her upstairs to let her relax and dress, why don't we do the same? Agreed, ladies?"

With unanimous approval, the ladies rose, and Highfield's study grew quiet once more.

Chapter 32

L t Steve Verrier was glad to be away from his post in Halifax for a few days. Since the beginning of the war, the Ocean Terminals complex had come under the control of Canada's military forces. During the last six months, his post with the RCN was at Pier 21. Although Pier 21, the immigration facility, originally served only civilian traffic, it now regularly served troopships. With military traffic added to an increasing number of passengers and cargo delivered from large ocean liners, the port was never quiet. Furthermore, Canada's intercontinental railway system delivered and received goods and passengers directly at the docks, keeping the Port of Halifax busier than ever.

Of course, military security was operating under unprecedented strict levels. During the Great War, German U-boats had targeted shipping from Nova Scotia, but today's Kriegsmarine was sending U-boats to sea in ever-increasing numbers. Known to wait at sea in groups called Wolfpacks, any ship that left port, including unarmed merchant and passenger ships, had become targets for their torpedoes. For Lt Verrier, no day was routine. The Port of Halifax had to be battle-ready, and even though he served his duty ashore, his training and knowledge of shipping schedules were crucial to Canada's national defense. He was fortunate to be granted three day's leave for Michelle's wedding.

Steve was especially pleased to introduce his girlfriend, Brenda, to his family in Charlottetown. He had only known her for about six months but was already thinking about the future. They had met in Halifax at a pub that he and his friends frequented regularly, far from the rowdy places nearer the docks, uptown in location, quality, and patronage. No sailors were allowed within, only officers and local civilian patrons.

The first time he saw Brenda, she stood out from the crowd immediately, with her blonde hair swept into a French twist and her bright blue eyes. Steve didn't approach her that night because she was with another man, a civilian by his dress. The second or third time he saw them together, he learned her companion was her brother, Edward, who was doing his duty to watch over his younger sister.

Steve and Brenda had seen each other several times before he learned that she had moved east from Ottawa almost two years ago, shortly after her mother died. He also learned that her father had died when she was very young. Edward had moved to Halifax two years earlier than Brenda. At twenty-five and with no reason to stay in Ottawa, Brenda followed her dream of living near the sea and settling in a milder climate than Ottawa could offer. Her brother's description of Halifax convinced her that the Maritimes could provide a warmer climate and everything else she craved. Not yet ready for a place of her own, Brenda shared an apartment with Edward, not far from the port, where both worked in the offices of one of the largest commercial shipping companies.

Steve was looking forward to showing Brenda off at the rehearsal dinner tonight. Although he had introduced her to his family at home, they needed more time to get to know her. He hoped everyone would be as impressed with her tonight as he was. He planned to pick her up at the Old Town Hotel in an hour.

Unknown to Steve, when Brenda Kimble moved from Ottawa to Halifax, she left behind not only her family home but also her family name. Born Brenda Ilse Kimmel to Hans and Freda Kimmel, she had lived among immigrants in German communities in Canada since birth. Her father, a German naval officer captured during the Great War, had been imprisoned in Canada for two years until the war ended. She never forgot the treatment she endured as a German growing up among Canadians after the war. A deep, gnawing bitterness lay just below the surface, hidden only by her well-disguised hunger for revenge.

Shedding her German surname at her mother's death, Brenda chose Kimble, a name of Anglo-Saxon origin. Also unknown to Steve was that the man she had introduced as her brother, Edward, was not her brother. The man who called himself Edward Kimble had been born Ernst Hoffman in Germany. Disguised as a student, Hoffman, secretly an agent of the Third Reich, had emigrated to the United States more than six years ago. Known then as Ernest Duncan, he was a naturalized American citizen who practiced long-learned linguistic skills that allowed him to hide his true nationality. Formerly a clerk in an art supplies store in Charlottetown, he had disappeared in less than a day to follow an assignment in the West. Returning to the Maritimes now as Edward Kimble, he scheduled commercial maritime traffic at the docks in Halifax. After hours, he transmitted maritime traffic data to German off-shore agents for use by the Kriegsmarine. Brenda, still resenting the treatment she and her family endured in Canada after the Great War, was happy to work closely with him.

There was one last thing that Steve would never have suspected. Brenda and Edward played brother and sister by day. By night, however, they were lovers.

Chapter 33

With Susan and Michael's wedding and wedding rehearsal still a recent memory for many, Michelle and Grayson's wedding rehearsal spanned only a comfortable and relaxed half hour. Fr. Hunt was his usual jovial self, helping everyone to enjoy the formalities of the rite. As could be expected, Armand had the most difficult task—preparing to surrender his daughter to a waiting groom. Anna stood faithfully by him to offer her support. When all were satisfied that they had adequately rehearsed their parts, the wedding party left St. Peter's for the dinner Grayson had arranged at the Hotel Charlottetown. On the way, Steve stopped to pick up Brenda at the Old Town Hotel while Emily and Andrew followed the rest of the wedding party to the hotel dining room.

Although several in the group had only recently met Michelle, Grayson, and the Highfield family, one would be hard-pressed to find a more comfortable gathering. The conversation and laughter flowed freely among a grateful group who thoroughly enjoyed their nearly two hours at their tables. When Michael and Susan stood to offer a final toast, everyone joined them with champagne flutes in hand.

"A couple's journey to happy moments like these," Michael began, "can sometimes be long and convoluted, often due to old assumptions we make about ourselves, our families, and others throughout our lives. Our marriage vows require us to leave many of those old assumptions behind, to begin anew and entrust ourselves to another and the guidance of one larger than us," he said, looking at Susan as she nodded in agreement.

"Now, Michelle and Grayson," Michael said as he turned to them, "you found a way to keep your engagement shorter than most." Pausing to acknowledge the laughter that ensued, Michael said, "But I know you haven't taken any shortcuts through the process that has prepared you to marry. Now, having no secrets from yourselves or each other, it is plain that you are ready to take your vows, and we," he said, acknowledging all the guests, "now stand to raise our glasses to your union."

After the toast, when all had taken their seats, Grayson and Michelle stood together, hand in hand, happy to address their family and friends.

Grayson began, "Though not a stranger to the Moncrieff family, I am an entirely new commodity to the rest of you here on this beautiful island. I must thank all of you," he said, "especially Anna, Armand, and Steve, for receiving me so warmly." After a pause, Grayson continued, "I must also tell you that from the moment I met this beautiful woman," he said, looking at Michelle, "I knew I had discovered the treasure I had long sought. I should have been overjoyed, but instead, I must confess, I was terrified." Over everyone's laughter, he continued, "You see, I was smitten, and I knew I would never be satisfied with another. But what if she wouldn't have me? What if I wasn't the one she had been waiting to find? If she wouldn't have me, I knew I should remain forever bereft," he said.

Squeezing his hand to interrupt him, Michelle looked at Grayson, then back to their guests and said, "What Grayson didn't know was that I had recently discovered something, too. I discovered I couldn't engineer my happiness by chasing down the wrong man. I had to trust that the right man would appear someday, and I would know him in a moment. There was a better plan afoot." Then, turning to Grayson, she said, "We found each other, darling," and, turning back to their guests, she added, "and just so all of you know, Grayson wasn't the only one smitten that day!"

Amidst a room filled with laughter, Grayson and Michelle faced each other. Grayson didn't wait until the morning for Fr. Hunt's invitation to kiss the bride. Amidst cheers and tears, their family and friends celebrated Grayson and Michelle's happiness.

Morning arrived earlier than any member of the wedding party, especially the bride, might have chosen. Grayson and Michelle had scheduled family photos with Anna and Armand at nine o'clock. Susan had Michelle up and moving by seven, bathed and breakfasted by eight, and ready to drive to Charlottetown by eight-thirty. Once the photos were complete with her parents, the photographer had only minutes to precede them to St. Peter's for the service at ten o'clock.

Thankfully, traffic was sparse on this unusually warm November day, and Fr. Hunt had made everyone comfortable at the church. When they arrived, Michelle, happy to be guided by Susan's experience in formal affairs, relaxed and gave herself to the moment, a beautiful and gracious bride. Her attendants, too, comfortable in their roles, were all at ease. Even Grayson, bolstered by Michael at his side, traded the last of a groom's butterflies for the confidence he had already come to trust in his union with Michelle. The service lasted only minutes, and after the photographer completed the last round of photos, the church emptied the wedding guests into their cars for the short drive to Highfield and the wedding reception.

Of course, after their luncheon, Highfield's Victrola provided music for dancing. The bride and groom weren't ready to leave their guests behind until Michelle threw her bouquet, which somehow found Emily's waiting hands. In a shower of rice and flower petals, Grayson and Michelle ran to their waiting car. When it disappeared around the last corner in the driveway, Michael raised his voice to speak over all the guests, asking for their attention.

"Just one announcement," he said over the hum of the happy crowd. "Grayson and Michelle request that you gather at the front entrance in forty-five minutes for a surprise. Until then, please enjoy your wedding cake before you return."

Grayson had taken no one but Michael into his confidence regarding his final surprise for Michelle on their wedding day. Of course, she expected Grayson to drive to their hotel, but he had other plans, which he didn't reveal until they drove through the security gates at the RCAF airfield in Charlottetown. When they arrived, he parked the car, turned to his puzzled bride, and handed her a small gift-wrapped box.

"Oh, Grayson," she said. "Another gift? I'm already spoiled, but I can't fathom why we're here and why you are handing me another gift."

"When you open it, you'll understand," Grayson answered, "and it will be only the beginning of surprises for today."

Michelle tore the wrapping paper off the box, opened it, and parted the tissue paper to reveal a pair of leather flight goggles.

"For flying?" she asked as she turned excitedly to Grayson.

"Of course, darling," he laughed. "Hurry now. Our flight suits are waiting in my office, and some airmen are warming the aircraft. We're flying to the island's west end for our first night away, but we have a shorter mission first. Here, give me your hand."

Michelle followed Grayson to his office, and moments later, they ran to a waiting bi-plane in their flight suits. With their bags stowed within, Grayson helped Michelle into her seat and secured her flight harness. Once Grayson was in the cockpit, they taxied out to the airstrip.

Ever the adventurer, Michelle's few worries yielded to Grayson's confidence, and she guessed his plan—a flyover at Highfield. Michael, the only partner in Grayson's scheme, had all the wedding guests waiting as Grayson and Michelle flew in from the west, banked to circle Highfield twice, and swooped down to only a hundred feet above the crowd. All their guests could see the bride and groom smiling and waving. Then Grayson banked the aircraft to the west toward their honeymoon destination, pulled back on the stick, and took the bi-plane high into the sky as everyone on the ground waved farewell.

Even in their flight suits, the temperature at altitude was chilly, but Grayson and Michelle knew they'd find a way to warm up once they reached their destination, a short distance and a few minutes away.

Chapter 34

S ir Richard Moncrieff paced the floor of his office at SIS headquarters on Broadway in London, hoping for news from the Dutch embassy. Overnight, German Gestapo and SS officers had crossed into Venlo, a town in the Netherlands on the German border, and seized two SIS agents. Both agents were well-known to Sir Richard. Sigismund Best, who had served SIS since the Great War, and Richard Stevens, a multi-lingual officer formerly of the British Indian Army, were now in German hands.

In Munich, just a day earlier, an attempt had been made on Hitler's life. The details were still lacking, but it appeared that a mistimed explosion at a beer hall where Hitler was celebrating led to the abduction of the two SIS officers. At the same time, the RAF was bombing Munich, but Hitler was able to escape both attacks. Although Sir Richard knew SIS operatives were not responsible for the blast at the beer hall, he also knew Hitler would not require evidence before condemning the two captured SIS officers, now in German custody.

The only good news of late had come from the US. President Roosevelt had signed amendments to the US Neutrality Act that allowed Britain to purchase arms on a cash basis, delivered without aid from ships flying US flags. Sir Richard knew that gold from the UK was already in vaults in Canada to pay for the arms Britain sorely needed. He also knew that the Royal Navy had ships in the North Atlantic to protect merchant vessels from German U-boats. His sons, Boyd and Nigel, were aboard those ships.

With the war in Poland reduced to a German occupation mission, Sir Richard knew the Nazi Wehrmacht would soon turn its eyes toward Belgium and France, with the UK as its ultimate target. Neither France nor the British Expeditionary Force on the continent was equipped with arms or numbers to face the German war machine. While conscription was swelling the ranks of British military forces, a war-trained force was not yet available. Nazi preparation for war had been going on for years, giving Germany a clear and decided advantage. If the Germans got to the English Channel, Sir Richard feared for the destruction the Luftwaffe could bring to the UK. Three weeks earlier, they had bombed the UK, first attacking ships off Rosyth, and then the fleet anchored at Scapa Flow. With German airfields established in occupied territories closer to Britain, future attacks could prove unstoppable.

Reports of German atrocities continued to come in, especially those aimed at Jewish populations. Hitler's troops moved thousands of Jews from Austria and Czechoslovakia to concentration camps that were in Poland. Other purported anti-Nazi groups targeted by Hitler, notably university professors and clergy, had also been captured and imprisoned. At one university in Poland, German troops captured more than 150 professors in a single day, leaving them beaten and imprisoned before removing them to German custody elsewhere. Sir Richard had to wonder where the evil would end.

In the late afternoon, as the last sunlight waned in the west, Sir Richard stopped pacing and sat at his desk. Reaching to his right bottom drawer, he retrieved the bottle of Dewars and a glass. He poured two fingers and looked out his west window to toast the sun's last rays. Of course, looking to the west also meant looking toward his Angela, an ocean away at Highfield. Susan and Michael were there, too, of course, but Angela's face was always the one he craved when the world was out of control and when he needed reasons to believe that the insanity would cease. He had never been more grateful for the inspiration to secure a safe home for Angela now that England faced the current Nazi threat. Others had looked at him quizzically then, but now they admired his foresight. Of course, he knew from whence the inspiration came.

His inspiration had come during a moment of prayer. It might seem an odd combination to some, prayer and the glass he was holding in his hand tonight, but he believed the one who heard his prayers understood completely. Sir Richard also trusted that his customary second pour most nights enjoyed the same understanding. After he shared the angst that each day brought him, Sir Richard often needed a moment to quiet his heart and mind so that he could stop and listen. You see, prayers were never one-way conversations. "Be still and know that I am God," he quoted to himself. He nodded and sat back in his chair. He waited silently, listening for the one voice he didn't want to miss.

Chapter 35

Before Sir Richard returned to London following Michael and Susan's wedding last spring, he alluded to some British plans to protect children's lives when war ensued. With growing concern in the UK concerning Luftwaffe air strikes, British families had been evacuating children from potential German bombing targets since 1938. Special efforts were afoot in industrial centers and cities like Manchester, Belfast, and Liverpool. Of course, London was always considered Germany's prime target, and many London families had already evacuated their children from the city. Nearly 1.5 million children from the south and east coasts of England and the Channel Islands had found refuge in "reception zones" in the country's more rural areas under Operation Pied Piper. Sir Richard's news that the Children's Overseas Reception Board had developed plans to evacuate children to Canada as early as the coming spring was of particular interest to Highfield. Prince Edward Island was one site chosen to receive evacuees.

Michael and Susan's experience locating adoptive families for the four orphans who arrived with Susan from Ipswich last year had been entirely positive. In the face of need, Prince Edward Island's people had proven warm-hearted and generous. The children who found homes here last year were thriving among their new families. As Michael looked forward to larger numbers of children arriving from England, he formed a plan for specific ways Highfield could help.

Highfield had more than eighteen acres of pasture, producing more hay than Michael needed to feed its livestock. He considered taking eight acres of pasture and dedicating them to the two acres currently cultivated for vegetable gardens. Of course, cultivating ten acres would require additional labor, but Michael had a plan for that, too.

He wanted to build two cottages to house young people who needed jobs from early spring to late fall each year. Michael knew that PEI had never fully recovered from the Great Depression, and many people needed work, especially young people. With one cottage for young women and another for young men, Highfield could provide a place for them to live and work while waiting to find adoptive homes. Even after many in PEI had offered to serve as host families, evacuees might need work that Highfield could provide. He was sure the products of their labor would find ready markets, both on the island and the mainland.

His initial plans for each cottage included eight bunks, a simple lavatory, and a small gathering area. He also planned an outdoor shower area at the rear of each cottage, accessible from an interior door for privacy. With adequate lumber already milled and waiting, Michael was sure the construction, including the necessary plumbing and electrical installations, could be completed in less than three months. The cottages could be ready for the next planting season if construction started soon. He had prepared a few simple drawings indicating the locations he was considering adjacent to some of the outbuildings and some elevations to give Susan and Lady Moncrieff an idea of how the cottages would look. If they approved, he was sure Emily would be willing to draw a complete set of plans. First, however, he needed to speak with Susan.

"So, you think there's a good chance that children evacuated from home will arrive here this spring?" Susan asked as she poured her second cup of tea in the kitchen that morning.

"It seems likely," Michael answered. "Of course, homes may be available across Canada, but initially, destinations not far from Halifax will likely be the first where the children will arrive. I hope we can provide a place ready to welcome them here at Highfield."

"And the new gardens could provide them with income and produce to help with expenses at their family homes here. That way, no one would be burdened?" Susan asked.

"Exactly," Michael agreed. "How do you think your mother will receive such a plan?"

"I'm sure she'll be delighted. Why don't we talk with her at lunch?" Susan asked.

"Fine," Michael agreed. "I'll dedicate a little more time this morning detailing these sketches. If your mother agrees, I'll ask Emily to help with the full plans."

"Brilliant," Susan said. "I can't wait to see what Mother has to say."

Michael left his drawings in the study for the moment because he needed to stop at the sawmill first thing this morning. Luc and Joseph were helping Jacques mill fenceposts from some black locust logs that had been seasoning for almost a year. Black locust resisted rotting better than any other species on Prince Edward Island. Highfield was fortunate to have several healthy stands of black locust trees, some as tall as sixty feet. Highfield's pasture and garden fences always needed a ready supply of fenceposts, and today was the day Jacques had chosen to mill a hundred or more into six and eight-foot lengths.

There was nothing Jacques enjoyed more than working with his sons. They were, of course, adopted sons in the world's view, but not to Jacques. Luc was his by way of Jacques' marriage to Doris, Luc's mother. Joseph, an orphan from Ipswich, England, had emigrated from England with the Moncrieffs. When Jacques and Doris married, however, her children and Joseph became the sparkles in Jacques' eyes each morning. The two boys had become young men, quiet, caring, well-trained, and multi-skilled under his tutelage. Jacques had every right to be proud of them.

Michael drove his Ford flatbed up the North Path, struggling through the wet mud made by yesterday's rain and two inches of wet snow that followed it overnight. As he approached the sawmill almost half a mile from Highfield, he was surprised to hear the roar of the sawmill engine cease. Michael waited to hear it start again but was surprised when it didn't. Jacques' common practice was to ready all the logs for milling so that once he started the engines, the mill could run in full, two-hour shifts. This silence after less than an hour meant something was wrong.

As Michael turned off the North Path into the mill yard, the sight before him took his breath away. At the base of a well-stacked pile of eight-foot-long locust logs, he saw the torso of a young man face down in the snow and mud, his legs buried under three or four logs, each over a foot in diameter. Above him, twenty or thirty more logs in the pile were ready to follow the first. Jacques and the other young man struggled to secure the logs without bringing the whole pile down on top of them. As Michael leapt from his truck, he was able to identify Joseph on the ground, moaning, while Luc worked frantically with Jacques.

"You're a godsend, Michael," Jacques shouted. "I need you to unhitch the tractor from the PTO and drive it here, bucket first. We need the tractor to hold this pile back before they come down. Luc and I can't hold them much longer."

Michael knew what Jacques needed and had the tractor un-hitched minutes later, bucket up, and forced into the lowest logs that threatened to fall next. Then he joined Jacques and Luc as they struggled to lift and prop the logs on the ground to free Joseph's legs. Cold, wet, and only semi-conscious now, Joseph could only mumble between groans of pain. It was clear his injuries were severe. Jacques and Michael carried Joseph to Michael's truck bed using their coats and some stray lumber sticks to make a stretcher. Jacques climbed onto the bed, doing what he could to comfort Joseph, while Luc rode in the cab with Michael.

"How did it happen, Luc?" Michael asked.

"I'm not sure, Mr. Moreland," Luc began. "The logs were all cribbed up the way we always do. You saw them at the yard's edge, piled up against that big white pine, didn't you? Joseph was walking by when we heard a crack, and part of the white pine came down on the pile. That was just enough to snap some of the cribbing, I think, because then the logs came down on him," Luc said as he began to cry. "I couldn't do anything but watch; it happened so fast. I was so afraid that the logs would keep coming and bury him there in the snow and the mud."

"I'm sure it was horrible, Luc," Michael said. "It's always horrible when we feel helpless. We're going to get Joseph to the hospital as quickly as possible. I'll need your help to do some things as soon as we get to Highfield."

Looking up from his tears, Luc nodded and said, "OK, Mr. Moreland."

"First, we have to keep him warm," Michael began, "so as soon as we arrive, I need you to go into the house through the back kitchen door and into the servant quarters where my room used to be. Gather all the blankets from both bedrooms and bring them to me outside. We'll be taking Joseph to the hospital in the sedan. Jacques and I will get Joseph into the back seat and cover him with the blankets you bring, OK?"

Luc nodded, "OK."

Michael continued, "Your mother will probably be in the kitchen, so you'll need to tell her that there's been an accident, and Jacques and I are taking Joseph to the hospital. Ask her to telephone the hospital to let them know we are on our way. All right, Luc?"

"But, she'll want to go to the hospital, too, Mr. Moreland; I know she will," Luc said.

"I'm sure you're right, Luc," Michael said. "I'm also sure Miss Susan will gladly drive her. It would be best if you came with her, too, Luc. Can you do that?"

Luc nodded and said, "I can do that, Mr. Moreland. I've done it before."

At that moment, they arrived at Highfield. Michael and Luc climbed out of the truck at the back door.

"OK, Luc," Michael said. "Blankets first, right?"

"Right," Mr. Moreland. "I'll be right back."

Michael shared his plan with Jacques as he ran toward the garage to get the sedan. He pulled up to the back of the flatbed and opened the car's rear door as Luc returned with the blankets and his mother. Doris looked into Michael's eyes for reassurance. He answered her without having to speak a word. His eyes and his nod told her all she needed to know.

Joseph was awake but unable to speak intelligibly. Shivering and in shock, he could do nothing more than endure Michael and Jacques' efforts to wrap him in blankets and slide him into the back seat of the sedan as gently as they could. As they drove away, Michael watched Doris and Luc in the rearview mirror as they hurried back into the house.

Chapter 36

When they arrived at the Accident Room at the hospital, Dr. Mac-Millan was already on hand, ready to receive Joseph. Once out of the car and on a gurney, the doctor and his team rushed him inside to begin treatment. Jacques followed Joseph while Michael parked the car away from the ambulance entrance.

Michael was leaving the car when he saw Susan's cabriolet turn into the hospital driveway. He waved to catch her eye, and she pulled her car into a parking space beside him. Doris, Emily, and Luc were in the car with her.

"They've just taken Joseph into the Accident Room," Michael said to Doris. Jacques is with him."

"Follow me, Doris," Emily said, hurrying her to the main entrance doors, "I can take you straight to Jacques."

As Doris and Emily rushed ahead, Michael and Susan gathered Luc up and hurried behind them. Still wet and cold, Luc shivered as they entered the hospital doors.

They sat for a few minutes until Emily returned to take them to the Accident Room waiting area, where coffee and tea were available. Michael was quick to get a hot cup into Luc's hands. It was almost an hour before Dr. MacMillan arrived to report on Joseph's injuries.

"Jacques described how the accident happened. Joseph is a fortunate young man. All his injuries will heal, though it will take some time." the doctor said.

It turned out that Joseph had a broken leg, a dislocated hip, several minor lacerations, and some severe bruises. One doctor sedated Joseph while Dr. MacMillan set and cast his leg and got his hip back into place. He was sleeping now while they were treating his lacerations and icing the bruises to limit swelling. It would be a day or two before

Joseph would be ready to have visitors, and his leg would be in a cast for the next eight weeks or so. Thankfully, Dr. MacMillan was confident he would make a full recovery.

Just then, Doris and Jacques appeared with Emily. Luc rushed to Jacques, who gathered him into his arms in a welcome embrace that assured him that all would be well. After thanking Dr. MacMillan and Emily, Jacques sent Doris and Luc home with Susan while he and Michael drove back to Highfield.

"I don't understand it, Michael," Jacques said. "I know a good-sized limb came out of that tree and landed on those logs, but nothing like that could have been enough to splinter the cribbing and set those logs free. Nothing."

"I hope you're not blaming yourself, Jacques, because no one else is," Michael said.

"I'd just like to take a look out at the mill to find something that makes sense. If you hadn't come when you did and hadn't gotten the tractor bucket on that pile," Jacques said, "I don't know if we'd have been able to save him. That lad must have a guardian angel watching out for him."

"I'm sure he does, Jacques, but it could just as well have been you, Luc, or me under those logs. What would you say to us taking another look out there now to try to make sense of it all?" Michael asked.

"I'd say let's get this car back in the garage, start your truck, find our way back through the mud, and have a good look while the sun still shines," Jacques answered.

Michael parked the car in the garage but took a few minutes in the kitchen to make ham and cheese sandwiches while Jacques poured two tall mugs of apple cider. Knowing they couldn't drive the rutted path to the sawmill with full mugs in their hands, the men took a few minutes to assuage their hunger and thirst. Refreshed, they returned to the truck and turned into the mill yard a few minutes later.

With the tractor bucket still stabilizing the pile of locust logs, Michael and Jacques pored over the pile and the cribbing without risking another avalanche. It didn't take long for them to find something they could not have predicted.

Two vertical members, each six inches thick, had been braced to hold the pile of logs in place. Both had shattered about two feet from the ground, causing the logs above to roll down and trap Joseph. There was no reason for them to shatter like that unless someone had deliberately weakened them somehow. One look at each member told the same tale.

"Look, Michael," Jacques said, surprised. "Someone has back-cut this one. I see four kerfs from a thin blade like a pruning blade, almost halfway through over a four-inch span."

Michael looked at the shattered crib at Jacques' feet and then back at the one in front of him. It, too, had shattered due to four back cuts designed to weaken it enough to break under a load.

Looking again at the pile, Michael traced his way past the pine bough that Luc had described. It was half of a forked trunk, one not likely to break and fall under the weight of the previous night's light snowfall. Michael climbed over the pile to reach the butt end of the pine trunk. Once more, he found a series of saw cuts waiting to release one tree fork onto the log pile below.

For a moment, neither man wanted to believe what his eyes told him. Someone had planned and executed an ambush intended to inflict a potentially fatal injury. An innocent boy was its victim, but who was its intended target? Who wanted someone at Highfield dead, and why? While neither man spoke, a quiet rage rose in each. Both bolted toward the base of the pine tree.

"This was the trigger," Michael said, pointing at the broken fork. "Either he made his cuts and was willing to wait for nature to take its course, or he was here to make the final cut and watch the tree fall. I'm betting he was here."

Footprints in the melting snow at the base of the tree proved Michael right. With the roar of the sawmill engine, no one would hear the final strokes of a handsaw on the fork of the white pine. In the excitement that followed, the perpetrator could easily make his escape. The footprints in the snow led north, and other footprints confirmed where their enemy had come in, probably before dawn, under cover of darkness.

Michael's mind went to his SIS training. He was facing a well-informed adversary who had an opportunity through reconnaissance. Michael knew that terrorists planned, but they also depended on opportunity. Something recent had given this enemy information about when, where, and how he could attack. Furthermore, the enemy didn't care who he victimized. Michael was confident the target was simply Highfield. Someone hated Highfield, or what Highfield stood for, or the man who owned Highfield. He hated enough to murder.

Michael was sure the enemy was not from Prince Edward Island. He was not even Canadian. His target was Sir Richard and his family, but ultimately, his target was Great Britain. This enemy was a Nazi. A Nazi on Canadian soil, acting alone. The question was, "Where did he get his intelligence?" Michael had the answer as soon as the question met his mind.

Chapter 37

Armand saw the look on Michael's face when he entered Verrier's Hardware. He took off his leather apron and waved Michael upstairs. Armand poured two cups of coffee while Michael removed his coat, revealing the shoulder holster that held his Walther PPK. Michael placed his coat on the back of the chair and sat at the kitchen table. As Armand eyed the pistol Michael carried, Michael looked back at him and nodded.

"I never thought I'd have to carry this regularly," he said, indicating the gun.

"It must be serious, Michael," Armand said, "it's written all over your face."

"Attempted murder," Michael said. "Thank God it wasn't successful."

After Michael had recounted the entire story of the sawmill "accident," he finished with his theory.

"The perpetrator is a hothead, an egotist who thinks he's beyond discovery. There is nothing subtle in his actions," Michael said. "He thinks he's subtle, of course, but that's because he is sure everyone else is stupid. He's a classic narcissist."

"So, you've got an idea where we look next?" Armand asked.

"Yes, and that's where I need your help," Michael said.

"Anything. Michael, anything," Armand answered.

"All right. I've gone over the last six months at Highfield. Beyond local and well-known friends, Highfield has had only one recent guest whose past we can't confirm," Michael said.

"And that is Brenda, I must assume?" Armand asked.

"Exactly," Michael answered.

"I understand completely," Armand said. "How would you like to proceed."

"In the interest of time," Michael began, "we need to contact Steve immediately. We need to know everything he can tell us about her. She may have been lying to him since they first met, or she may be an innocent woman who has fallen under the charms of the enemy, but it will be up to us to sift through whatever he can tell us."

"I understand," Armand said.

"I'm sure this won't be easy for you, especially because Steve doesn't know your status with SIS," Michael said. "You'll appear to be a nosy father, asking what will seem like a lot of impertinent questions."

"Perhaps," Armand answered, "but I'll get Anna on the phone, too. A mother's curiosity can be irresistible to a son, you know."

"Let's do it, then," Michael said. "We need to know several things up front. First, while at Highfield, did Steve and Brenda take a walk, perhaps up a path in the woods? Did they happen upon anything interesting? Second, does Steve know if she has any close male friends or relatives nearby? If so, has Steve ever met them? Those questions alone may be all we need for a start," Michael said.

"Consider it done," Armand said. "Anna talks with Steve at least once a week, sometimes twice. I think tonight might be one of those nights."

"Thanks," Michael said. "I'll be waiting to hear. And let's use the radio. I'm not ready to trust the telephone."

"Understood," Armand said, "understood."

Michael shook Armand's hand and turned to use the stairway to the street where his truck was parked. As he drove away, Anna took her place at Armand's elbow.

"It's him again, isn't it?" she asked.

"Him?" Armand asked.

"Yes, Armand, you know. The young man who killed his father, the young man I saw later on the train?" she asked.

"We don't know, Anna, we don't know yet," he answered.

"A man who could kill his father could certainly set a random death trap for someone else. Yes, Armand, I heard it all, and it's terrifying," she said.

"That's precisely why we have to help, Anna. The Nazis spread terror, and we cannot let them terrorize us. If this girl is using Steve, we have to find out so that she can be exposed. Otherwise, neither he nor we will ever be safe," Armand said.

Anna stopped to breathe deeply for a moment. Twenty years of captivity still had a hold on her. When she had calmed, she said, "Yes,

Armand. I promised myself I would never be a prisoner again. Neither will my children be prisoners. Let's call Steve right now."

Armand radioed Michael an hour later to confirm that Steve and Brenda had walked up the North Path to the fire tower. On the way, they stopped at the sawmill. Furthermore, Steve had met Brenda's older brother, with whom she lived. He was about six feet tall, with fair hair, a fair complexion, and blue eyes. His name was Edward. Steve also identified the company where they both worked, scheduling commercial shipping and working closely with the RCN at the port of Halifax.

Armand was sure that Anna was correct. Michael was, too. The next morning, after conferring with Sir Richard in London, RCN officers contained the building where Edward and Brenda Kimble were employed. They were arrested, taken into custody, and secured in private cells in Halifax.

An investigation into files discovered in Edward Kimble's office and others found at his flat revealed a regular pattern of conveyance of shipping records, procedures, and schedules, including merchant, passenger, and RCN shipping, to enemy communication destinations on both land and at sea. The discovery of those records led to the arrest and detainment of several other German sympathizers, as well as the immediate development of measures to secure the shipping data at the port in Halifax.

Chapter 38

Two weeks after their wedding, Michelle and Grayson were satisfied
that they had feathered their nest well enough for Michelle to declare
a holiday from their labors. One call to Susan and Michael brought the
couples together for dinner at the newlyweds' home. Michelle couldn't
wait to show Susan everything she and Grayson had done to make a
lovely furnished home their own.

When Michael and Susan arrived and rang the doorbell, Grayson
answered the door with a hammer in his hand.

"Whoa," Michael laughed, his hands in the air, "we come as friends,
not foes!"

"Oh, this?" Grayson said, looking at the hammer. "M'lady found
room to hang one more picture, and I'm just returning from the scene of
the crime. Oops," he said, realizing Michelle might overhear him. Then
he said through his laugh, loud enough for her to hear, "And that room,
oh, it never looked better!"

"What's that, darling?" Michelle asked as she descended the stairs
behind him, her hands posed to strangle him. She laughed, though, and
let her arms collapse over his shoulders as she stopped one step above
him and kissed his cheek.

"Men seem to have no decorating sense at all. Have you noticed,
Susan?" Michelle asked. "It's as if the caveman's walls are still made of
stone, which no hammer and nail can pierce. But I'll have him civilized
eventually, don't you worry!" she laughed.

All Grayson could do was turn toward Michael's understanding eyes
and roll his own as he surrendered to his bride.

"I give up, darling, now that I've perfectly pierced every wall. Give
me a moment to pour our guests an appropriate glass of wine, and the
tour will be yours to guide," he laughed as he led Michael to the kitchen.

The ladies started upstairs as Michael and Grayson opened a bottle and found four glasses.

"Do you know how many little nails it takes to hang curtains in a house with twenty-two windows?" Grayson moaned. "Because," he elaborated, "it's not only the sheers that go behind the curtains, the valances above, and the tie-backs. Then there are the shades and, I don't know, Michael. It's just bigger than I could have imagined," he said, shaking his head.

"Maybe we should open a second bottle, Grayson," Michael laughed. "If we stay here, they'll get hungry and find us eventually, and we'll be well-oiled when they do!"

"That's the best idea I've heard all day," Grayson said with his glass in the air. "Here's to you."

The women's voices got louder as Susan and Michelle came downstairs for the first-floor tour. When the ladies had almost completed their circuit, Grayson and Michael joined them while offering flutes of prosecco.

"Well, Susan," Grayson said, "hasn't she done a masterful job?"

"It's lovely, Grayson, and Michelle was happy to give credit where it was due. She said she couldn't have done it without you," Susan said.

"Then I'm flattered enough to finish this wine, get the car, and drive us to dinner. Shall we?" Grayson asked.

Hearing no objections, they were soon on their way to dinner. Almost an hour later, when they finished dessert, Michelle asked, "What's new at Highfield? I know it's only been two weeks since I last saw it from the air, but it seems like months."

Susan looked back at Michael, who nodded and began, "We've had a bit of excitement, and not all of it pleasant."

"Really?" Michelle asked, "How so?"

"Unfortunately, some of it had to do with Steve's girlfriend, Brenda, and someone who reached back into your mother's past," Michael began, "but please bear with me as I explain."

Michael recounted Joseph's injury at the sawmill. He went on to explain how he and Jacques had discovered the evidence that proved the attack was intentional. Michael finished by recounting Brenda's arrest with the mastermind, Ernst Hoffman, the son of Michelle's mother's twenty-year captor, Conrad Hoffman.

"Hoffman and Brenda were actively involved in espionage that compromised the entire port of Halifax. Of course, Steve was an innocent victim. Hoffman's attack at Highfield compromised a huge German presence in Halifax. For the first time in over a year, ships can sail in and out of port with increased security," Michael said.

Michelle sat quietly, obviously concerned for her brother, Steve.

"Steve must feel so betrayed. She used him so freely, and all the time, she was living with a German conspirator. Beyond feeling betrayed, though, he probably feels guilty for not seeing through her lies," Michelle said.

"Yes," Michael said, "but you should know that Steve is under no suspicion from the RCN or the port authorities. They know him only as a victim, victimized just as they were," Michael finished.

"And Hoffman," Grayson asked, "what is his fate?"

"He's being guarded twenty-four hours a day. He's a naturalized citizen of the US, part of his cover for many years. It's not likely he'll ever be charged for his attack at Highfield. Proving his part in that incident would be difficult; however, the proof of his espionage at the port of Halifax is damning. Still, Canada and the United States will have to decide whether to charge him and if he will stand trial," Michael said. "It will be some time before he and Brenda face a judge or jury."

"Nonetheless," Grayson said, "the whole incident proves there is an active Nazi presence in Canada, in Halifax, and as close as Charlottetown."

"That's correct," Michael agreed. "We need to remain vigilant."

"Michelle," Susan said, "are you all right? I hope you know that no one faults Steve in any way."

"I'm just upset," Michelle admitted, "and the fact that this Ernst Hoffman has such close ties to my mother and her twenty years as a prisoner makes me uneasy. He murdered his father, isn't that right, Michael?" she asked.

"That's what the official reports indicate," Your mother was correct when she thought she recognized him on one of the trains that brought her home to you. Now, though, he is under twenty-four-hour guard. He won't be able to hurt anyone anymore," Michael said.

"That's my only comfort, Michael. Thank you," Michelle said.

Michael said no more, especially nothing about his intention to visit Ernst Hoffman in his cell in Halifax. The folly and amateur nature of the attack at Highfield didn't fit with Michael's understanding of the disciplined mind of a Nazi officer of Hoffman's rank. There was something that felt personal about Hoffman's assault that made Michael curious. There might be an opportunity for redemption that Michael could not ignore. He couldn't rest just yet. He needed to confront Hoffman. He hoped he could do so soon.

Chapter 39

Michael arrived at St. Peter's for morning prayer earlier than usual on Monday. After attending the early mass on Sunday, he spoke with Fr. Hunt and made an appointment to talk with him. Another early riser like Michael, Fr. Hunt had suggested meeting at seven o'clock. Michael brought some warm scones that Doris had baked and some peach jam, a product of Highfield's orchard. He knew Fr. Hunt would have the coffee ready.

"So, Michael," Fr. Hunt began, "what is it that's stealing your peace?"

"Is it that obvious?" Michael asked.

"We've known each other too long to let that tired look around your eyes go unnoticed. How can I help?" Fr. Hunt asked.

Michael began, "Do you remember a year or two ago when I was involved in an altercation at the Cask and Cork? I had been able to stop an angry man from hurting any more people than he already had."

"Of course," Fr. Hunt said. "It was Jacques, now one of your closest friends."

"That's right, Father. Well," Michael continued, "when I saw you in church the following Sunday, you seemed very concerned for me and told me something I've never forgotten. You told me I was a peacemaker, the kind of man Jesus called blessed."

"Yes, Michael, I remember that," Fr. Hunt nodded.

"But you were worried for me because you said that peacemakers are often called to pay a price," Michael said.

"That's been my experience," Fr. Hunt began. "Peacemakers make sacrifices to ensure peace for others. Sometimes, the price for those sacrifices is dear. Is there some current circumstance on your mind?"

"Yes," Michael said, "but it's a long and convoluted story affecting many people close to me."

"Is it something you can share?" Fr. Hunt asked.

"With you, Father, of course," Michael said, "but you might want to pour yourself a second cup. There's a lot to tell."

Fr. Hunt filled both of their cups as Michael began. "I'm sure you recall the details of Anna Verrier's kidnapping and twenty-year captivity. What few others know is that the German POW who kidnapped her had a son who had been tracking his father on this continent for years. He wasn't seeking a happy reunion. The evidence tells us that he came either for revenge or at the orders of superiors who sent him to kill his father. While he was attacking his father, Anna made her escape."

Fr. Hunt nodded, "I see. Please go on."

"Just weeks before that day, that young man was living in Charlotte-town and working at the art supply store For Art's Sake. Nurse Emily from Highfield shopped there, and it was clear that he had been overly friendly with her, inviting her to use his first name and offering to deliver her purchases to her home. Flattered but overwhelmed, Nurse Emily did her best to keep their relationship at a business level. To my mind, the man craved a relationship, but by chance, several of us encountered him one afternoon on the train. Though we never had the opportunity to speak, we all felt strangely ill at ease and suddenly suspicious of his intentions. He seemed to recognize our suspicion because he disappeared overnight, abandoning his job and the room he rented in town. He also abandoned his principal occupation, which involved mapping the shores of Prince Edward Island for his employer in Europe. That was when he traveled west to the United States in search of his father," Michael said.

"I would guess his employer is German?" Fr. Hunt asked through knowing eyes.

"Yes, Father," Michael said. "We were wrong if we thought we would not encounter him again. When he left the US, he returned to Canada under another assumed identity, engaged a young woman as partner/conspirator, and, together, they found employment at the port of Halifax. Recently, however, for reasons we cannot completely comprehend, we believe he plotted a covert attack against Highfield. In the end, one of our young men suffered some serious injuries."

"Will the young man be all right? He will recover, won't he?" Fr. Hunt asked.

"Yes, Father," Michael said, "we believe he will fully recover. But here's where my dilemma lies. Of course, I want to hate this enemy. I'm sure he aimed the attack at Highfield, at Sir Richard and his family, or against me, and not at an innocent boy. But there's a missing piece in this puzzle. This man's primary mission involved tracking and reporting shipping traffic to his employer. The attack at Highfield doesn't fit in. I'm not sure his superiors ordered it. So, I have to ask what would make a well-trained, single-minded man under authority commit a rogue act that could potentially endanger his primary mission. There had to be some emotional hook that made him do something no superior asked of him. That rogue act in Charlottetown led directly to his discovery and immediate imprisonment, not for the attack here at Highfield, but for a much larger danger he posed to the commercial and RCN shipping in Halifax."

"So, what is it that you aren't entirely sure you should do, Michael? That's your question, isn't it?" Fr. Hunt asked. "You're trying to solve a problem here, right?"

"I think I'm supposed to visit him in Halifax. I think I'm supposed to confront the man. His irrational decisions endanger him again and again. Those decisions point me to a victim with an injured mind and spirit," Michael said. "Yes, he has done some evil things, Father," Michael said, "but somewhere behind this irrational attack, I see a sobbing boy, not a heartless murderer. It's almost like someone possessed. Jesus helped possessed people, didn't he? What if this man is possessed by a past ruling his present, too?"

"There's the peacemaker I was talking about, Michael. I can't give you an answer, and I can't tell you what you should do. But," Fr. Hunt said, "you and I both know someone can."

"Yes, Father," Michael said, "we do."

"Are you willing to ask him, then?" Fr. Hunt asked.

"Yes," Michael said, "but, please, Father, would you come to the rail to pray with me as I do?"

"Of course, Michael," Fr. Hunt said, "of course."

Chapter 40

Ernst Hoffman, alias Ernest Duncan, was sitting in his cell at the RCN port authority building in Halifax on the morning when a uniformed RCN seaman escorted Michael to a chair outside his cell. Hoffman raised his eyes, and a look of disgust turned into a sneer as he spoke.

"If it isn't the wealthy Brit from the hilltop house in Charlottetown. Come to gloat, have you?" he asked.

"How do you know me?" Michael asked.

"Well, doesn't everyone in Charlottetown know you, the rich, smart, giant-slaying Brit from Highfield?" Hoffman asked.

"But we've never met, have we, Mr. Hoffman?" Michael asked, "At least not in my memory."

"It's Mr. *Duncan* to you, Mr. Moreland. Please don't forget that I am a naturalized American citizen, kept here in Canada only as long as it will take the American embassy to have me released. Uncle Sam takes care of his own, you know," Hoffman smirked.

"Fine, Mr. Duncan," Michael said, "but I don't believe we've met before. How do you know me?"

"Do you think the Secret Intelligence Service in London is the only European agency with eyes and ears on the world? That kind of arrogance and stupidity makes it so easy for Britain's enemy in Europe to outsmart her at every turn. I know who you are, Mr. Moreland, I know who employs you, and I know why you're here," Hoffman sneered.

"So, why am I here?" Michael asked.

"Why?" Hoffman asked. "Because you want to know why you and yours were targeted."

"That is correct," Michael answered, "but that's only part of my purpose for being here."

"So, you're the curious sort, Mr. Moreland? Then, tell me. What is it that you want to know?"

"I am curious to learn why a man with your education, training, and skills succumbs so regularly to his emotions, letting them lead him to sabotage his primary missions consistently," Michael answered.

"I don't know what you're talking about," Hoffman said, turning his back and pacing to the rear of his cell.

"I have to assume that your primary mission involves tracking and reporting commercial shipping and naval traffic to and from Halifax for Nazi Germany. Staging an ambush at a portable sawmill on an estate on Prince Edward Island nearly two hundred miles away appears incongruous. I believe that ambush could have been your idea, or it was the brainchild of an over-ambitious superior, Mr. Duncan," Michael said.

"Is that it?" Hoffman asked as he faced the wall. "That's why you came here today?"

"Not entirely, no. There was also the previous mission you sacrificed to your emotions, the mapping mission of ports and points-of-entry on the island. You sacrificed that mission to a few moments of familiarity with a nurse from Highfield whom you met at an art supply store," Michael added.

"Fascinating, Mr. Moreland," Hoffman said, "but is there more?"

"Yes," Michael answered. "I'm wondering what drove you to take your father's life."

"Fascinating once again," Hoffman said with a laugh, "but a failure in the facts. I didn't take my father's life. I didn't have to. He died before I had a chance to touch him when he stumbled and fell to the ground, clasping his chest and breathing his last. I had only the simple task of binding him and placing him in a slough to feign his murder."

"But you wanted him dead. Is that not true?" Michael asked.

"Oh, yes. I'd wanted that for years, ever since he forced me to watch as he beat my mother bloody and ever since he made her watch when he beat me. Would you like to see the scars, Mr. Moreland?" Hoffman asked.

"I believe you," Michael said, "and I am sorry you and your mother endured such pain. I'm also sorry you've felt driven to inflict it on another."

"What do you mean?" Hoffman asked. "I've never hurt anyone in that way."

"I beg to differ," Michael said. "A sixteen-year-old boy named Joseph would also have to differ, Mr. Duncan. You see, his legs were crushed under a falling pile of locust logs, resulting in a compound fracture and a dislocated hip. He'll remain hospitalized until he heals sufficiently and learns to walk again. He wonders what he did to earn such injuries. Did you wonder about that, too?" Michael asked.

"I did not intend a sixteen-year-old boy to be injured," Hoffman said quietly. "That attack wasn't aimed at children."

"The boy was an orphan, abandoned by his parents, newly adopted by a family here that loves and cares for him. They, too, ache for the pain he endures. Were you once an innocent boy like Joseph?"

"Why would you care, Mr. Moreland, you who have never wanted for anything?" Hoffman asked.

"Is that why you meant the attack for me, because you think I've never wanted for anything?" Michael asked. "I don't think you know me as well as you think you do."

"Really?" Hoffman asked. "Surprise me then. Tell me something we don't know about you and your SIS in-laws in London."

"My father went to war before I could speak," Michael said, "and came back with wounds that never healed. My mother died of Spanish flu a week after he returned from the trenches. I was six years old. I lost my mother and the better part of my father to war and illness. Yet I will freely admit that I never knew the pain you endured from a man like your father. You are a survivor, Mr. Duncan, one worthy of admiration," Michael said.

"Oh, that is rich," Hoffman scoffed. "You admire me for surviving?"

"Yes, I do," Michael said. "But, I also believe that the injuries you suffered at your father's hands drove you into worse hands, Nazi hands. They are using you now and will deny they knew you when you come to trial. You do know you are expendable in their minds, don't you? If you intended your attack at Highfield to impress your superiors, I believe you will find your superiors will remain unimpressed."

"What do you mean? No one has denied me. No one will," Hoffman said.

"Your father knew he could never return to Germany after the Great War. After he escaped the POW camp, he knew he could never go home. He was a failure in his own eyes. He always had been. That's why he beat you and your mother. He knew no one in Germany would honor his sacrifice, so he took care of himself on this side of the ocean—at least until you intervened," Michael said. "We both know he abandoned you years before he went to war, just as your Nazi superiors have abandoned you now."

"So you think I'll face abandonment again?" Hoffman asked.

"They abandoned you the day you became a US citizen, Mr. Duncan. You are no longer German to them. They will never attempt to rescue you. You will never return to Germany," Michael said. "Neither will the US defend you. You were plotting the demise of US merchant and US Navy ships at sea. You are alone and in prison, accused of war crimes. You will never live outside a cell again unless . . . ."

"Unless what? I'd love to hear your logic," Hoffman laughed.

"Unless you take your life back from the father whose cruelty defined you. I'm sure his father defined his life. He could not give you a gift of a father's love because he had never experienced such a gift himself," Michael said. "Until you forgive him, he continues to rule your life, even from his grave. How long are you going to let him win, Mr. Duncan?"

"Oh, and it's that simple?" Hoffman asked. "Take back my life, forgive the man who scarred me, stole my innocence, abandoned me to pain?" he asked.

"Yes," Michael said, "or you can let him win, which means the Germans who command you will win, too. You could be in prison until you die, the way your father died, looking over his shoulder until his last breath."

"So, you think it's that simple?" Hoffman asked.

"No," Michael answered, "I *know* it's that simple. I've had to war with my own demons, Mr. Duncan, just as you can choose to war with yours. You can also choose to remain a victim in your own mind, claiming you were just following orders or trying to impress your superiors by attacking the home of an SIS agent from London. One thing is sure, though. No one will listen. But," Michael said, rising from his chair, "I won't keep you any longer. The authorities here know how to contact me. If you'd like to talk again, they can arrange it," Michael said. With that, he stood to leave.

"I never meant to hurt that boy," Hoffman said as Michael turned from the cell and began to walk away."

"I believe you, Mr. Duncan," Michael said over his shoulder as he walked down the corridor to the door. "I hope I'll hear from you soon."

Michael was almost to the door when he heard Hoffman say, "There's one more thing you might like to know, Mr. Moreland."

Michael stopped to listen. Eventually, he returned to his chair outside the cell. It was nearly an hour before he continued to his car.

Michael had a long drive home to Highfield. Before he left Halifax, though, he stopped to see Steve, who was still badly shaken by Brenda's betrayal and the attack she aided at Highfield. Before leaving Halifax, Michael called Fr. Hunt to fill him in on his conversation with Hoffman. Then he got into the sedan and drove west. It would be a late night before he found his bed at Highfield.

Chapter 41

When Michael turned onto the driveway at Highfield, he craved only one thing—a light waiting for him in his bedroom window. He rounded the last bend in the driveway and was not disappointed. A light shone from his second-floor window on the west side of the house. He downshifted and hit the gas pedal as he urged the Ford sedan up the hill and parked outside the kitchen door. The sedan would have to wait outside overnight because Michael wasn't taking another minute to garage the car. No, he ran up the back stairs, hoping to find Susan waiting for him.

Susan was awake and standing at their bedroom door as he hoped. Simon heard his master's footfall on the stairs and thumped his tail on the floor as he lay in his bed in the corner of the bedroom. As Michael rushed down the hall, he dropped his coat and gathered Susan into his arms, warmed by every part of her that he pulled to himself in their embrace. He felt he had been gone for days, but hours always felt like days when they were apart. He hadn't stopped to eat on the two-hundred-mile trek home, but even now, he didn't crave anything the kitchen might provide. He had traveled over some unknown ground today into the mind of a man driven to madness. He needed someone who could understand, someone who could listen as he mumbled and murmured and tried to make sense of the unfathomable angst that leads a man to plot murder. Susan would listen; he knew she would.

His arms still wrapped around her, Michael began to rehearse the last twelve hours, like an ancient mariner whose heart compels him to rehearse his story. Susan led him downstairs to the kitchen, where there was no chance they would be overheard and where she could find something for Michael to eat. He rambled on as he ate, clearly troubled by the man he discovered in the cell in Halifax.

Michael did his best to recount his conversation with Hoffman. Though there were parts he didn't yet understand, others seemed remarkably clear.

"I was sure I heard the voice of evil, Susan," he began. "For an all-too-long moment, there was not a hint of remorse and certainly no apology for the injuries he had caused to an innocent young man like Joseph. In time, though, I discovered he was playing a well-rehearsed role. He was expecting something hard and unforgiving from me that didn't materialize. I believe he was confused by the lack of condemnation that his practiced attitude and training could challenge and withstand. He had a cache of answers but was confused when I didn't ask the questions he expected."

"So what changed?" Susan asked. "You said you heard the voice of evil."

"That's right, Susan," Michael began. "I heard that voice for a moment, but it didn't last. A more hardened man would not have entered the conversation. I believe Ernst Hoffman is an injured man, not a hardened one. Oh, his injuries are real. His wounds are deep. His hatred has its reasons, sound ones. Still, there was one remark that stuck in my mind. He said, 'I never meant to hurt that boy.' I heard genuine regret in his voice. That one remark gave me a reason to hope for his soul."

"But Michael, you said you heard the voice of evil. What did you see in him that you believe can be redeemed?" Susan asked.

"His father shamed and beat him for years. But a generation earlier, his father faced the same shame and even worse abuse. The injuries followed the generations to the present day. Before I left our conversation, he wanted me to know that he regretted Joseph's injuries. A colder man would never care. Somehow, Hoffman does," Michael said.

"Meaning?" Susan asked.

"Meaning, I don't believe he is the walking evil that many Nazis are. He still values life. His primary goal is not to injure and kill indiscriminately. He still has a soul," Michael said.

"But he came to our home," Susan said, "he laid a trap designed to maim or kill. He could have killed you, Michael," she cried. "Are you ready to forget that?"

"No, Susan, I'm not. But I'm also not ready to believe an injured man can't find healing. He wasn't always callous. I believe him when he says he didn't kill his father, the man who left him and his mother physically and emotionally scarred. We both know how his father tortured

Anna. To please his superiors in Germany, Hoffman had to make his father's death look like murder."

"I'm thinking back to Jacques Boucher, Michael," Susan said. "At least, I'm trying to. You told me Jacques deserved a second chance. I wasn't sure then, but now I would trust him with my life. However, I'm not ready to believe in someone like Ernst Hoffman."

"And I'm not asking you to. I have to be true to myself, though. I must wait to see if he contacts me and wants to talk again. There have been people who didn't give up on me. I can't give up on Hoffman yet," Michael said. "Besides, he told me one more thing, something he didn't have to reveal."

"What was that?" Susan asked.

"The attack on Highfield wasn't a rogue move on his part," Michael said. "I was wrong. He was following orders. The Nazis want to threaten your father, attacking him here in Canada, where he will feel helpless to defend his wife and daughter. They want to break his concentration. They want him to fall into worry and fear, compromising his work at SIS in London. Ernst was just the pawn following their orders."

Michael surprised himself by using Hoffman's first name. Somehow, it seemed hopeful in a world that needed a reason to hope.

"I have an idea that may help to redeem something from all this chaos, Susan," Michael said. I need to share it with your father before I can tell you anything more. Please trust me. It's not a secret; just a story that's not ready to be told."

With his appetite assuaged, Michael and Susan cleared the table, leaving the dishes for the morning. Susan took Michael's hand as he followed her up the back staircase to the west wing and their bedroom. As they entered the room, Michael scooped Susan into his arms and backed toward the door that her foot reached out to close. Their kisses had already begun as he deposited her in their bed, shed his traveling clothes, and hurried to find the shower he sorely needed after a day that started in the barn before sunrise. When he returned to her, her arms were waiting for him. She was ever content to remain the willing prisoner of his embrace, overwhelmed by his energy and kisses wherever he planted them. Later, when their hunger for each other was satisfied and weariness overcame them, they abandoned all thoughts of the day to lie silently in each other's arms, sharing their heartbeats and each breath. Sleep came eventually, for nothing more could keep them awake tonight.

Chapter 42

"Armand," Michael said, "we both know that Conrad Hoffman was an evil man, capable of atrocities. Anna has testified to his cruelty and still bears the scars of her imprisonment."

"And?" Armand asked.

"That's why I wasn't surprised when his son alluded to tortures throughout his childhood, tortures that both he and his mother endured," Michael added.

"So," Armand asked, "what makes you think Ernst Hoffman or Ernest Duncan, or whatever he calls himself, can help us today?"

"I think he ran to the Nazis in his teens when he had nowhere else to go, but I'm sure he's still searching for someone who will believe in him," Michael said. "With some encouragement, I think he could turn to our side."

"But he's been reporting the arrival and departure of every ship that sails in and out of Halifax to the Germans for months. With his information, the U-boats have been busy sinking merchant shipping in the waters around Britain, hoping to starve the Brits and shackle the industries that keep their military supplied. Those U-boats will be here soon, and Hoffman is the German setting up the shooting gallery for them," Armand said.

"That's right," Michael agreed, "but if he doesn't maintain regular contact with the Nazis, they will either abandon him or send someone to dispose of him. Here lies an opportunity for us. I believe we could convince him to sell those same wares to two markets."

"Tell me more," Armand said, leaning forward.

"He's been sending his reports to the Germans once or twice a week to avoid discovery. They haven't yet missed a single contact from him, even though he's been in a cell for several days. If we can convince him that his superiors will abandon him or find a way to kill him, I believe he'd be ready to work for us," Michael said, "and the Germans won't know anything."

"How do you see that working?" Armand asked.

"For a promise of future freedom, Hoffman would have to agree to continue to radio German intelligence as they expect him to," Michael began, "but now the reports he sends them won't be entirely accurate. Shipping dates will be off by a day or two. He'll misreport the cargoes and alter the reports of courses that the ships and convoys will take. So far, he has given the Germans coordinates for every convoy that has sailed from Halifax. The Kriegsmarine has plotted the sailing time from Halifax to the waters north and west of the UK and has deployed U-boats to wait there. However, when Hoffman is working for us, the intelligence he sends the Nazis will be full of holes."

"I see," Armand said.

"At the same time," Michael continued, "he will provide us with intelligence concerning enemy ships like U-boat locations and courses for other German vessels sailing west."

"I understand your plan," Michael, "but are you sure Hoffman can be convinced to change sides?" Armand asked.

"I should know that soon, Armand," Michael answered. "The Admiral has authorized me to begin that conversation with him."

"He'll have to remain a prisoner," Armand insisted.

"That's right," Michael answered, "until the war's end. Only then will his performance be assessed to determine if he has earned his freedom."

"A double agent, then, Michael," Armand marveled. "I hope we have men of sufficient caliber surrounding him to ensure he doesn't dupe us. Suffice it to say, it may take some time before we know if a plan like that can succeed."

"I'm walking on uncharted ground, too, Armand. I'm sure we'll find out together," Michael said.

"When do you meet with him again?" Armand asked.

"Tomorrow, Armand," Michael said. "I'll be in Halifax in the afternoon."

"And returning?" Armand asked.

"Tomorrow night," Michael answered, "or perhaps the next day. Don't worry, Armand, you'll hear everything I can tell you as soon as I return."

"I'll be waiting," Armand said as he offered his hand.

Michael took his hand and pulled Armand into an embrace. These men had been through too much together to stay at arm's length. The next day would bring them even closer together.

Chapter 43

B ecause Michael was leaving for Halifax in the morning, he had scheduled a late-night conversation by radio with Sir Richard tonight.
First, he had to report on the events at Highfield and his first interview
with Ernst Hoffman. Second, he needed to suggest his plan to harvest the
Germans' trust in Hoffman—if he could successfully convince him to
become a double agent. Third, Michael needed to seek Sir Richard's mind
on heightened security at Highfield now that Hoffman had admitted the
Germans knew of Sir Richard's interest there.

Radio transmissions were slow, limited by the number of relays
between Canada and London. It would mean a long night for Michael.
However, it was a night he would endure for Highfield and the unnum-
bered sailors whose lives depended on him to convince Ernst Hoffman
to swear allegiance to the UK's cause.

Michael's perch at the radio console in Highfield's attic provided
all the comfort a radio operator could expect—food, water, and coffee
for the sake of its caffeine. A cot stood nearby, but Michael dared not lie
down to doze. He needed to stay awake and ready for the radio transmissions that arrived at random intervals.

After hearing Michael's assessment of his conversation with Hoffman, Sir Richard agreed that Michael should invite him to work with
SIS for the duration of the war. Sir Richard summarized Michael's observations, confirming that Hoffman qualified as one whose psychological
status could be labeled "injured." The injuries he endured at his father's
hand, both physical and emotional, the injuries he observed visited upon
his mother, and the subsequent abandonment he endured had made him
a ripe target for the transference of his need for parental bonding to those
who recruited him to serve the Third Reich. Michael was free to encourage him to join the cause of the UK in the current conflict.

During their radio conversation, however, Michael learned more about some darker discoveries SIS agents had discovered in Poland, Germany, and Austria. The Third Reich was systematically capturing and re-locating Jewish populations from their homes, moving them to several remote locations, and housing them in work camps. Families were separated, while many young men were captured, killed, and buried in mass graves. The evil originated at the top echelons of the Third Reich, but the enforcement of such evils fell to those with boots on the ground throughout Europe.

Although Michael's SIS training had included studies into the wartime minds of officers and foot soldiers, his personal experience was limited and went back to the Great War. His father returned from combat an injured soul, but one whose physical and emotional injuries still allowed him to remain a father to his son, to work competently at a productive occupation, and to care for others. Michael knew of other men who lived not far from Clifton Manor, his boyhood home, whose injuries were more serious, men who were scarred deeply and lived sadly at a distance, never the same men who once left for war. However, Michael had never encountered men like the German and Russian troops Sir Richard described, men with souls so seared that the lives of innocent women, children, and young men meant nothing to them. He could not imagine those who ordered the killings that filled mass graves and the burning pyres where fires consumed the bodies of innocents.

To Michael, the stakes never seemed higher. Three thousand miles away from the European continent, he needed to do all he could to defeat the evil of the Third Reich. Tomorrow, he would meet again with Ernst Hoffman, an Oberleutnant of the Third Reich and an accomplished spy. By the end of the day, he needed to persuade Hoffman to transfer his allegiance to the UK.

Injured souls, scarred souls, seared souls—they were all men, like Michael, whose hearts beat and who breathed as he did, but whose souls ached from some outside force that threatened to twist them into the unimaginable. Michael felt small and out of his element as he considered his conversation with Hoffman the next day.

As he left the attic for the comfort of his bed, Michael promised himself a stop tomorrow for Morning Prayer at St. Peter's and another conversation with Fr. Hunt.

Chapter 44

S ir Richard Moncrieff was at his desk earlier than usual on a Monday morning in late March 1940. He was reviewing a communique from Michael that his staff had just decoded. Only a few weeks after the surprise attack at Highfield, Michael's work with the Nazi agent in RCN custody in Halifax had been successful. The German Oberleutnant responsible for executing the assault at Highfield and compromising shipping in and out of Halifax was now in Britain's employ. As a double agent, his recent work for the Allies, painstakingly scrutinized by RCN and SIS operatives, was already proving fruitful. Michael's intuition had proven correct. The value of such a foreign agent in Allied hands was without measure.

Apart from the war, Sir Richard was encouraged to learn about some changes at Highfield that Michael had been able to accomplish with the help of several local workmen. The cottages Michael had planned were nearing completion, thanks to a mild winter. Jacques Boucher found several local fishermen whose boats were ashore for the season to help in the construction. Michael had revised the original plans to include a small kitchen in each building and a larger common area for dining and recreation. Highfield was expecting the arrival of the first group of evacuee children sometime in mid-April. Both cottages would be ready for their new residents by then.

As Sir Richard watched the war on the continent, his intelligence sources reported that Hitler's interest was moving toward Denmark and Norway. Meanwhile, Russia had secured its hold on Finland by a peace treaty signed in Moscow after one hundred and five days of Soviet attacks. While those negotiations were underway, France and Britain had signed an agreement promising that neither would seek peace with Germany separately. Sir Richard feared that Germany would soon turn west toward France and Britain, but some encouragement from an un-expected source heartened him.

For all that the Prime Minister had been unable to accomplish for Britain's defense as Germany prepared for war, he had been able to bolster two vital defense initiatives already showing promise. First, recognizing that a German attack on Britain would begin in the air, Chamberlain had encouraged an initiative bolstering the production of British warplanes and accelerated training of pilots and ground crew. His second initiative, one still in development, was a matter of highest secrecy.

Along Britain's east coast, a series of timber towers, some over 240 feet tall, seemed to have grown out of the ground overnight and stood like sentinels looking toward the continent. Hastily equipped with a cache of experimental radar equipment, British scientists updated the new tech-nology constantly. Almost daily, technicians discovered more about this exciting new radar equipment. Specially trained teams of men and women manned each tower, though many were neophytes engaged in defending Britain through an utterly unfamiliar science. With the use of radar in the hands of skilled operators, it was possible to detect a German air attack while the Luftwaffe was miles away, giving the RAF time to send their fighters into the air to meet the enemy somewhere over the Channel. Given the name Chain Home or CH for short, this initiative for using radar had already shown great promise for Britain's defense.

At the same time, new aircraft production had finally found its pace. Among the latest fighter planes, the Submarine Spitfire and the Hawker Hurricane showed the most significant promise for success against the Luftwaffe's Messerschmitt Bf 109. More than a year ago, SIS intelligence had warned of an overwhelming German advantage in numbers of ready aircraft. The Luftwaffe had access to more than a thousand Messer-schmitts at the beginning of the war. Britain was fighting to catch up with the production of fighter planes in two cities that were sure to be among Germany's first bombing targets—Itchen and Woolston. The RAF had to be ready with fighters to defend the production of aircraft desperately needed from those factories. Beyond numbers, though, SIS intelligence had learned that the Messerschmitt was faster at high altitudes than its RAF adversaries and also carried more armament. The one good piece of news Sir Richard welcomed each day was that the Wehrmacht's concen-trated attention in Poland hadn't waned. Each day that Germany's war efforts remained in the east was a boon to Britain's desperate efforts to increase aircraft production and train pilots.

Sir Richard's thoughts concerned his son Nigel, who had recently transferred to the HMS Ark Royal. The aircraft supplied to aircraft carriers at sea bore no resemblance to the RAF fighters now in production. The Fleet Air Arm where Nigel flew depended on the aged, though dependable Fairey Swordfish, a bi-plane with a canvas-covered fuselage lovingly labeled "a string bag." Lt Nigel Moncrieff was somewhere in the North Atlantic today, either flying reconnaissance or flying with a cache of bombs or torpedoes that made the Swordfish effective against U-boats at sea. Against a German Messerschmitt in the air, however, the aged bi-planes would stand little chance of survival.

Meanwhile, Sir Richard's younger son, Lt Boyd Moncrieff, was sailing in convoy across the Atlantic, bound either for Halifax in Canada or returning to British waters. Both of his sons were aboard torpedo targets for the dreaded Nazi U-boats, a reality that kept Sir Richard's prayers on target, too.

Sir Richard's thoughts returned to Highfield, Angela, Susan, and Michael. "I am a most fortunate man," he said as he sat at his desk. He leaned back in his chair to look at the photo of Highfield that Boyd had taken on Susan and Michael's wedding day. Boyd had captured a candid shot of Highfield with his father and mother standing at the front door looking toward the setting sun in the west. Sir Richard longed for the day when he would return to Highfield, when war was behind them, and when he could again enjoy his home away from home.

"Someday," he said as he stood and approached the photo in its walnut frame. "Someday, I will walk through your front door again and embrace you, my darling, Angela. Until then, God keep you," he said quietly. He stood for another moment before bowing to the grand lady in the photo, his arm outstretched and blowing her a kiss.

Chapter 45

"It's hard to believe that Joseph has been in a cast for eight weeks now," Susan said. "Now that it's off, I hope he can forget what's behind and look forward to life without a wheelchair."

"I agree," Michael said as he drove out of the Boucher's driveway, "but I'm sure his youthful impatience will need curbing. He needs to follow the doctor's orders and take things slowly. I'd wager that the crutches will help for the first week or two, but soon, he'll be itching to abandon them, too."

"Now that the snow is finally gone and the days are getting longer, we'll all be able to get outside while there's still some afternoon sun," Susan said. "I'm sure Luc will keep an eye on him when Doris and Jacques are busy."

"Speaking of busy," Michael began, as he steered the sedan toward Charlottetown, "I have three stops to make in town after I deliver you to Dr. MacMillan. How long do you think an annual physical examination will take?"

"When I spoke with Emily yesterday, she advised me to plan on a full hour," Susan said. "Will that be enough time for you to finish your errands?"

"I'll make sure it is," Michael said. "I'll be sitting in the waiting room when the doctor has finished with you."

Michael drew the sedan up to the curb outside the main entrance to Charlottetown Hospital and walked Susan through the lobby to Dr. MacMillan's waiting room. With a customary public peck on the cheek, he left her sitting in her camel melton coat in a brown leather armchair. She was sorting through the magazines on the side table when he disappeared through the lobby doors.

Michael's regular rounds took him to the post office, the telegraph office, and the newsstand. Today, though, he needed to see Armand at Verrier's Hardware. However, when he stepped through the door, he was surprised to find Michelle at the cash register where he first met her almost two years ago.

As she looked up when the doorbell rang over Michael's head, he said, "Mrs. Royce, what a lovely surprise. I haven't seen you at that register in some time. What brings you back to your familiar old haunt?"

They laughed together as she answered, "Well, Mr. Moreland, I won't be here much longer. Since my father and mother are enjoying a late breakfast at Tea for Two, I volunteered to keep the home fires burning. But what brings you in today?"

"Nothing unusual," Michael said, "just some cabinet hardware for the kitchens in the two cottages at Highfield. We expect our first British evacuee children in less than two weeks."

"That must be exciting for you," Michelle began, "greeting new folks with that same British vocabulary and accent from your homeland. But where is Mrs. Moreland this morning?"

"Susan is with Dr. MacMillan," Michael said, as Michelle's face turned into a frown, "but not to worry. It's only a long-scheduled routine examination."

"Thank you for nipping my worry in the bud," Michelle said. "I'm afraid it's automatic. Now, let's have a look at some hardware."

A few minutes later, after Michelle filled Michael in on Grayson's student pilots' progress at the airfield, Michael had a box filled with brass hinges and pulls for the kitchen cabinets and drawers. Armand and Anna were coming in just as he headed for the door.

When their greetings were complete, Anna disappeared to the apartment upstairs while Armand and Michael retired to his office.

"Everything is quiet, Armand," Michael began, "almost too quiet."

"I agree," Armand said, "but we can be happy about the situation in Halifax. I monitor nothing but good news there."

"May it ever be so," Michael said, nodding in agreement. "How good can come out of bad is amazing. Now we have to hope that the enemy doesn't discover that their man at the docks in Halifax has become *our* man."

"Yes," Armand said. "We need them to continue trusting the data he provides. Thankfully, he knows his freedom at the war's end depends on what he can do for us now. His American citizenship also helps our cause. He needs to keep both Canada and the US happy. Otherwise, where can he go?"

"Exactly," Michael agreed.

"So, I hear you're welcoming guests from England soon?" Armand asked.

"That's right," Michael answered, "and I'd best be heading back to get this hardware installed," he added, holding up the box he carried. "I'll be on my way."

With a final wave to Michelle as he left the store, Michael was in the sedan and on his way to Charlottetown Hospital to pick up Susan. After parking the car, Michael passed through the main entrance doors and the lobby and arrived at Dr. MacMillan's waiting room just as Susan and the doctor returned from his examination room. Susan was wearing a look on her face that Michael could not decipher, somewhere between shock and surprise.

"Michael," Dr. MacMillan said as he reached out to shake Michael's hand, "you're right on time."

"Thank you, doctor," Michael said, and looking again at Susan added, "I trust everything is in order?" asking more of a question than making a statement.

"Oh, yes, Michael," Dr. MacMillan said, "but it's fortunate we're meeting like this. If you have a moment, I need to explain some details about your wife's examination today."

"Of course," Michael said.

"Wonderful," the doctor answered, "please follow me to my office."

Concerned and a bit confused, Michael followed the doctor to his office with Susan on his arm. Michael and Susan took seats opposite the doctor's desk.

"Michael," the doctor began, looking at Michael's worried face, "there is nothing to concern you about Susan's examination today, except for . . . " he paused as he looked for words.

"Except for what?" Michael said, leaning forward, his eyes riveted on the doctor.

"Except for her diet," Dr. MacMillan answered.

"Her diet?" Michael asked. "Why should I be concerned about her diet? Susan eats well, and we grow most of our food. Doris is an excellent cook, and we lack for nothing."

"I'm not concerned about the quality of her diet, Mr. Moreland," the doctor said. "All her tests show that she is healthy and eating well."

"Then what is your concern with her diet?" Michael asked.

"It's not really a concern, Michael," Dr. MacMillan said as he abandoned his professional demeanor to become a friend. "It's just that Susan is eating for two now."

Michael's jaw lost its tension, and his shoulders relaxed as he exhaled in relief. He turned to look at Susan, whose eyes were now smiling. They nodded together as Michael raised her hands to his lips and leaned ever so slightly forward, letting their foreheads touch before their eyes met again. Michael's lips found hers, their first kiss as expectant parents.

Dr. MacMillan sat back in his chair, content to sit as long as these two cared to celebrate. He knew Michael would suddenly have a dozen or more concerned questions about how to care for Susan, but he was no stranger to those queries. When Michael had all the answers he could hold, they left the doctor at his door. As he spirited her to their waiting car, Michael surrounded Susan with his whole being.

Chapter 46

F lt Lt Grayson Royce waited by the telephone at his desk at the RCAF airfield in Charlottetown. On a Friday afternoon shortly after four o'clock in late March of 1940, an RAF envelope lay open on his blotter, its typed contents still in his hands. After reading every line twice, he was about to read the letter a third time when he stopped, dropped it on the desk, and walked to the window.

The airfield was empty. Flight training was over for the day. All the aircraft were in the hangar where the maintenance crews had just begun their shift, preparing the planes for tomorrow's exercises. Though officially off duty, Grayson wasn't ready to leave the airfield yet. He was waiting for a telephone call from Michelle, but the letter on his desk held his thoughts captive as he looked out the window.

Almost any other RAF Flight Lieutenant would have been honored and overjoyed at the contents of the envelope on the desk. Promotions weren't easy to find under most circumstances, but they often became more prevalent during wartime. The numbers in every branch of British military service were growing. At every level, the military needed officers to lead those men. So, it was no surprise that the letter on Grayson's desk announced his promotion from Flight Lieutenant to Squadron Leader.

Instructors like Grayson rarely wore the insignia of Squadron Leaders. As Sqn Ldr Royce, especially during wartime, Grayson could expect to lead a squadron of men into the air, but not in training aircraft. They would be in fighters like the RAF's new Supermarine Spitfire or the Hawker Hurricane, searching the skies for Luftwaffe bombers escorted by squadrons of Messerschmitts. Every RAF officer knew his most important task was the defense of their homeland, Nazi Germany's prime target from the sky. With this promotion, Grayson knew his days on Prince Edward Island were ending soon.

Only months ago, he had longed to take to the skies as a fighter pilot, ready to pit his skills against the enemy for the sake of King and Country. But now everything had changed. He would no longer be risking only *his* life now. He looked again at Michelle's picture on his desk. Now, it was *their* life he would be risking, the life they had planned together. Even more, though, the telephone call he awaited might bring another reason, one he was ready to celebrate before the letter appeared on his desk.

He felt a sudden grief, not for himself, but for Michelle. She was the one who would be alone, fearing the worst, unable to control a single detail of life without him. Michelle was not ready to be alone. Fate had left her abandoned as a child. She would not be ready to face Grayson's abandonment, no matter how necessary or how honorable it might be.

New orders did not accompany the letter announcing his promotion, so he did not know how immediate his exit from the island might be. Still, he was sure the orders were forthcoming, perhaps arriving with the surprise and urgency of his last orders, leaving him only enough time to pack his bag before a ship took him across the ocean to England.

Just then, the telephone rang. Grayson had the receiver in his hand before the first ring ended.

"Michelle?" he asked.

"Yes, Grayson," she said, taken aback. "I expected to hear your usual 'Lt Royce speaking.' You caught me off guard."

"I'm sorry, Michelle. I'm just anxious to hear your news. Please, tell me what the doctor had to say," he asked.

"Can't you see me smiling through the telephone, darling?" she teased.

"Then you are . . . " Grayson began.

"Expecting?" Michelle asked.

"Yes," Grayson said. "Please don't hold me in suspense."

"Yes, Grayson!" Michelle squealed with delight. "The doctor said everything is just fine, and we can expect to be parents in early October!"

"Does anyone else know yet?" he asked.

"No one but the doctor and his nurse," she said, "but I heard from Susan just as I walked in the door. She and Michael have invited us to dinner tonight. She said something about some news to share but wouldn't add a word to soothe my curiosity. Of course, I didn't say anything about our news, so if you agree, they can be the first to know. I told her I would call her back after I spoke with you."

"Well, how do you feel, darling? Are you sure you're up to a night out?" he asked.

"Of course, Grayson. I'll burst if I don't tell someone soon, and apart from Mom and Dad, Susan and Michael would be my first choice."

"Well, let's go out and celebrate our announcement with them," he said.

"I'm so glad you agree," Michelle said, "I'll call and tell Susan we'll be delighted to have dinner with them. They should be here in just half an hour. Tell me you can make it by then," Michelle urged.

"I'm clearing my desk as we speak," he said, "and I'll be home as quickly as possible." Then, with unusual enthusiasm, he added, "I hope their news is something we can celebrate, too, because I'll be ready."

Surprised by his excitement, Michelle laughed, "Grayson? Is that you? I don't know what's gotten into you, but I'll take it! See you soon, sweetheart!"

Sqn Ldr Royce smiled as he hung up the telephone. Michelle's voice could light up any moment for him, as it had just now, especially with the good news from the doctor. Looking again at the letter on his desk, though, he shook his head. He had to find a way to deal with the news sitting there and settle his heart before he could share it with her. Until then, it was his secret, and secrets had no place in their marriage. He had to find a way to tell her.

He promised himself he wouldn't let anything dim the joy that burned so brightly for them tonight. Tonight, they needed to celebrate.

Chapter 47

Michael and Susan were crossing the street in front of St. Peter's after a visit with Fr. Hunt. Michael could hardly keep himself from hovering over Susan, keeping guard, offering his hand at the curb, then his arm, shielding her from invisible traffic, cautioning her every move. She wasn't used to his constant and persistent attention.

"Michael Moreland," she spouted, "I am not made of crystal; you don't need to wrap me in cotton for fear of breakage! Of course, I love your attention and care, but not all of it, all the time! Yes, I am with child, but our child is many months from arriving. Please save some of your energy for a day when I truly need it."

Michael had to laugh. "Please forgive me," he began. "I don't mean to overwhelm you. It's just that I have no experience at all with women who are expecting, and everything in me wants to do all I can to care for you. I don't know how much is enough or too much." Then, taking a breath, looking down at the curb, shaking his head, and looking up again, he smiled and said, "I will do better."

It was Susan's turn to laugh. "I know you will," she said as she hugged his arm. "We'll do it together. That's what Fr. Hunt told us, isn't it? We'll become parents together—but not all at once and certainly not today!"

"Point well made and taken, Mrs. Moreland," Michael said with a slight bow. "Now, dear wife, your chariot awaits. Allow me to open your door."

Smiling and shaking her head, Susan entered the sedan, and Michael closed her door. They would be across town in a few moments to pick up Grayson and Michelle.

"Mother has had a busy week," Susan said. "I've not seen her this enthusiastic about any of her interests as she is about the Canadian Red Cross Society."

"I could hardly believe how filled the driveway was on Saturday afternoon when she hosted their meeting," Michael said. "Will there be a meeting here every Saturday?"

"No," she answered. "The Summerside Town Hall is their primary meeting place. Women all over Prince County are busy providing knitted items, blankets, refugee clothing, hospital supplies, and quilts."

"Well, your mother loves hosting folks at Highfield, and by the numbers, folks enjoy coming here," Michael said.

"I'm sure part of the appeal is simple curiosity, but more and more, we are becoming less like strangers and more like neighbors here. I know that makes Mother happy," Susan said.

"When the group of evacuees from England arrives, I'm sure we'll have other local folks as guests. I hope that good homes are available for all the children who need them," Michael said.

"Don't forget," Susan said, "before next year at this time, we'll have a new little stranger of our own."

"How could I forget, Mother?" he asked. "That's when I'll become Papa."

"Papa?" Susan asked. "I don't know if I'll ever get used to that."

"I'm leaving 'Father' to your father, Susan," Michael said, "and, for the moment, we will remain just Susan and Michael. Here we are at the Royce residence."

Michael had no sooner opened the driver's door when Michelle and Grayson arrived at the car.

Grayson laughed as he opened the door for Michelle, saying, "Michelle has a nose for news, Susan. I hope you're ready with something good. Once I opened the front door, I had to run to keep up with her on the way to the car!"

"Oh, stop, Grayson," Michelle laughed as she slid into the car, "it's just that women don't like keeping secrets from each other."

"Or is it that women *can't* keep secrets?" Grayson asked as he joined her.

"Oh, we can keep secrets," Susan said, "but that's always less fun. It's better if we share them."

"I notice you're not saying anything, Michael," Michelle chided. "What are you hiding?"

Michael looked at Susan and raised one eyebrow as if to say, "Shall I?" Susan waved her hand, palm up as if to say, "Be my guest." Finally, Michael ended Michelle's suspense.

"To answer your question, Michelle," he said as he looked at Susan and smiled, "We are not hiding anything that shall not be fully revealed in a little less than eight months."

The back seat of the Ford sedan nearly exploded as Michelle erupted in laughter and cheers, bouncing up and down in excitement. Michael was glad he hadn't started backing out to the street, for he was sure he would have had trouble keeping the car on the driveway amidst all of the high-pitched squealing and laughter coming from the rear of the car. Michelle finally calmed enough to take a breath. Then, summoning her greatest reserve, she looked at Grayson and said, "Well, Susan, we should probably tell you that I had a doctor's appointment this afternoon . . . "

Susan's eyes grew large as she took a breath and opened her mouth, but no words came out. Instead, Michelle, unable to hold back any longer, said, "And perhaps the hospital maternity ward can arrange for adjoining rooms so we can be together!"

It was Susan's turn to erupt in laughter and cheers as she climbed halfway over the front seat to hug Michelle while the two giggled together in joy.

Although the women's voices never quieted during the twenty-minute drive to the Port O' Call restaurant, Michael and Grayson said all they needed to each other in a momentary glance in the rearview mirror. Grayson offered his smile, a thumbs up, and a congratulatory hand on Michael's shoulder. Michael matched Grayson's smile with his own and added his nod of congratulation.

Once at their table, the celebration continued when Grayson ordered a bottle of prosecco and offered a toast. "To Susan and Michael and their offspring yet to be revealed: May your child enjoy Susan's beauty and intellect along with Michael's ingenuity and tender heart." With their glasses still raised, Michael added, "And may Michelle and Grayson enjoy all the blessings God has in store for their new family, a child filled with Michelle's sparkle and abounding in Grayson's calm courage."

The conversation over dinner never strayed from all the preparations that parents of first-borns must make. "Michael already has plans to install a door between our bedroom and the adjacent bedroom in the Servants' Quarters," Susan began. "That room will become the nursery."

"Oh," Michelle began, "At that end of the hall, no one in the other bedrooms will ever hear a baby."

"Exactly," Susan said, "and the kitchen and laundry are just down the stairs whenever we need bottles or diapers."

"We haven't begun to plan yet," Michelle began. "You've got to come over tomorrow, Susan, so I can catch up. With only two of us at home, we have rooms to spare, but I'd love for us to put our heads together," Michelle said.

Somehow, the two couples managed to look at the menu and eat dinner. While they waited for dessert, the women visited the Ladies' Room. Once they were out of earshot, Grayson turned to Michael.

"I need to share some news with you, Michael," he said, "news I haven't been able to share with Michelle yet."

"Are you sure?" Michael asked, "Because . . . "

"I need to tell someone," Grayson interrupted, "and I will share it with Michelle as soon as we are home tonight. Please bear with me now, Michael. I need to tell someone I trust."

"Of course," Michael said. "I'm glad to listen."

After telling Michael of his promotion, what he believed the future would hold for him during wartime, and his concerns for Michelle, Grayson looked down a moment before looking back at Michael.

"It's too big for me, Michael, beyond me. I don't know what to do," he said.

"I can't begin to offer any advice, Grayson," Michael began, "I've never had to look forward to anything so serious and all-consuming. But, I know someone who I trust will be able to help."

Lifting his head to look at Michael, Grayson asked, "Who?"

"Fr. Hunt, Grayson. I believe he will be able to give you some perspective so you don't feel so lost," Michael said.

"You think so?" Grayson asked. "What would he know about fighter pilots going to war or leaving expectant wives behind?"

"Probably nothing," Michael admitted, "but I believe he'll be able to offer you more than you are expecting, and from my experience, I've never been sorry when I've spoken with him."

"All right," Grayson said, nodding, "Perhaps I can call on him tomorrow if he is available. I'm afraid I haven't spoken to him since our wedding. He was a caring, helpful cleric, then. Perhaps he'll be able to help me now."

The drive home was quieter than the drive to the restaurant. Although a calm exhaustion seemed to surround the ladies, they lacked no subject for conversation, especially when preparing for their new arrivals. Once Michael and Susan were alone for their return to Highfield, Susan surprised Michael with some news.

"I think something is going on with Emily and Dr. MacMillan, but I don't know just what yet," Susan said.

"What makes you think that?" Michael asked.

"Well, just after she returned from the hospital this afternoon, perhaps fifteen minutes before we left to pick up Michelle and Grayson tonight, she knocked at our door while I was dressing," Susan said. "You know how careful she is never to intrude on us, but when she saw that I was dressing to go out, she asked if she could speak with me when we returned tonight. She should be waiting when we arrive."

"And you have no idea what's on her mind?" Michael asked. "Your intuition is usually quite dependable," he said, smiling.

"Well, not exactly, Michael," Susan said, "but they have been seeing each other more regularly—and exclusively—for several months now."

"And you expect the next step is imminent?" Michael asked.

"Ordinarily, I would," she answered, "but both have the habit of surprising me. I'm not ready to make any predictions at the moment."

"Well, darling, whatever it is," Michael smiled, "when you find out, don't leave me in suspense too long, all right?"

"Of course not," she said. "After all, we have no secrets, have we?"

"On that count," Michael said, "let me tell you about my conversation with Grayson. By now, Michelle should know everything I know."

Chapter 48

Michael and Susan arrived at St. Peter's for morning prayer on a chilly Saturday morning in late March. A few other parish members were present, but they also saw Grayson and Michelle seated near the back of the church. The sisters filed in and intoned the first antiphon only a moment later. When the service ended, Michelle joined Michael and Susan while Grayson walked to the front of the church to speak with Fr. Hunt. A moment later, Fr. Hunt and Grayson turned toward the hallway leading to Fr. Hunt's office.

While waiting in the narthex, Michelle said, "Grayson told me about his promotion last night and his worries for me and our baby if he has to report for active duty."

"I'm glad he could tell you," Michael said. "I'm sure it was difficult news to bring and to receive."

Michelle nodded. "Of course, I want him safe here at home, but we've always known the RAF might call him to active duty. Now, though, it seems he's carrying an impossible burden. I've never seen him so overwrought, so dark. He hardly slept all night, tossing and turning and talking in his sleep."

"I've known Grayson from childhood, Michelle," Susan said. "Even as a boy, I remember him as an over-achiever, terribly serious, dedicated to caring for his mother and sister. But since he met you, I've seen a more relaxed and happy Grayson than I've ever seen before. I hope his worries are only temporary. Perhaps Fr. Hunt can help him shed them."

Meanwhile, Grayson was sitting stiffly in one of the leather armchairs in front of the mahogany desk in Fr. Hunt's office. Though trying to relax, he leaned forward in nervous anticipation as Fr. Hunt took his seat. He took a moment to tell Fr. Hunt about his promotion to Squadron Leader, ending with, "When the war broke out, Michelle and

I expected the RAF might call me to combat duty someday. This promotion signals that day may be very soon." Then he looked down and sat, folding and unfolding his hands.

Fr. Hunt nodded and said, "I understand, Grayson. Please go on."

Grayson continued, "Well, now we have a baby on the way, and this promotion means I could be leaving Michelle for duty in Europe any day now. I fear I can't be the husband and father I need to be, nor the pilot and Squadron Leader I need to be, and I certainly can't promise her I'll come home whole and well."

Fr. Hunt paused a moment, considering Grayson's concerns. Then he stood and walked to a painting on his wall. Pointing to it, he said, "This is a copy of a painting of St. Francis preaching to the birds. The original was painted in Italy by an artist named Giotto in 1299."

With a quizzical look, Grayson nodded as Fr. Hunt continued, "Birds are a favorite of mine, Grayson, as they were of our Savior. Jesus spoke about birds often. He said, 'Consider the birds of the air. They neither sow nor reap, yet your heavenly Father feeds them.' He also told us that no bird falls to the ground without the Father knowing."

After considering a moment, Grayson said, "I don't understand, Father," shaking his head. "What have those birds to do with me?"

Fr. Hunt reached for a smaller frame hanging on the wall beside the painting of St. Francis. He offered it to Grayson, saying, "A young man you know gave this to me some time ago. You may find it helpful, Grayson."

The frame was small and held a single page of fourteen lines. Grayson took a moment to read it.

Until He Dies

With hollow bones a bird learns how to fly
Not once despising frame all delicate,
But pushed without the nest his wings to try,
Fast finds the air till flight's inveterate -
And pauses not to ponder nor to care
How fragile are his limbs amidst his flight,
But boldly lifts his wings upon the air
And mounts the wind all ignorant of fright.
And so each day, until he dies, he lives!
He soars aloft, aloud, and all replete,
Content with gifts that his Creator gives,

His weakness making all his life complete.
Who curses frailty wisdom needs implore,
For only those whose bones are hollow soar.

When Grayson looked up from the frame, Fr. Hunt said, "A bird's hollow bones, his 'frailty,' the poet says, enables him to fly."

"Yes," Grayson said, "it's remarkable."

"And birds are not created to carry burdens, are they?" Fr. Hunt asked.

"No," Grayson answered.

"Tell me, Grayson, when did you first want to be a pilot?" Fr. Hunt asked

"The first time my father took me up to fly with him. I think I was six years old. I knew then that I had to fly," Grayson said.

"And did you consider then that flying was dangerous, that equipment could fail, or that you might crash?" Fr. Hunt asked.

"It never crossed my mind," he said, "I simply knew that I had to fly."

"And flying a fighter plane in combat, Grayson," Fr. Hunt said, "requires every ounce of concentration you can muster, correct?"

"Yes, Father," Grayson agreed.

"So, would it be fair to say that a fighter pilot should leave every other burden aside when he enters the cockpit on a mission?" Fr. Hunt asked.

"Yes," Grayson answered, "that would be correct."

Fr. Hunt said, "Grayson, as I remember, your father died when you were a boy. Is that correct?"

"Yes, that's correct, Father, in the Great War."

"And were you ever charged with being 'the man of the house' in your father's absence?" Fr. Hunt asked.

Grayson didn't hesitate. "Yes, I was," he began. "Father gave me that assignment when he left home on the troop train. I also remember him saying, 'Make me proud, Son.' I've tried to make him proud all my life."

"And after his death," Fr. Hunt asked, "were you ever reminded of that charge at home?"

"Often, Father," Grayson said, "regularly. But what does that have to do with the present conversation?"

"A great deal, Grayson," Fr. Hunt said, looking at him through understanding eyes, "because you're living under an impossible burden today. You've believed the lie that you're supposed to be able to bear it."

"What do you mean?" Grayson asked.

"With the best of intentions, parents often saddle their children with impossible burdens. No boy can shoulder the one your father gave you," Fr. Hunt began. "You've struggled to live up to it since you were six. Now, as a man, you're trying to take on further burdens you cannot bear."

Grayson sat, looking at Fr. Hunt, trying to understand.

"A bird doesn't know that many of his bones are hollow, Grayson. He is born to fly. Mortals like you and I have spirits that are supposed to soar. Unfortunately, we often take on inappropriate burdens; our parents deliver some, and we choose others for ourselves. But we were not made to bear them. We forget that we are only men. We rail at ourselves, saying 'I should be able to . . . ' and we live burdened and guilty."

Fr. Hunt paused as Grayson looked up at him.

"Now that you're married and you and Michelle are expecting a baby," Fr. Hunt said, "perhaps it's time you let God relieve you of some of those burdens."

"But, I am an RAF pilot during wartime, Father. I may have to ship out any day. How can I care for my wife and child or look forward to our future when my life may be required of me in battle at any time?" Grayson asked.

"That's a perfectly reasonable question from a man who took on an impossible burden as a boy," Fr. Hunt began, "a man who has struggled for years to fulfill an impossible role. The problem, Grayson, is that those futile years have left you desperate, fearful, and joyless."

Grayson took a moment before responding. Then he looked at Fr. Hunt and said, "I don't know what to do, Father. I've never lived any other way."

"I would also venture to guess that you've sworn to yourself you would never abandon your wife and child as your father did. Would my guess be correct, Grayson?" Fr. Hunt asked.

Grayson looked up and nodded as his eyes filled with tears.

Fr. Hunt leaned forward and spoke quietly. "When you lead a squadron into battle, Grayson, God will go with you. But you must abandon the orders you've given yourself and learn to listen only to his still, small voice. Attune your ear to the one who gave you the passion to fly. No sparrow falls to the ground without his knowledge, and he has promised that you are worth far more than many sparrows. He knows every hair of your head, Grayson."

Grayson nodded as Fr. Hunt continued.

"God has provided you with a remarkable intellect, superior training, keenly honed skills, and first-class aircraft. Now, you must sacrifice the impossible responsibilities you continue to assign yourself. Your safety and that of the men who follow you will depend on the ear you give to him," Fr. Hunt said, pointing toward heaven. "Both in and out of battle, you must listen for his still, small voice. And never doubt that the same one who guards you in the air will also guard Michelle and your child here. You must relinquish that burden, too. Give it to the one who has promised to bear it. He will not leave you, Grayson. He will not forsake you."

As Grayson looked up, Fr. Hunt said, "Think on these things, and let's talk again soon."

Rising, Grayson offered his hand, and Fr. Hunt received it with both of his, saying, "Soon, Grayson, soon."

"Thank you, Father," Grayson said, and the two men left the office to make their way to the nave, where Michelle was waiting at one of the kneelers. Grayson joined her there, and she took his hand while Fr. Hunt offered a blessing for them. As he prayed for Grayson to abandon the burdens of his boyhood, Michelle felt Grayson's shoulders begin to tremble, and she heard him begin to sob quietly. Several minutes later, he looked up at Michelle, who hugged him long and tight. Never had they been closer in mind, heart, and spirit. With Fr. Hunt's blessing for them and their child, they left the church with Susan and Michael.

As they approached the street, Grayson said, "I had no appetite for breakfast earlier this morning, but I'm ready to eat now. Would anyone else care to stop with me at the Yeoman's Board?"

"Well, it's almost ten o'clock, and my breakfast is more than four hours old," Michael said. "I know I could eat something, and since our wives are both eating for two . . . " Michael said, eyeing Susan and Michelle.

"I'll be happy to join you," Michelle smiled, "and Susan?" she asked, "You won't desert me, will you?"

"Try to keep me away," Susan laughed as they walked toward their cars together. "Besides, Michelle," Susan said, "I need to tell you the latest about Emily and Dr. MacMillan."

Even the men were intrigued now, and the two couples wasted no time driving to the restaurant.

Chapter 49

L t Boyd Moncrieff chose to remain below decks as a storm raged in the North Atlantic. Steaming east toward the UK in early March, the Revenge had continuously sailed the North Atlantic in convoy for several months. Her last convoy bound for Halifax included another well-guarded shipment of gold sent to pay for more military supplies from the US. That convoy was one not easily forgotten. While the convoy formed in early February, the Revenge collided with a British tanker, the SS Apalachee. Though the damage to the Revenge was light, repairs forced her to remain at Halifax for several weeks.

Now bound for Liverpool, the Revenge sailed with convoy HX19, helping to guard some forty-five ships, the majority British but with others from France, Norway, Panama, and Greece. Their cargoes varied from crude oil, benzine, and other petroleum products to wool, grain, wheat, and lumber. A lifeline for the UK, convoys like these delivered products essential to the war effort while remaining prime targets of Nazi U-boats. Constant airborne reconnaissance and radar helped to keep the convoy safe, and Lt Boyd Moncrieff's role as Chief Communications Officer was essential.

He had only recently learned that his elder brother, Nigel, had been transferred to the HMS Ark Royal. Some months earlier, when Nigel was aboard the HMS Furious, their ships had passed each other in the North Atlantic. However, the Ark Royal was somewhere in the North Sea now, and Nigel was likely in the air on reconnaissance or launching torpedoes and dropping bombs from a Fairey Swordfish or one of the newer Blackburn B-24 Skuas.

Though the Revenge had spent significant time in port, Boyd had enjoyed only a few hours of shore leave. He was ready to trade his sea legs for a pair more accustomed to Mother Earth when they arrived in the UK, but the constant German threat at sea promised no guarantee for shore leave, especially anywhere near the UK. Those waters were the prime hunting ground of the Kriegsmarine.

Meanwhile, Lt Nigel Moncrieff, sailing with the Fleet Air Arm aboard the HMS Ark Royal, had recently returned from the South American coast where the Ark Royal had been searching for German commerce raiders. Arriving in Devonport while escorting the damaged HMS Exeter, the Ark Royal proceeded to Portsmouth, where she re-fueled and took on supplies. The Ark Royal had steamed for Scapa Flow with some new personnel aboard.

Air time in the cockpit was a regular duty for Lt Moncrieff, as surveillance in the U-boat-infested waters around the UK was constant. Fortunately, flying a Blackburn B-24 Skua with its closed cockpit design was more comfortable than the open Fairey Swordfish. More capable as a dive bomber than a fighter, the Skua had proven an effective weapon against the dreaded U-boats. Nigel longed for the day his squadron would bring the battle to a German cruiser or battleship. There, the Skua could prove its mettle in short order.

At the same time, Sir Richard Moncrieff was pleased to follow his sons' ships at sea, one advantage a retired Royal Navy Rear Admiral in SIS could claim. Although he had no authority that could affect their service or their safety, the knowledge of their whereabouts helped to keep his anxiety at bay.

Other matters he was following at SIS brought him sparse comfort, though. The war brought a few small victories in February—the RAF shot down a Luftwaffe bomber over British soil near Whitby, five German U-boats had been sunk or lost at sea, and German aircraft bombed and sank their own Leberecht Maass, killing 280 aboard. In a rescue effort, the German destroyer, Max Schultz, sank after hitting a mine, taking 308 German seamen to their deaths.

Beyond these small victories, however, were the darker, unreported evils—another Jewish ghetto established in Poland, further Soviet mass deportations of Poles to Siberian prisons and labor camps, and Czech Jews forced to close their businesses under Nazi rule. Sir Richard feared the next wave of revelations his operatives would report. The evils of the Nazis, followed by those of the Soviets, were beyond his comprehension.

Meanwhile, though, the regular correspondence he enjoyed from Highfield remained the brightest part of every day. He loved hearing that Angela was thriving and enjoying more and more of the local life in Charlottetown. Now that Susan was expecting, he was beginning to enjoy thoughts of retirement and the time it would bring to enjoy grandchildren. Michael's ingenuity continued to keep Highfield thriving as the estate became increasingly self-sufficient while helping the local economy by producing crops and offering employment to families still in need following the Great Depression.

Sir Richard's mind went back to the Great War. Compared to the present conflict, that war seemed simple. The Great War was merely a conquest fueled by nationalism and pride that forced most of the world into war. Four imperial dynasties fell when the war ended. Few who lived through those years believed civilization would endure such a war again.

But now, the ideologies weren't only a reflection of pride or nationalism. The evil today demanded the subjugation or annihilation of peoples based only on their bloodline and birthright. Sir Richard could think of no darker evil than the one he discovered every day in the continued reports from SIS operatives in Germany, Poland, and Russia.

He reached to his bottom drawer for his bottle of Dewars and closed the dossier he had finished reading. "No more tonight," he told himself. Instead, he chose to open his top drawer, where he kept Angela's letters and those from his children in a leather portfolio. He read and sipped for the next thirty minutes—read and re-read—before securing each letter again. Then he holstered his Walther PPK, donned his overcoat and fedora, turned off the desk lamp, and locked his office door for the night. Tomorrow would be another day.

Chapter 50

On Friday after lunch, Emily called Highfield to speak with Susan. Fortunately, when Emily rang, Susan was passing the telephone on her way to the laundry. After their hellos, Emily explained the reason for her call.

"Andrew has asked me to help him with an errand for his mother this afternoon. I shall probably be an hour beyond my usual return time if that seems all right with you," she said.

"Of course," Susan said, "but I hadn't heard his mother was in town. What a surprise."

"Oh, she isn't," Emily said. "Andrew has only just returned from a short visit to Quebec. I understand she hasn't been entirely well over the past two weeks and isn't ready to leave the house yet. She gave him a task that requires a jeweler, and he decided to use a local jeweler he found here on Grafton Street rather than one in Quebec."

"I'm so sorry to hear that Andrew's mother isn't well, Emily. Please tell him I was asking for her," Susan said.

"I will," Emily promised, "and I will see you no more than an hour after my usual time."

Susan suspected nothing unusual until after dinner that night at Highfield. Only three were left at the table enjoying dessert—Emily, Susan, and Lady Moncrieff.

"So," Susan began, "was your errand with Andrew successful?"

"Yes, I believe so," Emily said, "but we shan't know for sure until the jeweler finishes his work."

"What sort of work is required?" Lady Moncrieff asked.

"Well," Emily began, "Andrew's mother has several rings that need attention. They are all quite beautiful. One, with a large ruby, requires re-setting. The stone is loose, and Andrew's mother fears she may lose it. Two others need to be re-sized. It seems his mother's fingers are smaller than they once were. All the rings had been gifts from Andrew's father years ago."

"I've never visited that jewelry store," Susan said. "Did you see many fine pieces?"

"Oh, yes, Susan," Emily said, "but I have no experience at all with fine jewelry, so I found myself quite ignorant among so many beautiful pieces. I suspect Andrew sensed my discomfort, so while the jeweler examined his mother's rings, he suggested I enjoy trying on some beautiful ones from the jeweler's case. There were other rubies, emeralds, and sapphires, I think they were called. Andrew insisted I try on several until they found one that fit perfectly. I must confess, I felt like a princess, but I'll not have to worry about wearing such beautiful things. A nurse's hands are not made for lovely rings."

Susan's eye found her mother's, and both turned back to Emily, who was busy enjoying a chocolate-covered macaroon with her tea.

"Emily," Lady Moncrieff said, "what size was the ring that fit perfectly?"

"I believe it was a size 6," Emily answered. "The gentleman at the counter heard the British in my voice and offered to interpret the British size, which he told me would be a size L," Emily said. "Interestingly, it was the same size as two of Andrew's mother's rings."

"Emily," Susan began, "have you wondered why Andrew needed your help for his errand? As you describe it, his task seems rather straightforward and one he could have accomplished without your help, doesn't it?"

"Now that you mention it," Emily said, "I must agree. He really didn't need my help for anything," Emily said.

"Except for one thing," Lady Moncrieff said.

"One thing?" Emily asked.

"Yes," Lady Moncrieff agreed. "Your presence was essential if he hoped to learn your ring size."

"My ring size?" Emily asked. "Why would he need to learn that?"

"Yes," Susan agreed, asking, "Why would any man who professes his love for a woman need to know her ring size?"

Emily's eyes grew large as she looked at Susan, Lady Moncrieff, then back at Susan.

"You don't think?" Emily began, stopping to put her hand over her mouth lest her conclusion reach their ears. "So it was all a ruse?" she exclaimed, "and," after a second thought, "his mother was aware of his plan as well?" she asked.

"I suspect so," Susan nodded. Emily looked from Susan to Lady Moncrieff, who joined Susan's nod.

"A ring for me?" Emily said quietly, nearly breathless, looking from face to face again. Then, making a further discovery, "An engagement ring?" she dared to suggest.

"I would suspect so," Lady Moncrieff said. "I would say in all probability that Dr. MacMillan was shopping for an engagement ring. I am pleased that you could be of such fine assistance to him," she said, smiling.

Transfixed momentarily, Emily put her half-eaten macaroon back on her plate and sat quietly, looking at her left hand and staring at a ring not yet on her finger.

"May I offer one small piece of advice, Emily?" Susan asked.

Removing her eyes from her hand, Emily looked up and answered, "Of course, Susan."

"If we are correct," Susan began, "you must remain completely amazed when Andrew presents you with a ring. That is a moment he will have long anticipated. He will want to surprise you."

Emily, still in a state of shock, could only smile and nod.

The next day, while sitting at the Yeoman's Board enjoying breakfast with Michelle, Michael, and Grayson, Susan said, "And that's all the news I have to report concerning Emily and Dr. MacMillan. Her innocence is most entertaining, wouldn't you agree?"

"Yes," Michael began, "but another surprise is almost equally entertaining."

"Which is?" Susan asked.

"That you could wait until morning to tell anyone, darling," Michael laughed.

Michelle laughed, adding, "Susan has always been the very model of patience and discretion, Michael. You know that."

"I dare not disagree," Grayson said. "But, Susan, you must promise to inform us when the next shoe drops. Promise?" he asked.

Susan raised her right hand with a smile and said, "Promise!"

Chapter 51

The arrival of spring in 1940 saw many changes at Highfield. Chief among them was the arrival of thirteen evacuee children from England. Lady Moncrieff, well-known in Suffolk, England, for her work supporting orphanages on Britain's east coast following the Great War, had contacted several social welfare agencies in Suffolk near Clifton Manor. Together, they had been able to sponsor and arrange to evacuate several hundred children to Canada. Among them, thirteen "guest children" were currently bound for Highfield, where two new cottages awaited them. Several host families on Prince Edward Island had already applied to house a child, so the Highfield family anticipated hosting all thirteen only temporarily.

Earlier in the year, Michael had noticed a new maturity in the Boucher children, making Luc, Joseph, Ingrid, and Patrice true partners in the daily work it took to keep a working estate going. The arrival of thirteen guest children, six boys and seven girls, provided one more opportunity for them to prove their mettle.

The guest boys ranged in age from six to fourteen and the girls from eight to fifteen. They arrived at Highfield on a bus chartered by Lady Moncrieff, who was on hand to greet each of the children. All seemed travel-weary from their overnight train ride from Halifax, so while Luc and Ingrid delivered their luggage to the cottages, Lady Moncrieff hosted lunch for them at Highfield. Michael and Susan had added every leaf to the dining room table to accommodate all their guests.

"Ladies and gentlemen," Lady Moncrieff said from the head of the table, "Highfield is delighted to welcome you to Prince Edward Island. While we deliver your trunks and cases to your cottages, I hope you will enjoy lunch here with me. First of all, though, I hope to learn all of your names and where your homes are in England. My assistant," she said as she indicated Patrice, who waited with a notebook and pencil in hand, "will keep a record for me so that I will soon be able to remember all of you."

Though tired and a bit disheveled, each of the children found his way to the head of the table and politely offered his name and that of his town or village, the older children helping the younger. Patrice smiled for each, especially when she needed help spelling village names like Aldeburgh and Pettaugh. Their first task completed, the children were back in their seats and ready to enjoy a lunch that included a savory shepherd's pie, cold apple cider, and a warm custard tart.

With their appetites satisfied, the boys followed Luc, and the girls followed Ingrid to their cottages. Newly finished, the cottages still smelled of fresh paint, while every room enjoyed brightly colored curtains against walls and ceilings of warm white. Susan had chosen coordinating bed-clothes and towels, shades of blue for the boys, and warmer colors for the girls. While the children were still at lunch, Patrice prepared bed cards for each bed, neatly inscribed with each child's name. Under each pillow, she also left a Hershey's chocolate bar and a pack of chewing gum. Luc and Ingrid had been sure to keep the fires burning in the woodstoves so each room was warm and comfortable.

Later that afternoon, when the children had settled in their rooms and there was still plenty of afternoon sun, Luc and Ingrid gave them a tour around the grounds. Although there was a lot to see, the children enjoyed the livestock most, especially Abe and Billie. Before the sun was too low, Susan gathered everyone for photos at Highfield's front door, the stable, and their cottages.

"Your family and friends in England will want to see where you landed in Canada," Susan said, "so we'll have some photos available for all of you to send back in a letter later this week. I teach at the school that you can just see across the east pasture," she said as she pointed. "That's our next stop, where I have paper and pencils for all of you so you can begin your letters tonight."

It was obvious that the children were already beginning to feel more comfortable at Highfield. They were not as quiet, were eager to ask questions, and seemed genuinely excited by everything the estate had to offer. One of the younger boys, a lad named Philip, asked, "May I stay here until the war ends, please? I don't want to go anywhere else. I want to stay with the horses." Susan could only answer, "We'll have to see, Philip. There are still lots of adventures ahead for all of us."

Lady Moncrieff met the children again at dinner, where each found a place card with his name inscribed at his seat. Patrice had prepared a chart at the head of the table for Lady Moncrieff so that she could recall each child's name from her place. When she asked about their afternoon, the children showed no hesitance in responding. That Lady Moncrieff seemed to have memorized their names made them feel even more welcome and at home. She guided the conversation to learn something new from each of the children as Patrice made notes about their families and homes in England, their expectations of Canada, and especially what they missed most since they boarded the ship in England. After hot chocolate and shortbread completed their meal, Luc and Ingrid escorted the children to their cottages.

Later, Lady Moncrieff, Susan, and Michael sat together in front of the fireplace in the study.

"I can't imagine traveling across the Atlantic at the age of six without my family," Lady Moncrieff said as she sipped her cordial. "I hope each of them found something here today to comfort them after such a journey."

"I'm sure we shall see some tears and homesickness over the next days," Susan said, "but from my brief observations, most seem to be looking forward rather than backward."

"The majority are from orphanages. Is that not true?" Michael asked. "Perhaps they will miss little of their lives in Suffolk."

"That may be true, Michael," Lady Moncrieff said. "For them, the future may look brighter than their past."

"I hope those who came from warm homes find warm ones here," Susan said, "and I am glad we can provide a first stop for them."

"For several," Lady Moncrieff began, "the stay here may be short. The Red Cross is arranging interviews with prospective parents for several younger children tomorrow afternoon. Those children may find families as early as tomorrow evening."

"I hope that is so, Mother," Susan said, "though little Philip already won my heart when he asked if he could stay at Highfield until the war ends."

"Until the war ends," Michael said, looking into the fire with his snifter in his hand. "May it be soon," he said, addressing the ladies and lifting his glass. In turn, they lifted their glasses and echoed in unison, "May it be soon."

Chapter 52

On a Monday morning in early April, Michael drove the flatbed into Charlottetown to make regular stops at the telegraph, post office, and bank. The telegraph office was more of a habitual stop now that most communications from London arrived at Highfield by radio. No telegrams awaited him today, so Michael proceeded to the post office. Among the letters in Highfield's box was one addressed to Michael from Attorney Leighton in Quebec. Letters from his lawyer used to appear every quarter, but they had been arriving monthly for some time. The Moreland Radiator Cooling Shroud's success resulted in several new licensees, all announced in letters posted in Quebec, each containing a bank draft.

Michael was not accustomed to handling money and certainly not to personal wealth. His father's position as the superintendent of Clifton Manor often included budgets and ledgers that later fell to Michael to manage. The Moncrieffs had always treated his family as their own, and under their care, even in the most trying of times, his family had lacked for nothing. Now, though, Michael's financial status had changed dramatically. A simple invention inspired by his father's penchant for problem-solving provided more income for his family than he could have imagined.

When Michael returned to his truck, he sat with his elbows resting on the steering wheel while he opened the envelope. He scanned the usual cover letter from his lawyer and looked at the enclosed bank draft. Not believing his eyes, he leaned closer and looked again. He sat back against the seat and made a quick mental calculation. The monthly check in his hands was the equivalent of more than ten years of an average Canadian household's income.

Two nights earlier, he and Susan had discussed some needs at Highfield. The three-year-old Ford sedan that came with the house when Sir

Richard bought the property in 1937 was used primarily for errands most days. Often, it was unavailable when Lady Moncrieff wished to shop in town. When not busy at the sawmill, the tractor was always in demand at two or more other places in the fields. Michael's flatbed was also shared all over the estate, sometimes forcing him to borrow Susan's cabriolet for errands in town. They had agreed that an investment in vehicles was overdue. As Michael looked at the check in his hand, he said, "The time has come. Here is the answer."

Michael's next stop was the bank, where he deposited the check and verified his bank balance. He stopped in the flatbed to take a notepad and pencil from his attaché. Making a few calculations on the notepad, he nodded for his own benefit, returned the notebook to the attaché, and drove toward Freeman Ford.

Although Steve Freeman, the owner of Freeman Ford, had become a friend and trusted businessman, Michael always made Bill Stewart in the Parts Department his first stop whenever he stopped at the dealership.

"Michael Moreland," Bill said when he saw Michael come through the door, "I haven't seen you since your wife drove away in that red cabriolet. How have you been?"

"Well, Bill, as a matter of fact, very well. Going to be a new dad this fall, in case you hadn't heard," Michael said.

"No, I hadn't heard," Bill said with a smile. "Congratulations, Michael!" he added as he offered his hand.

"How about you, Bill? Doing well, you and Mrs. Stewart?" Michael asked.

"The best," Bill said. Then he lowered his voice to say, "We've come into some unexpected income. A check has appeared in the mail on the fifteenth of the month for the past four months. The envelopes are posted from a law office in Quebec. They won't tell us anything about the source. Anyway, it's enough money to buy that new blue coupe outside that's wearing my plates," he said proudly.

"I'm happy for you, Bill. I saw it when I came in. It's a beauty," Michael said.

"We think so, too," Bill said, "but you didn't come here today to look at my new car. What can I do for you?"

"I need to speak with Steve today. We're keeping our vehicles at Highfield pretty busy these days. We need another car and maybe another truck at Highfield. Is Steve in today?" Michael asked.

"Sure is, and you know where," Bill said as he pointed toward the showroom.

Steve Freeman was sitting alone in the showroom. Monday wasn't usually a busy day at Freeman Ford. He was glad to hear from Michael, though, and he had immediate solutions for two out of three of Michael's needs.

"I have a 1940 Deluxe sedan right here on the showroom floor. It has the flathead V-8, you know well, hydraulic brakes, and something you've never seen. The shift lever is mounted on the steering column so that the front seat easily seats three," Steve said.

"What do you call that color," Michael asked as he walked around the car.

"It's called Claret Maroon," Steve said, "a welcome addition to the available colors this year. Take a look under the hood. You may recognize something there."

Michael had to smile. He knew what Steve meant.

"I expected to see that cooling shroud, Steve, and there it is. But I also need to see one on a new platform stake body truck," Michael said.

"I have two parked behind the garage, Michael, in your choice of red or green," Steve said.

"And what about the tractor and all the implements?" Michael asked.

"Give me a few days on those," Steve said. "They're not in my regular line, but a dealer in Moncton owes me a favor. I'm sure he can supply what you need."

"All right," Michael said. "Let's look at the numbers, and if your pencil is sharp enough, perhaps you'll be delivering two out of the three to us at Highfield tomorrow."

"Follow me to my office," Steve said as he smiled and turned toward his open door.

Susan was glad to hear about the expected delivery scheduled for Tuesday morning, but she and Michael decided to surprise her mother. After one look at the sleek, shiny, maroon sedan with its mohair upholstery, Lady Moncrieff scheduled a premier afternoon drive with Michael and Susan. Michael had chosen green for the new flatbed to avoid the red of Susan's cabriolet. Jacques and Luc were overjoyed when they saw the new truck and heard about the new tractor and implements.

"We won't be waiting for Michael to return with the truck anymore," Jacques said. "And now we can park one tractor at the sawmill while the other is in the field, Luc! We'll get twice as much done."

Michael had to smile. He looked at Susan, his expectant wife, beaming as her mother sat in her new car, enjoying the new car smell and the roomy interior. Jacques was busy showing Luc the engine in the new flatbed and telling him about all the work the new harrow, hay baler, and other implements would help accomplish in the fields.

Michael couldn't have foreseen any part of the prosperity and blessing he enjoyed today and every day. He deserved none of it, but he knew where it came from. The war and its evils overshadowed every day, of course, but today, all he could do was count his blessings and be grateful.

Chapter 53

On a Friday morning in early May, Dr. MacMillan telephoned Highfield and asked to speak with Lady Moncrieff. Susan answered the telephone and found her mother reading the newspaper in the dining room.

"Mother, Dr. MacMillan would like to speak with you on the telephone. Shall I tell him you are in?" Susan asked.

"Yes, Susan," Lady Moncrieff answered. "Please tell him I will be available in just a moment."

Lady Moncrieff's conversation with the doctor was brief, and Susan could hear only one side. All Susan heard her mother say was, "Yes, I believe I could meet with you then. I'd like to include two others in the conversation if you don't mind," and, "Of course, I shan't say a word."

Susan was ablaze with curiosity. When her mother hung up the telephone, Susan was full of questions.

"Mother, can you share the nature of your conversation with me? Did it concern your medical condition?" Susan asked.

"Oh, no, dear," her mother answered, "it had nothing to do with that at all."

"Well, can you tell me who you want to include in a conversation?" Susan asked.

"My, Susan," her mother said, "I'd forgotten how keen your memory is when capturing half of a conversation." The smile that followed her remarks only served to fuel Susan's exasperation.

"Mother, you're being cruel now. Please tell me something!" she pleaded.

"All right," her mother said. "I'll ask you to find Michael, and when he finds it convenient to join us for a few minutes, bring him back with you to the study, where I will meet with you." Then Lady Moncrieff retired to the study, smiling and shaking her head in disbelief.

Susan began her search for Michael immediately. His truck was nowhere in sight, and she feared he might have driven into Charlottetown on an errand. Upon further investigation, however, she found him lying underneath the old tractor in his coveralls, surrounded by tools. Luc was in the tractor seat, his foot on the clutch pedal.

"Oh," Susan said, "there you are. Michael. I need you to come to the house right away. Mother is waiting."

Michael heard only a voice underneath the tractor but couldn't distinguish the words. He answered, "What did you say, Luc? I couldn't hear you."

"No," Luc shouted. "It wasn't me."

Michael interrupted before saying more, "Then just keep your foot on the clutch until I tell you to let it out."

Exasperated, Susan called, "Michael, Mother needs you at the house."

Hearing Susan's desperate voice, Michael crawled from under the tractor. His face, dotted with spots of oil, peeked out at her.

He answered, "Susan, what about your mother and a mouse?"

"Not mouse, Michael," Susan said. "House. Mother needs to see us at the house."

"Now?" he asked. "I need to adjust this clutch and get cleaned up before I dare return to the house."

"It must be important, Michael. She had a call from Dr. MacMillan. She wants to see us in the study. She's there now," Susan said.

"I understand," Michael said. "Give me just a few minutes to get cleaned up, and I'll meet you there."

Thankfully, Michael's coveralls kept the rest of his work clothes from the worst of the ground underneath the tractor. He took only a few minutes to clean his hands and face before he hurried into the study where Susan and Lady Moncrieff were waiting.

"I'm sorry to keep you waiting," Michael said as he caught his breath. "Please tell us why the doctor had to call you."

Sensing his concern for her, Lady Moncrieff said, "Michael, please don't be alarmed. His call had nothing to do with my medical condition, as I told Susan."

"Then you aren't unwell?" Michael asked.

"Not at all, she said. "That's why I asked Susan to find you and ask you to talk with me when convenient."

Michael looked toward Susan, but he needed no words. He answered her guilty shrug with a weary shake of his head.

"Well," he said, "here I am. What did Dr. MacMillan have to say?"

"He was asking to speak with me concerning Emily," Lady Moncrieff began. "Though he didn't say as much, my intuition tells me he wants to ask for her hand in marriage. Lacking parents to whom he might apply, it appears he is calling here."

"I'm not surprised," Michael said. "He is smitten, and, as always, he remains ever the gentleman."

"I asked if he would mind if I included two others at our meeting," Lady Moncrieff said, "and he was quite agreeable. Would you and Susan be available this evening at seven?" she asked as she glanced at Susan.

Michael looked to see Susan nodding her head vigorously. "Of course," Michael said, turning back to Lady Moncrieff. "We would be happy to attend." Then, looking intently at Susan again, he added, "I've got to get back to the barn now. I have a job I need to finish before lunch. Will you excuse me, please?"

"Of course," Lady Moncrieff nodded.

With a last look toward Susan, Michael managed to hide a smile as he shook his head and returned to the barn.

Andrew had said nothing to Emily about his visit with Lady Moncrieff. When Simon barked to announce the arrival of a car in the driveway after dinner that night, Emily was surprised when she looked out the window to see Andrew's car.

"Andrew is just arriving at the front door," she said to Susan as she turned from the window. "I can't think of why he would arrive without calling ahead," she said.

"Not to worry," Susan said, "he called earlier today to speak with Mother. He is coming to speak with her. Michael and I are joining them."

"I hope he hasn't discovered anything to signal that Lady Moncrieff is not well," Emily said.

"Emily," Susan said, "I can assure you his visit has nothing to do with Mother's health. Perhaps I'll have more news after our conversation." With that, Susan left Emily in suspense as she walked briskly toward the study. A moment later, Patrice led Andrew to the study door.

"Dr. MacMillan," Lady Moncrieff said, "how pleasant to have you call at Highfield."

"The pleasure is all mine," he said, "and I hope you will address me as Andrew. Once away from the hospital, I enjoy leaving the professional behind."

"Of course, Andrew," Lady Moncrieff said, "I understand completely. Michael and Susan lack the advantage of hearing our conversation on the telephone. Could you explain the reason for our meeting this evening?"

"Of course," Andrew said as he turned to Michael and Susan. "I've come to speak with you about Emily and her future at the hospital. During the last year, she has developed a training program for our nursing staff, which has proven more successful than we could have imagined. Others she has mentored have proven to be natural teachers, relieving Emily of many of her teaching duties. With a promotion to an administrative position, she will enjoy a higher salary and a significant reduction in hours required at the hospital."

"So," Susan said, "she'll be able to spend less time at the hospital and more time here at Highfield?" Susan asked.

"Well, yes," Andrew said, "her hours at the hospital will decrease. However, I was hoping that she could also reduce the hours she spends at Highfield unless, of course, Lady Moncrieff, you require her attendance for medical care."

"As you know, Andrew, "Lady Moncrieff began, "I have enjoyed an amazing recovery since coming to Highfield, and the symptoms of many of my ailments have all but disappeared. I call on Emily for care only very rarely now."

With the beginning of a smile, Andrew said, "I could not be happier for the wonderful improvement in your health," Andrew said. "And since your health is so much improved, you give me great hope for my own."

"You are not unwell, are you?" Michael asked. "Your health is not compromised nor your life threatened by some disease or ailment, I hope."

"There is only one ailment I can report to you at Highfield, you who have taken Emily in as a member of your family," he said, "so I will confess this," he said as he leaned toward Lady Moncrieff. "I cannot live without Emily as my wife. I have come here this evening to beg for her hand. I seek only your permission to ask her to marry me."

Lady Moncrieff paused to look briefly at Susan and Michael before turning to Andrew to say, "I will freely admit, Andrew, that your request comes as no surprise." Then, extending her hand and smiling, she said,

"I will also freely admit that we," she continued, looking at Michael and Susan, "are completely delighted to grant your request."

As Andrew kissed Lady Moncrieff's hand, Michael and Susan stood to congratulate him. The excitement of their laughter escaped through the study doors and reached Emily in the library, where she stood looking out into the hall. A moment later, though, Susan was at her side to escort her to the study, where Andrew waited alone.

When Michael returned from the wine cellar with an appropriate bottle for celebrating, Emily and Andrew were ready to join their friends in the drawing room. A lovely gold ring with an oval-cut ruby flanked by two diamonds sparkled on Emily's left hand. Between their tears and smiles, it was obvious that Emily and Andrew had never been happier. Furthermore, they had already decided to ask Fr. Hunt if his schedule would accommodate a wedding before the end of summer.

Later that night, as Michael and Susan prepared for bed, Michael sat in his chair in the corner, deep in thought.

"What is it, Michael?" Susan asked. "Something on your mind?"

"Yes, something's on my mind, and I'm afraid it has to do with jealousy," he said.

"Jealousy?" she asked. "Say on, please."

"Emily's ring," he said. "There was a time when we couldn't afford nice things, but times have changed. I think it's time I bought you something sparkly for your left hand, and maybe something for your wrist and something to hang around your neck, too. Would that be all right?"

"Of course, that would be all right, Michael," she said as she sat on his lap and kissed his cheek. But then she grew quiet, wrinkled her nose, and said, "There's just one problem."

"A problem?" he asked. "What's wrong with a man buying jewelry for his wife?"

"Nothing," she said, "nothing at all."

"Then what could the problem be?" he asked. "Surely we can find a solution," he said, sitting erect, his voice full of concern.

"On second thought," Susan said quietly, "there would be no problem at all, as long as . . . " she hesitated.

"As long as what?" Michael begged as she stood, walked to the mirror, and reached for her right earlobe.

"As long as you don't forget the earrings, darling. You left out the earrings," she said with a pout.

She had done it again, and shaking his head, he had to join her laughter. As his shoulders relaxed and dropped in relief, he leapt up to sweep her into his arms and kiss her before carrying his expectant wife to bed. Before he tucked her in for the night, though, he made a trip to the kitchen and returned with her chamomile tea. She was asleep shortly after he retrieved her empty cup, snoring her little snore, one secret he vowed he would never disclose.

Chapter 54

When Denmark fell to the Nazis in early April, Sir Richard Moncrieff knew the "Phony War" had ended. Russia's attacks on Finland and Germany's concentrated attacks on Norway kept the war relatively quiet in the Low Countries and France for precisely a month. However, at dawn on May 10, the invasions of France, the Netherlands, and Belgium began. One might say the echoes of the artillery attacks sounded in London because, by evening, Prime Minister Neville Chamberlain had resigned. Within hours, Winston Churchill, at the request of King George VI, had accepted the post as Britain's next Prime Minister.

Luxembourg fell to the Nazis in one day, while the Netherlands fought bravely for five days before surrendering. In France, the Wehrmacht concentrated its forces in Sedan, hoping to capture the bridges at the Meuse River. A German victory there left a clear path to the English Channel.

Sir Richard's encouragement on this May morning in London came from the Prime Minister, a personal friend, and a friend of SIS. Winston Churchill was no stranger to military service, having wartime experience serving the Royal Navy and the Royal Army. One of his first acts as Prime Minister was to address the House of Commons with a speech devoid of his predecessor's weakness. Saying, "I have nothing to offer but blood, toil, tears, and sweat," he went to work immediately, contacting President Roosevelt with a request for ships, aircraft, and anti-aircraft guns. Although Roosevelt lacked the authority to provide for those needs immediately, Churchill's request did not fall on deaf ears. Churchill left the conversation assured that support from the United States would be forthcoming. Sir Richard was encouraged over the next two weeks when the new Prime Minister remained in regular contact with SIS, eager to receive reports from Sir Richard's operatives in the field. Both men relied on SIS sources as their eyes and ears on the front lines, where they continued to intercept Nazi communications, observe and report troop movements, and support resistance efforts.

With the Wehrmacht hastening daily toward the Channel, Sir Richard remained satisfied that his decision to evacuate his family from Clifton Manor had been a wise one. He lifted Lady Moncrieff's picture from his desk and reached for the pocket-handkerchief in his breast pocket to brush the dust from its frame. During wartime tensions, he and many of his senior officers couldn't risk the cleaning staff eying the memoranda on their desks. Looking at several teacups and saucers that remained stacked here and there, he smiled when he thought of how Angela would react to his irregular cleaning schedule, which left her photo so dusty.

"Perhaps it's a good thing that you are not an eyewitness to my negligence, darling, although tonight I so wish you were here to chide me," he said, smiling. "Chide away, my dear. It would be as sweet music to these ears."

An ocean away in Canada, Lady Moncrieff had just finished lunch in her room and was enjoying her second cup of tea. Michael had brought her the newspapers from Charlottetown. The headlines of the war took her thoughts back to the Great War.

When Sir Richard joined the fleet, Nigel and Boyd were toddlers. Susan was born two months later. Thankfully, their staff included a nurse and a governess for the children, allowing Lady Moncrieff to attend to the business of running the estate in her husband's absence. Busyness was often a welcome friend to a young mother whose husband was in constant peril at sea, with waters filled with mines, U-boats, and enemy battleships.

She had been happy for him when he received the call to SIS after the war. He was a born strategist who read the world as he read a chessboard. His service at SIS had kept him young and vital, giving him purpose after he retired from the admiralty. However, over two decades later, her old war fears were re-awakened. Though Richard wasn't at sea, she feared the Luftwaffe and the indiscriminate attacks they had brought day and night, decimating cities in Poland, Norway, the Low Countries, and France. Soon, she feared, Germany's Wehrmacht would send the Luftwaffe across the Channel to bomb London. She could only hope that SIS had evacuation strategies sufficient to keep her Richard safe.

Then, of course, Nigel and Boyd remained at sea, hunted by U-boats in the ocean while remaining Luftwaffe targets from the air. Her prayers were unceasing for her sons, though she dared not speak of her fears for them or Richard at Highfield. The household was ever-sensitive to the dangers the Moncrieff family endured. Their unspoken support and understanding were welcome sources of comfort where no other was available.

As she watched Susan grow ever more round with her baby, she was pleased that Michael's service to SIS would keep him at home at Highfield. Michael had become a father figure at Highfield since the war began. She knew that his understanding and maturity came partly from his experience during the Great War when his father served in the King's Artillery. Although his mother's death was not directly related to the war, Michael's loss of his mother, only days after his father's return from battle, left an immense emotional toll on the young boy. For one so young, the war and his mother's death had become one inseparable grief.

Today, Lady Moncrieff also found herself aching for Grayson and Michelle as they wrestled with their fears concerning Grayson's almost certain call to arms. The Moncrieffs had known the Royce family for years before any of their children were born. Grayson had always been another brother to Nigel and Boyd. To reunite with him on this side of the Atlantic during wartime made the union of their families all the stronger. Lady Moncrieff felt a mother's attachment to this man whose mother and sister were waiting for him in Derbyshire. Women's burdens in wartime had always been excruciating, but if her prayers could help, Lady Moncrieff's heart was willing to take on one more.

"Richard, Nigel, Boyd, and now, Grayson, Lord," she prayed. "Wherever you call them to serve you, may their guardian angels watch over and defend them. Bring them home rejoicing, I pray. Amen."

Chapter 55

Grayson's orders arrived on May 15, 1940, calling him to report to RAF Kirton in Lindsey, Lincolnshire, England. He was joining No. 71 Squadron RAF, a squadron equipped with Hawker Hurricane fighters and tasked with defending northern England from German air attacks. Unknown to many, No. 71 Squadron was also manned by American airmen, all volunteers in RAF Eagle Squadrons. Although the United States remained neutral, thousands of American airmen had traveled to Canada to join the Royal Canadian Air Force. Many were already serving in Britain, Finland, and France. Although the United States was not officially at war, Grayson would fly alongside American pilots eager to defend Great Britain.

Grayson was familiar with the airfield initially built during the Great War. Abandoned after the war ended, construction of the new airfield began in 1938, shortly before Grayson's transfer to RCAF training in Canada. He had spent several months in Kirton in Lindsey, assisting with plans for training facilities there.

Grayson felt a certain relief when his orders arrived. The waiting was finally over, and he and Michelle could begin to plan for her future at home without him. He could hardly think of her alone in their house, but neither could he see her returning to her parents' home. Both knew Highfield would receive her gladly, but neither felt at peace with that alternative. A week after his orders arrived, Michelle called him at his office with another thought.

"Grayson, I have an idea," she said. "I don't want to tell you over the telephone, so please come home as soon as you can."

Grayson wasted no time clearing his desk and driving home. When he arrived, Michelle had two cups and a pot of coffee ready. She poured Grayson's cup, then her own. He took his coffee black, but Michelle liked hers with one teaspoon of sugar and some milk. When she finally sat and dipped her spoon in her cup to stir, Grayson could wait no longer.

"Michelle, you've got me in suspense. What is this idea we couldn't discuss over the telephone?" he begged.

"I'm sorry to make you wait," she said. "It's just that I'm not sure you will like my idea."

"Well, you won't know unless you tell me, so please, let's hear it," he asked.

"All right," she began. "I went to the library to find a map to see where Kirton in Lindsey is in England." Michelle rose and went to the sideboard to pick up an atlas. She brought the massive volume to the table and opened it so they could see the page where she had placed her bookmark.

"Yes," Grayson said, pointing, "that's Lincolnshire, and," he said, pointing to Kirton in Lindsey, "the airfield is here."

"Exactly," she said, "and here, almost directly west through Nottinghamshire . . . " she said as she traced a route with her finger.

"Is Derbyshire," Grayson said.

"Right," she answered, smiling. "And Derbyshire is where your mother and sister live in New Mills, right here, correct?" she asked with her finger on the map.

"Yes, Michelle," he answered, "that's correct, but what is your point?"

"Well," Michelle began, "every time we've discussed the war and what you know about the most likely places the Germans might attack, you've said you are not worried about your mother and sister in New Mills."

"That's right. There is nothing in New Mills or anywhere in Derbyshire that would constitute a likely target for the Nazis to bomb, so I'm not overly concerned for my family's safety," he said.

"Exactly," Michelle answered with a smile, "and I measured the train route between New Mills and your base in Lincolnshire, and it's about ninety miles."

"That's correct, too," he said, "and I've traveled it many times, but what is your point?"

"It's this, Grayson," she said. "You've said you believe New Mills is safe from attack. You've shown me pictures of the town and your mother's house. It's clear that she has lots of room, and I've always wanted to travel to England and . . . "

"Are you telling me you want to go to England with me and stay with my mother and sister in New Mills?" Grayson asked.

"Yes, Grayson," Michelle answered, "that's precisely what I'm telling you."

Grayson sat for a moment, looking at the map, transfixed.

"Well?" Michelle asked.

"I would never have thought of it," Grayson admitted as he looked up from the map. "There is no doubt that New Mills is a more dangerous location for you and our child than Prince Edward Island, but you are also correct when you say I've not been overly concerned for my family's safety in New Mills."

Grayson sat quietly again, staring at the map. Then, pointing, he said, "They might attack Kirton in Lindsey or Ringway in Manchester, but both are miles away from New Mills."

A quiet moment later, with Grayson's eyes still locked on the map, Michelle broke the silence.

"So, darling," she said, as she stood and leaned over his shoulder, her cheek next to his as they looked at the map together, "would you consider my idea as a possibility? I can't be three thousand miles away from you when our baby is born, Grayson. I can't," she repeated. "But, ninety miles means we might be able to see each other sometime, and perhaps we *could* be together when our baby is born. Please tell me you'll consider it," she asked.

It was another moment before Grayson answered. When he broke his silence, he stood, put his arms around his wife, and drew her close. They held each other for a long moment before Grayson, his voice breaking, said, "I would never have thought of it myself, but . . . " As he hesitated, Michelle felt his tears on her neck. He began again, "but I cannot bear the thought of being an ocean away from you and our baby. I will apply for our passage tomorrow and pray that the RAF grants it so we can sail to England together."

Grayson received RAF approval for Michelle's passage to Liverpool one week later. After another week of closing up their home in Charlottetown and packing mere essentials, Sqn Ldr Grayson Royce and his wife boarded the Empress of Australia, an ocean liner converted to a British troopship in Halifax. The Royce family's wartime travel adventure was about to begin. Nine days later, they disembarked at Liverpool and planted their feet on British soil.

Chapter 56

B y June, Michael and Susan were already missing their two closest friends, but enough was happening at Highfield to keep their
minds busy at home. After an overwhelming response from local families, all but one of the guest children from England had found homes.
The oldest girl, Lois, would have been a lonely soul alone in the girls'
cottage had Ingrid not volunteered to move in to keep her company.
The two had become fast friends, and Ingrid had reached an age where
she welcomed a little distance from her brothers at home. They didn't
expect another group of guest children until the end of the month, so
Ingrid and Lois had the cottage to themselves until then.

Meanwhile, Emily and Andrew had just returned from visiting
Andrew's mother and sister in Quebec and were ready to announce a
wedding date. After meeting with Fr. Hunt at St. Peter's on Saturday after
Evensong, they arrived at Highfield Sunday afternoon to share their news.
Michael, Susan, and Lady Moncrieff met them in the west sunroom.

Their joy was palpable, and one look at the happy couple drew a
smile from every face. When Michael, Susan, and Lady Moncrieff sat on
the sofa opposite them, it was evident that Andrew was a bit nervous.
Sitting next to him on the settee and holding his hand with both of hers,
Emily began the conversation.

"We wanted you to be the first to hear about our visit with Andrew's
family in Quebec and our talk with Fr. Hunt," she said.

"Yes," Andrew added with a stitched-on smile, sitting like a recruit
at attention.

Emily looked at Andrew, expecting him to continue, but when he
said nothing more, she said, "Andrew's mother was very pleased to hear
of our engagement."

"Yes," Andrew nodded, looking first at Emily, then Lady Moncrieff, Susan, and Michael, before returning to Emily.

Again expecting Andrew to speak, Emily waited an instant before adding, "As was his sister, Irene."

"That's right," Andrew agreed, smiling but still at attention.

Looking at him again, Emily paused, but Andrew smiled and said nothing more.

"So," Emily said, "when we arrived in Charlottetown, we arranged a meeting with Fr. Hunt."

When Andrew turned to meet Emily's nod, turned to face the sofa, and smiled again, Susan could no longer maintain her decorum. She started to giggle, and her mother joined her. Michael's laugh was polite, but when Emily looked at Andrew and joined the laughter, Andrew's shoulders finally relaxed and fell away from his ears.

When their laughter subsided, Andrew finally said, "I have no idea why I am so nervous today. Everything has gone so smoothly. You have all been so gracious, Mother and Irene are so pleased, and Fr. Hunt couldn't have been more helpful. And here I am, wound tighter than my watch. I am about to marry the most wonderful woman I have ever met," he said, "and she seems happy to marry me. What do I have to be nervous about?" he laughed.

"Nothing, I suspect," answered Lady Moncrieff, "but formalizing any lifelong commitment is bound to raise our nerves a little, don't you think?"

"Of course," Andrew said, "so, leaving my nerves behind, let me tell you the rest."

"Say on," Michael agreed.

"Fr. Hunt has reserved the church for us on July 1. The hospital has graciously offered their conference room for our reception. It's large and has high ceilings and room for dancing on beautiful maple floors. Because it is adjacent to the kitchen, serving will be no problem," he said.

"Andrew's home is right next door," Emily added, "so we can return there after the service for pictures. The gardens are lovely this year. I'm sure the photos will be grand," she said, smiling.

"Mother and Irene will arrive three or four days earlier, and they will have their choice of bedrooms. I'm sure they'll be comfortable," Andrew said.

"And are your menus all planned?" Lady Moncrieff asked.

"That is one area where I hope I can ask you to help," Emily said as she turned to Susan. "I have some ideas, Susan, but I lack your experience. I'm hoping you will be able to help me."

"I'd be delighted, Emily," Susan said, sitting forward. "A wedding in July on Prince Edward Island offers a myriad of possibilities."

"But, there is just one other logistical issue where we hope Highfield can help," Andrew said. "We need a chef and a sous chef. Our hospital staff and students are happy to serve, but our kitchen staff has no chef qualified to prepare the quality of meal we'd like to serve. We'd like your permission to borrow some of your staff that day."

"I'm sure our calendar is clear on July 1," Lady Moncrieff smiled, "and I believe Doris and Alida will be overjoyed to offer their services. Would you agree, Susan?"

"Without a doubt," Susan nodded.

Emily and Andrew looked relieved, but the conversation wasn't over yet.

"Neither Emily nor I have made many close friends here on Prince Edward Island," Andrew said, "aside from a few professional acquaintances at the hospital." He paused before continuing, "Susan and Michael, we hope you will stand up with us at the wedding. Both of you have been enormously important to our relationship, as have you, Lady Moncrieff," he said, turning and addressing her.

"Yes," Emily said, "in so many ways, Lady Moncrieff, you have become a parent to me. Although I understand it is completely unconventional, I would like you to give me away if you would."

Lady Moncrieff looked at Susan and Michael and asked, "So what say we, one and all."

As they joined their voices, a resounding "Yes!" filled the study, and every hint of nervousness evaporated. During the laughter that followed, Michael excused himself momentarily to retrieve a bottle of champagne chilling in an ice bucket outside the study door. At the same time, Susan retrieved a tray of five flutes that happened to be waiting at the sideboard.

"To Emily and Andrew," Michael began, "and the life that shall be theirs together. May they always share the joy that fills this day."

A few moments later, Michael returned from the kitchen with a plate of raspberry thumbprint cookies, another of Doris's latest creations. While Michael refilled their flutes, Andrew devoured several cookies, commenting on the sweetness of the raspberry filling. As Emily nibbled politely, tasting the raspberry jam, her eyes met Susan's. Together, they lifted their glasses and shared a lady's knowing smile.

Chapter 57

"They've grown up on me, Michael," Jacques said as he reached for his coffee cup. "Seventeen is awfully close to eighteen when there's a war on, and both have notions of going to serve."

Across the table over breakfast at the Yeoman's Board, Michael nodded. "They're good boys, Jacques, but boys no more. You were a brave man to take on Luc, Ingrid, and Patrice when you and Doris married and then to add Joseph," he said, shaking his head and smiling. "No one who sees your family together now would doubt that each is your own because you've made them your own. That makes it all the harder to see them ready to leave the nest, doesn't it?"

"I suppose it does," Jacques said, "and Luc and Joseph are so different," he added as he poured syrup on his pancakes. "I know you've been busy at Highfield with the guest children, plowing, planting, and all, so let me tell you the latest."

"Say on," Michael said as he reached for his cup.

Jacques explained that Joseph had learned a great deal during the six weeks he spent in the hospital recovering from his injuries at the sawmill. With the help of a wheelchair, he visited several of the wards regularly and observed the operating theatre from the gallery. Feeding his interest, Dr. MacMillan encouraged Joseph to accompany Nurse Langdon and participate in parts of the nurses' training regimen. Joseph was a quick study, and on the children's ward, he proved to be a caring companion for many of the children who related well to him as a fellow patient. When his recovery is complete, Dr. MacMillan is ready to offer Joseph a further training program.

"Joseph has been spending twenty hours a week at the hospital for the last month, Michael," Jacques said with a smile. "They say he's a natural and especially good in the Accident Room, the first place he saw at the hospital when he was so badly hurt himself. So, now," Jacques said, "with the war on, he wants to train full-time and to serve where there's more need."

Michael heard a hesitation in Jacques' voice.

"Do you mean . . . " Michael began, but before he could finish, Jacques answered.

"Yes. He wants to join the army to serve as a medic. He has a soft heart, you know. He always has. He doesn't want to shoot back. He only wants to help the injured," Jacques said, "the way the nurses helped him."

The two men sat silently and took a couple more bites while the waitress filled their cups.

"That's a hard one for you and Doris to consider, Jacques," Michael said. "Has he asked you to sign the papers for a seventeen-year-old to serve?"

"Not yet," Jacques said, "but that's also where Luc comes in."

"Luc?" Michael asked.

"That's right," Jacques said. "Luc wants to serve, too, but his story is entirely different. He's been training at the shooting range with a veteran of the Great War."

Michael wasn't surprised. Luc and Joseph had learned to shoot at Highfield under his training, but Luc had shown a natural gift from the first day. He had a keen eye and a quiet, calm ability to wait for his breath and heartbeat to settle before squeezing the trigger. Once Michael introduced the boys to the scope when harvesting geese, he showed a particular aptitude for shooting at longer distances.

In time, Michael freed Luc to use a more powerful rifle than the .22 Remington the boys used for training. Highfield had been overrun with garden varmints in the spring. Using a Winchester Model 54 loaded with .220 Swift ammunition and a Redfield scope, Luc had been able to rid Highfield of twenty-six woodchucks that had ravaged the newly added gardens in the east pasture. From the blind where Luc sat, Michael observed him watch, wait, and then whistle to raise a woodchuck's head. Then, from more than two hundred yards, a single squeeze of the trigger dropped each woodchuck in its tracks.

"Luc and I visited the shooting range at Alexandra Point a month ago," Jacques said. "A veteran of the Great War from Port Huron, a man named Francis, was shooting with a sniper rifle. He was a quiet man and didn't say much, but we learned he had served as a sniper in France. Anyway, he saw the spark in Luc's eye as Luc watched him hitting bullseyes 400 yards away. I need field glasses to see that far, Michael," Jacques said.

Michael nodded as Jacques continued.

"Francis gave Luc a short lesson and then invited him to shoulder the rifle he used during the war. When two hundred yards was too easy for Luc, Francis moved him to three hundred yards. Luc did well for a beginner, so Francis offered to teach him. Luc has met him at the range every weekend since," Jacques said.

"So, Luc wants to join and serve as a sniper?" Michael asked.

"That's right," Jacques said. "He told me it's not that he wants to kill the enemy; he just wants to stop them from killing our men. He wants to save lives. So, both our boys want to join as soon as they can."

"I'm not surprised," Michael said. "On Sunday, when we read the news about the rescue of our soldiers from Dunkirk, we all knew the war was threatening to come to England. Canadians have always been a people of duty, Jacques, and you can be proud of Luc, a Canadian, and Joseph, a Brit, for wanting to do their part. Nonetheless, I can't imagine how frightening it must be for you and Doris."

"It is, Michael, it is," Jacques echoed. "I hope their training on this side of the ocean will take long enough for the war to end so that they're not needed overseas."

"We'll all hope for that," Michael said, "and pray for peace every day."

As Jacques and Michael drove home from Charlottetown, they rehearsed their histories with the two boys that time had made into men. In only a year or so, Luc and Joseph had learned so many new skills and helped provide so much of the care Highfield required. Beyond their hard work, however, they had learned to care for others and always remained properly respectful to the women, young and old alike. Their contribution to Highfield's welfare was regular, trustworthy, and came from grateful hearts.

Both young men were nearly a year away from the age when they could enlist without their parents' permission. Still unsettled with Michelle and Grayson's exit, Michael hoped Luc and Joseph wouldn't soon be leaving Highfield.

When Michael returned from breakfast with Jacques, he took the morning newspapers to the study but didn't bother reading them. Instead, he sat in one of the leather armchairs, using the quiet to take stock of everything that threatened to steal the peace at Highfield. Sir Richard in London and Nigel and Boyd at sea were of greatest concern.

Lady Moncrieff's heart was most closely tied to these three men, all living in harm's way. She tried to remain courageous, but Michael and Susan recognized the ever-present worry on her brow, the angst in her eyes, and the tremble in her voice, all symptoms of the burden that plagued her heart and mind. Between the weekly messages her husband sent to Highfield by radio, she relied only on vague newspaper reports of the war's effect on England. From what she could surmise, the Luftwaffe attacks would soon be raining bombs on London, where she feared Sir Richard would find no adequate protection. Just yesterday, she had commented on Sir Richard's goals for Highfield, which included a safe destination where his work with SIS could continue remotely.

"Richard spoke more than once about continuing his work here in Canada should London be threatened. Do you remember that, Michael?"

"Yes, ma'am," Michael had answered. "He planned to communicate by radio. I remember it well."

"To the best of your knowledge, Michael," she had asked, "is there anything here that would preclude that possibility?"

"I can think of nothing," he had answered, "nothing."

"Then I pray he will consider the option and that right soon," she had said. "Right soon."

Chapter 58

M any prayers were answered on Prince Edward Island when Michael confirmed by radio that the Empress of Australia landed safely in Liverpool at midnight on the third of June, 1940. By morning, troops were disembarking for transport to bases near Manchester and elsewhere in the north of England. Michelle and Grayson were among the last to leave the ship. Fortunately, they found a cab to drive them to Liverpool Central train station, where they began their fifty-mile trek to New Mills. Despite her lack of sleep overnight, Michelle's eyes rarely left the window at her seat. Once away from Liverpool and the towns nearby, she took in more and more of the countryside with its hills and rivers and the buildings in the villages that had so much history attached. The few photos of New Mills that Grayson had shared with her only hinted at Derbyshire's beauty.

"Darling," Grayson said, "the best is yet to be. You'll find the Peak District overwhelming."

"Grayson, you've seen Prince Edward Island, and besides Prince Edward Island, I've traveled no farther than Montreal. I'm already overwhelmed!" she laughed.

It was not a long ride by cab from the train station in New Mills to the tall stone home on Watford Lane where Grayson was born. As they drove, though, something about the streets and houses made Michelle feel small and out of place. The houses were all built of stone and seemed to grow larger as they approached their destination. When they arrived in the driveway, the sunlight dimmed as they sat in the shadow of the immense stone structure called Fletcher Hall, Grayson's family home. Michelle struggled to see the entire façade without turning her head while Grayson circled the cab to open her door. With only two duffel bags for luggage, Michelle and Grayson arrived at the front steps just as his mother and sister, Nancy, opened the door.

"Grayson!" his mother cried as she wrapped her arms around his neck to hug him. Coming to herself, she quickly turned to Michelle, saying, "My dear, forgive me, but he's been away too long this time." Then, extending her arms to Michelle, she said, "Welcome, Mrs. Royce! We are so happy to have you safely here."

Michelle had to laugh. "There can't be room for two Mrs. Royces here. Please call me Michelle."

"And I can't be Mrs. Royce among my immediate family," Grayson's mother said, "so I shall be Mildred, or, if you must, Mother Royce. Now, Michelle, please meet Nancy."

Nancy released Grayson to reach out to hug Michelle as they greeted each other by name and proceeded into the house.

Michelle's eyes grew wide as she entered the stone structure that looked large from the outside but even grander inside. The foyer alone was almost the size of her family's apartment, and the art and artifacts adorning the walls spoke of a long family history. She couldn't help feeling out of place again, but Grayson sensed her discomfort immediately and wrapped one arm around her shoulders.

"You'll get used to it, Mrs. Royce," he whispered. "Remember, though, it's all ancient history, left by people long dead. Our history is what we will make today and each day forward."

In that instant, Michelle remembered why she loved him so much. Her shoulders relaxed as she melted into him on their way to their second-floor bedroom.

Their bedroom was immense, with high ceilings, walls paneled in walnut, and two stone fireplace mantles adorned with framed photos and more history. The bedroom faced south and enjoyed two bathrooms, his and hers. To Michelle, their duffel bags looked so out of place.

Grayson caught Michelle's grimace as she looked at the bags.

"Are you ready to go?" he asked. "I'm sure Nancy has the car waiting outside."

"Car waiting?" Michelle asked. "Where are we going? We just arrived, Grayson."

"Oh," Grayson said. "I'm not going anywhere. You see," he said as he walked across the room to open a huge wardrobe filled with his clothes, "my wardrobe is full, but yours," he said as he crossed the room and opened a matching walnut wardrobe, "yours, my darling, is empty.

Nancy is ready to guide you to all the best shops that New Mills has to offer. You are not allowed to return until you can fill your wardrobe and every bureau drawer."

Though due in part to travel weariness, her tears were waiting—tears of weariness, yes, but also tears of gratitude and joy. She dared not think about her life a week from now when Grayson would report for duty. After that, she didn't know when she would see him again, but she would never forget how much she loved her husband, the man who always ensured she lacked for nothing. Their kiss might have lasted longer if Nancy hadn't called up the stairs.

"Are you ready, Michelle? The shops will close in less than four hours."

"Coming, Nancy, coming," she said as she dried her eyes, checked her lipstick, blew a kiss to Grayson, and rushed out the door to the staircase.

Grayson could only smile as he watched from their bedroom windows as the car rolled out the drive.

Chapter 59

I n early June of 1940, Sir Richard Moncrieff, like every SIS analyst, spent every waking hour monitoring the status of the Belgian, French, and British troops forced to the sea at Dunkirk. More than 300,000 soldiers were trapped there with their backs against the sea as German Panzer divisions advanced and the Luftwaffe planned their attacks on the defenseless troops. The evacuation plan for the troops brought only 8,000 Allied soldiers to safety on the first day. By the eighth day, however, more than 338,000 had found their way to Dover aboard Royal Navy ships, commercial vessels, fishing boats, and other small private craft, numbering more than four hundred.

Besides those evacuated from Dunkirk, France managed to rescue more than 25,000 French soldiers. Sadly, German forces took another 30,000 prisoners. German aerial bombing of Paris had begun simultaneously.

Every day, the Wehrmacht made further advances into France, forcing the French government to flee Paris on June 9. Meanwhile, the Italian dictator, Benito Mussolini, declared war on France and England, invading France within days. With the continued German assault on all fronts and Italy invading from the south, the French forces were overwhelmed. The Germans entered Paris unopposed on June 14.

With the fall of France, Prime Minister Churchill addressed the nation on June 18, saying, "The Battle of France is over; the Battle of Britain is about to begin . . . " On June 20, the Luftwaffe bombed Hampshire in the south of England. The worst fears of every British citizen were realized. The bombing of the UK had begun.

Sir Richard was not surprised to hear from the Prime Minister the following day. After gathering a sheaf of documents, Sir Richard summoned his driver, who delivered him to 10 Downing Street a quarter hour later.

In the spring of 1939, Sir Richard, serving as Rear Admiral Moncrieff, had planned and executed a trans-Atlantic Royal Navy training exercise originating in England and concluding in Halifax, Nova Scotia. The exercise involved a convoy carrying a mock cargo of gold bullion and securities destined for bank vaults in Quebec and Ottawa. No previous training exercise had required the level of secrecy that cloaked those ships and their cargo. The future of the UK depended on the flawless execution of its goal. That mission had provided Sir Richard with his first opportunity to visit Highfield.

In October of 1939, a convoy of several Royal Navy battleships, including the HMS Emerald, the HMS Revenge, the HMS Resolution, the HMS Enterprise, as well as the HMS Caradoc, sailed from Plymouth with a cargo of more than two million pounds in gold bars. Bound for Halifax, Nova Scotia, the convoy's cargo had been sent to purchase arms from the United States. In late June of 1940, the Prime Minister summoned Sir Richard to discuss another mission, this one imminent, code-named Operation Fish.

The Prime Minister's secretary ushered Sir Richard into the office where Churchill sat behind an expansive leather-topped desk. As no introductions were required, Churchill indicated a chair where the secretary guided Sir Richard. The Prime Minister began to speak immediately.

"I know you are well aware of the subject of our conversation," he said as Sir Richard nodded. "As you also know," he continued, "under the Emergency Powers Act, we required all British citizens to register their holdings at the beginning of the year."

"Yes," Sir Richard said.

"Those securities and two thousand tons of gold are being prepared for shipment to Halifax as we speak. The first convoy sails on the 24th," Churchill said.

"I understand," Sir Richard said. "How may my office be of assistance, Prime Minister?"

"It isn't your office I need, presently, Moncrieff," Churchill replied, "I have them always. I need but one person. I need you."

Surprised by Churchill's "I need you," Sir Richard responded, "I am at your service, Prime Minister. What do you require?"

"You were a large part of the planning of this operation from the beginning. With all the Admiralty in service at sea, you alone are qualified and available to advise and direct this operation." Churchill said. "The safe arrival of this cargo in Canada is of tantamount importance. We are placing the security of the UK in your capable hands, Moncrieff."

"I understand, Prime Minister," Sir Richard said. "All that I have and all that I am is at the disposal of my King and Country."

"There is one thing further," Churchill said. "The damnable Nazi Luftwaffe has already breached Britain's skies. We cannot risk losing your service to SIS to the next barrage of their bombs when London becomes their target. Therefore, would you please inform me of a few particulars?"

"Of course, Prime Minister," Sir Richard said. "What can I tell you?"

"I understand that you had the foresight to purchase an estate in Canada several years ago, one intended as an evacuation destination for your family but also equipped to maintain communications with SIS in London," Churchill said.

"That is correct," Sir Richard answered. "Highfield, as it is called, is located on Prince Edward Island, only several hours by car or train from the port of Halifax."

"And you have equipped Highfield to provide regular communications with SIS here?" Churchill asked.

"Yes," Sir Richard answered, "One of our trusted operatives has maintained contact from the island since the Great War. Thanks to his expertise, Highfield is well equipped and entirely able to maintain daily contact with our London office, Prime Minister."

"Have you any reservations about your ability to perform your SIS duties from that location?" Churchill asked.

Sir Richard thought briefly before responding, "Only in one regard, Prime Minister. Radio signals from three thousand miles involve delays as the signals are relayed. Communications will suffer some immediacy as a result."

"Those are delays with which we will learn to live," Churchill said. "Therefore, I shall be direct. Britain cannot risk losing your services in the event of a Nazi air attack here in London. We need you to accompany the convoy scheduled to depart Greenock, Scotland, in three days. Expected arrival at Halifax is July 1, where the RCN will transport you at all good speed to Highfield," he said, pausing to ask, "You did say, 'Highfield,' is that correct?"

"Yes, Prime Minister," Sir Richard said, "Highfield."

"I must advise you that you will sail on the HMS Emerald from Greenock in a convoy with less than ideal support. Your escort will include no more than three destroyers, all showing their age. As you know, our fleet is already committed on too many other fronts. You are also cognizant of the threats the damned U-boats furnish, with more than one hundred vessels sunk in the North Atlantic last month alone," Churchill said as he stood and offered his hand.

"I understand the risks involved, Prime Minister," Sir Richard said as he shook Churchill's hand, "and I thank you for this opportunity to serve at sea once again and from Prince Edward Island for the immediate future. We shall pray for the day when war no longer threatens the Commonwealth."

The Prime Minister's aide accompanied Sir Richard to the outer office, where a packet of orders awaited. His SIS driver met Sir Richard at the curb and drove him to his flat, where he sat briefly before considering how to pack for his trip. Somehow, those details seemed superfluous as he thought about the future at Highfield. The top-secret nature of his mission required that his planned arrival there remain unknown to all. How he wished he could share the news with Angela. He walked to his west window, looked toward the horizon, and said, "My darling, Angela, my dreams will come true in mere days. Once again, I will be by your side."

Chapter 60

E mily and Andrew's wedding day arrived like any other, but the first of July was particularly stunning on Prince Edward Island. The day boasted clear blue skies and a light breeze from the southwest. Highfield woke early and was soon buzzing as the women of the house attended to the bride. Andrew's sister, Irene, joined Susan to help Emily with all the details, and the trio reveled in the few hours remaining for them to prepare her for her wedding.

Meanwhile, Lady Moncrieff was happy to entertain Andrew's mother, Beverly. The senior ladies had discovered a common interest in gardening. Lady Moncrieff was delighted to provide a tour of her indoor and outdoor flower gardens after breakfast in the east sunroom.

Meanwhile, Michael had arrived at Andrew's home adjacent to the hospital before eight o'clock so they could enjoy breakfast at Tea for Two before dressing for the wedding. Michael produced a jar of Doris's raspberry jam as they sat at their table.

"A little something that Emily asked me to bring for your breakfast this morning," Michael said.

Andrew shook his head in wonder. "What could I have done to deserve a woman this thoughtful, Michael? Truly, I am a blessed man."

Michael nodded. "I know how you feel, Andrew. I share your sentiment. We have no deserving, yet we remain among the blessed."

As usual, Michael's day had begun early, so he made this breakfast, his second, a light one. Andrew, however, enjoyed scrambled eggs, sausage, waffles with maple syrup, home-fried potatoes, and two corn muffins well-buried in Doris's raspberry jam. Both men enjoyed second cups of coffee before they left the table.

Once back at Andrew's house, the men were dressed and ready by ten for the eleven o'clock service. Michael had borrowed Susan's cabriolet since the women planned to drive to St. Peter's in Lady Moncrieff's new sedan. By ten-fifteen, Andrew, every hair in place, sat in the passenger seat next to Michael. Ten minutes later, they arrived at the church.

Fr. Hunt greeted them and suggested they wait in the vestry while he finished preparing the altar for the service. When he returned, the organist had begun playing the prelude. A few minutes later, Fr. Hunt returned to say, "Gentlemen, the bride has not kept us waiting. Shall we?"

Andrew looked at Michael with wide eyes but turned to Fr. Hunt and nodded. Michael had to smile as he helped Andrew follow the priest to their places in the nave.

As Michael looked at the bridal party processing toward the altar, his mind raced back to his departure from the UK three years ago. He had left Clifton Manor in Suffolk for a year of SIS training in Scotland and New Zealand before traveling to Canada to assume his duties at Highfield. Another year passed while he readied the estate for the arrival of the Moncrieff family. Now, in the summer of 1940, he watched as his wife, blooming with their child, walked down the aisle of the church where they were married less than a year ago. Their marriage, a dream they shared separately but never believed possible, had come true. Now, Emily, Lady Moncrieff's faithful nurse, once resigned to life as a spinster, was a beaming, beautiful bride. He couldn't count the miracles he had witnessed in lives transformed among Highfield's noble, hard-working family.

Even his simple invention that kept Ford V-8 engines running cooler was providing his family with wealth he could never have expected. Yes, in Europe, a war was raging. Yes, the enemy had found a way to attack Highfield, an ocean away from England. He already missed Michelle and Grayson, who bravely dared to sail to England to live during wartime. At home, Michael feared for young men like Luc and Joseph, who looked forward to serving on the battlefield. In the brief moments when all these thoughts flooded his mind, though, Michael never lost his inner peace and confidence. Michael remained an ordinary man but a blessed man, one who had witnessed miracles. He trusted in the promise the author of those miracles had made *never to leave nor forsake* him. At this moment, in this church, his heart overflowed with assurance and peace.

Returning to the present from his brief reverie, Michael heard Fr. Hunt ask, "Who giveth this woman to be married to this man?" followed by Lady Moncrieff's firm and confident response, "I do." After lifting Emily's veil, looking into her eyes, and stretching to her full height to kiss Emily's cheek, Lady Moncrieff confidently placed Emily's hand in Andrew's and turned to take her seat. Just minutes later, the bride and groom had made their vows and exchanged rings. "What God hath joined together, let no man put asunder," Michael heard Fr. Hunt say. Once more, two had become one, joined forever as Dr. and Mrs. Andrew MacMillan.

With only thirty guests, the reception dinner was refreshingly informal. Emily and Andrew had chosen to feature seafood to please his mother and sister, who were unfamiliar with the local fare on Prince Edward Island. Appetizers included oysters on the half-shell and fresh shrimp, while the main course boasted broiled lobsters, boiled potatoes, fresh summer squash, and a salad of crisp garden greens. Emily got her wish for dessert—strawberry shortcake topped with whipped cream.

While enduring the academic rigors of a medical student in New York years ago, Andrew had allowed himself a diversion one summer—ballroom dancing lessons. To everyone's surprise, he and Emily had been practicing after hours at the hospital, and they made a very competent couple on the dance floor. Members of the hospital staff weren't shy for long, and Andrew's Victrola and supply of records was more than sufficient for the hour of dancing after dinner. Susan smiled to see Joseph cross the dance floor to ask Ingrid to dance while Luc partnered with his younger sister, Patrice. Susan was pleased that the last of their accelerated deportment lessons had already paid off. Michael and Susan joined them during a waltz, and Lady Moncrieff accepted Michael's request for one tour of the dance floor soon after.

As Susan watched her mother and Michael on the dance floor, she recalled the last time they danced together. It was almost a year ago when Susan and Michael were married. Susan was in her father's arms at the same moment, and when the couples met at the center of the floor, they exchanged partners to the delight and applause of their guests. It was a magical moment when her father and brothers found their way to Highfield for a family reunion she would never forget.

There were only threats of war a year ago, but now war lived in the back of everyone's mind every day. She thought back to her childhood and the Great War. Her father was at sea when she was born. Two years later, he came home at the war's end, and though her mother had often shown her pictures of Father, he was still a stranger to her when he arrived at Clifton Manor. Their early bond remained tenuous, and later, Father's work with SIS in London kept him away much of the time while she grew and became a young woman. Still, she missed her father, perhaps more for her mother than for herself, and she missed her brothers. She feared for all of them.

Susan remembered how often Father had spoken about his plans in the event that England came under attack. Highfield would remain a refuge for Mother and her, but it could also serve as a place where he could continue his work for SIS. Now, war had come, but still, Highfield was without him. "Oh," she said to herself, "to see him here again, for Mother, for Michael, and for me," and, with her hands holding her baby within, she added, "for his grandchild."

When Lady Moncrieff returned to their table, it was time for Susan to help Emily cut and serve the wedding cake. As Michael escorted Susan across the floor, Lady Moncrieff's thoughts took her back to her wedding day decades ago and the gallant young Royal Navy officer who had swept her off her feet. War was looming then, but few knew how imminent it was. Nigel came along a year later, and Boyd the following year. Though their father was away often, he returned on regular leaves until the war began. She found life difficult without him, even though he ensured she had a nurse for the children and, later on, a nanny. She could remember nothing more lonely than Susan's birth while Richard was away at sea. She had felt so bereft when he wasn't with her to celebrate Susan's arrival. She wrote to him daily but could never be sure Richard would see her letters. And here they were again, separated during wartime, but this time when Susan would deliver their first grandchild.

Of course, she missed Nigel and Boyd. Her mother's heart always wanted her boys close by, but the part of her heart that craved Richard's presence ached even more deeply. Today, she missed him selfishly for the comfort and confidence his presence brought her. She never felt more safe or whole than when they were together. Every hour of every day, she prayed for his safety in London, always looking forward to the day when she would enjoy his embrace again.

After the newlyweds had cut the wedding cake and enjoyed it with their guests, Susan took Emily away to exchange her wedding gown for her traveling clothes. Michael followed Andrew to gather his formal clothes, and a few minutes later, the bride and groom returned for one more photo before exiting in Andrew's car.

As the wedding guests waved goodbye to the bride and groom, Michael's thoughts returned to his wedding day. Men never enjoy wedding formalities the way women do. He remembered that he couldn't wait to escape the photos, the reception, and the dancing so that he and Susan could flee to the peace of the water and the Lady M. That day, he craved the wind and the solitude he felt as they sailed away alone. He felt a tinge of regret today, remembering their wedding day was the last day the Moncrieff family had been together. He especially missed Sir Richard.

Sir Richard had a vision for Highfield and trusted Michael to help him realize that vision. With Michael's skills and passion devoted to Highfield's completion, his home on PEI had become the safe haven Sir Richard had hoped it would be. Now, it was available should SIS need to send him there to continue his work away from the imminent danger of the Luftwaffe's bombs. However, what was more dear to Michael's heart was that Sir Richard had welcomed him into his family. In a matter of a few months, Highfield would welcome his grandchild. How Michael wished Sir Richard could be with them then.

The day had been neither long nor especially tedious, but by early afternoon, Susan was beginning to feel more like a mother and Lady Moncrieff more like a grandmother. When Michael suggested they return early to Highfield, both agreed gratefully. Michael was ready to be home, too, and he was pleased to help Lady Moncrieff and Susan into the comfortable back seat of the new Ford sedan. Susan left her cabriolet to the delight of Doris and her daughters. Once Michael had lowered its top, Susan tossed the keys to Doris, saying, "It's a beautiful day, ladies. The gas tank is full. Take the long way home. I would!"

On that same morning of July 1, 1940, while the bride and groom in Charlottetown were still in their beds, Rear Admiral Sir Richard Moncrieff manned the bridge of the HMS Emerald as tugs guided her through heavy fog to her dock at Halifax. During their crossing from Scotland, high seas in the North Atlantic had slowed their convoy, making them an easy target for German U-boats. Fortunately, the enemy had not detected them, and despite the weather delay, every ship in the convoy had arrived safely. When the Emerald was secure at her dock two hours later, Sir Richard left the bridge to dictate a radio communique coded *"The fish are at the dock."* The Emerald's communications officer immediately relayed the message to 10 Downing Street in London. The Prime Minister would have a rare reason to smile today.

When the HMS Emerald docked at nine that morning, the pier was alive with hundreds of well-drilled RCN personnel poised to unload and transport the ship's cargo to well-guarded trains bound for Montreal and Ottawa. With the cargo secure in the RCN's hands, Sir Richard's mission was complete, and once on the pier, two RCN officers greeted him and handed him a cache of documents sent from SIS during his journey. Then, they escorted him to a waiting staff car, where the driver stood at attention, saluting Sir Richard as he approached. The car was running and ready to drive west with its lone passenger. As Sir Richard settled into the back seat for the seven-hour drive, he addressed his driver.

"Does the Able Seaman driving this car have a name?" he asked.

"Yes, sir, Admiral, sir," the driver replied. "Able Seaman Nelson, sir."

"Nelson?" Sir Richard asked. "A descendant of Admiral Horatio Nelson of Trafalgar fame?"

"No, sir," the driver answered with a smile. "I am the lone descendant of Homer and Irene Nelson of Manitoba, Canada. Our family has no former history with the Navy. The only water on our farm is in a small pond the ducks enjoy, sir."

"I see," Sir Richard replied, "but they did give you a first name, Able Seaman Nelson, did they not?"

"Oh, yes, sir, Admiral, sir. It's Daniel, sir. Able Seaman Daniel Nelson."

"Very good, Daniel. Thank you. I know we have a seven-hour drive ahead of us, but I made this voyage on one previous occasion, approximately one year ago. We were able to complete the journey in six hours then. I have every confidence you will be able to match that record. Are you up to the challenge, Daniel?" he asked.

Sir Richard could almost see the smile that appeared on his driver's face. The smile was even more evident in his voice.

"Yes, sir, Admiral, sir," he began. "I have carefully studied the roadmaps provided and will make every reasonable effort to equal or break last year's record, sir."

"Excellent, Able Seaman Nelson," Sir Richard answered. "I have adequate work to keep me occupied here in my attaché, but you may also note my confidence in your driving skills by the sounds of sleep you hear coming from the seat behind you. I will rely on you to wake me if circumstances require my attention."

"Understood, sir," Daniel said, still smiling.

It was almost three hours later before Daniel spoke again. At a crossroads near Oxford, they were approaching a small variety store. The gas pump out front held a sign that read "Welcome Travelers."

"Begging the Admiral's pardon, sir," Daniel said, "but I need to make a brief stop ahead to top off one tank and empty another, sir.

Perhaps the Admiral would care to stretch his legs? We'll be only a very few minutes, sir."

"And our location relative to our destination?" Sir Richard asked.

"We passed the halfway point some ten minutes ago, sir," Daniel said. "If we take no more than five minutes here, we should arrive ahead of schedule, sir."

"Then no more than five minutes it is, Daniel," Sir Richard said as he closed his attaché and secured his morning's reading matter. "And, yes, I shall seek a moment of comfort within as well," Sir Richard said as Daniel pulled up to the attendant at the gas pump.

Once on the road again, Sir Richard smiled as he leaned back in his seat. "To sleep, perchance to dream," he thought, "but with an ending happier than Hamlet's," he smiled. "Tomorrow morning, I will wake next to my Angela at Highfield." He closed his eyes and was asleep in minutes.

Driving home on Suffolk Road, Michael stretched to look into the rearview mirror at Susan and Lady Moncrieff sitting in the back seat of the Ford sedan. When he glanced in the mirror at the driver's door a moment later, he shifted his attention elsewhere. A car following them for the last several miles had suddenly sped up and was about to overtake them. Its driver was nearly on their bumper, flashing his headlights and blowing his horn. Michael slowed to let the car pass, but as he did, the driver turned to the right in front of him, screeching to a halt and forcing Michael into the soft gravel on the road's right shoulder. Shaken in the back seat, the ladies cried out, but before Michael could speak, two men leapt from the car with guns drawn. One approached Michael's door, while the other ran to the rear passenger door on the opposite side of the car. Michael recognized the pistols they brandished—German Lugers.

"You must leave the car at once and come with us," the man said as he pulled Michael's door open, waving the gun in his face. The Walther PPK in Michael's shoulder holster was calling him, but as Michael stepped from the car, the gunman seemed to read his mind.

With the Luger's barrel pressed against Michael's chest, he said, "I'll take that," and reaching inside Michael's jacket, he seized the PPK. "SIS always wears them there, you know," he said, smiling.

At the same moment, Michael heard the second man open the back door and shout, "Come with me, ladies. Now! You need to come now!" With one eye on the gunman, Michael said, "Do as they say, Susan. Just do as they say."

Both women were in tears as Susan helped Lady Moncrieff to the door and out of the car to the man waiting there. Waving his gun, he directed the women toward the front of the car where Michael stood at gunpoint.

"Hands behind your backs, *now*," the leader demanded, his gun again in Michael's face, "Hands behind your back," he repeated as he waved his gun at Susan and Lady Moncrieff. As the prisoners complied, the second man handcuffed Michael's left hand to Susan's right, and with a second pair of cuffs, he handcuffed Michael's right hand to Lady Moncrieff's left. Helpless to resist, Michael could do nothing as the men blindfolded all three prisoners with pieces of coarse black fabric and forced them to walk forward and into the back seat of their running car. Sitting at gunpoint, three prisoners felt the car lurch forward as it sped away.

At that moment, a faraway voice called, "Admiral? Admiral, sir? Admiral, we're in Charlottetown, sir, just off the ferry. Are you awake? Are you all right, sir?" his driver asked.

Opening his eyes from the cold sweat of his dream, Sir Richard took a moment to gather his wits before saying, "Awake? Yes, quite awake, thank you. Where are we?"

"We're in Charlottetown," Daniel repeated. "We just arrived on the ferry. I didn't want to wake you, sir, but the streets on the map are somewhat crowded. I may need your help with directions, sir."

Fully awake now and reaching for his handkerchief to dab at the cold sweat on his neck and face, Sir Richard said, "Of course, Daniel. We don't want to jeopardize your opportunity to break our record, do we? Let's get on with it, then."

In truth, Sir Richard was still shaking within. His dream had felt too real. He had read hundreds of reports of thousands in Europe kidnapped, imprisoned, and often killed. The Nazis had already discovered Highfield and had been bold enough to level a clandestine attack there only months ago. They could attempt another at any time. Though he hoped his presence in Canada would not further endanger his family, one thing was sure: Highfield would need to embrace a new discipline of vigilance that he and Michael would work to develop.

Able Seaman Nelson smiled as he started the car. Although Sir Richard had visited Charlottetown on only one occasion in the past, his memory did not fail him today. With the help of his turn-by-turn instructions, they found Suffolk Road within minutes. As they turned into Highfield's driveway, Sir Richard said, "The driveway is one-half mile long, Able Seaman Nelson. By my watch, you will only achieve our six-hour goal by letting the horses run."

"I hear you, loud and clear, Admiral Moncrieff," Daniel smiled as he downshifted and hit the gas pedal. "Loud and clear, sir."

Sir Richard opened his attaché to retrieve a calling card and a pen. He wrote on the back of the card, "Able Seaman Daniel Nelson—top-rate man. I hope to see him again, should the need arise." Reaching over the back seat and tapping Daniel's shoulder, Sir Richard handed him the card.

"Upon your return to Halifax, Able Seaman Nelson, please deliver this card to your commanding officer."

A glance at the card left a smile on Daniel's face that would last all the way back to Halifax.

Chapter 61

I t was almost three o'clock when Michael parked the car in the garage and ushered his passengers safely indoors at Highfield. In preparation for early afternoon showers, the house had been closed all day and needed air. After passing through the kitchen and the dining room, Lady Moncrieff and Susan took refuge on the porch at the front entry, where they could enjoy the afternoon breeze coming out of the west. Meanwhile, Michael was busy indoors, opening windows on the first floor. Intent on opening the second-floor windows as well, he was halfway up the main staircase as Susan left her mother on the porch to return to a settee in the foyer.

As Lady Moncrieff turned to follow Susan, a distant motion in the driveway caught her eye. Peering intently, she saw a car approaching along the farthest turn of the driveway. As she shaded her eyes to take another look, she recognized the unmistakable gray of an RCN staff car. Red dust billowed behind the car, telling her the driver was in a hurry. Calling over her shoulder to Michael and Susan, Lady Moncrieff asked, "Are we expecting visitors from the Navy today? A staff car is racing up the driveway."

Michael and Susan joined her at the door and stepped onto the porch together, studying the approaching car, but no one could fathom why an RCN car would be arriving at Highfield in such a hurry. As the car drew to a halt at the end of the front walk, a uniformed driver got out and sprinted to the back of the car to open the trunk. Lady Moncrieff and Susan looked at each other again, still puzzled. Seconds later, the driver closed the trunk and reappeared carrying a gray sea bag. Hoisting the bag to his left shoulder, he reached to open the rear passenger door before stepping back, snapping to attention, and saluting his passenger.

Lady Moncrieff's eyes opened wide as the lone passenger exited the car. She recognized the uniform of the Royal Navy officer who returned the driver's salute, and before he could turn to face her, she was already hurrying down the porch steps toward him.

Whatever weariness Lady Moncrieff had felt moments earlier had disappeared. Susan followed as her mother and father rushed into one another's arms. As Lady Moncrieff dissolved into tears of joy, Susan caught up and joined them with Michael close behind.

Immediately aware of the bloom in his daughter's face and figure, Sir Richard opened his arms to hold Susan as only a doting grandfather could, already charmed by the new life she carried within. Michael, too, surprised and overjoyed at the same moment, dispatched any thought of the customary handshake he typically shared with Sir Richard. No, today, their long-awaited embrace was full and strong. The family shared joyful tears, immersed in the fresh afternoon breeze. As Michael retrieved the Admiral's bag, Sir Richard was busy trying to answer all the ladies' questions concerning how he came to arrive at Highfield that day. The top-secret nature of his mission left him little he could divulge, of course, except that he would serve SIS from Highfield for the foreseeable future.

Lady Moncrieff, Susan, and Michael had long since learned that secrets often lie and are better brought to light. Today, however, they willingly embraced Sir Richard's tenet: "For the sake of King and Country, some secrets lie still."

Safe within Highfield's four walls that afternoon, only one thing mattered—Sir Richard was with his family again, and nothing could make Highfield more content.

Common Terms and Abbreviations

Blitzkrieg	"Lightning War," the military offensive strategy used by Germany in WWII
HMS	His Majesty's Ship
Kriegsmarine	the navy of Nazi Germany from 1935–45
Luftwaffe	the air force of Nazi Germany from 1935–45
Nazi	the National Socialist Party led by Adolf Hitler that ruled Germany from 1933–45
Oberleutnant	Upper Lieutenant, the highest lieutenant rank in the German armed forces
OSS	Office of Strategic Services, the United States equivalent of Britain's SIS
PEI	Prince Edward Island
RAF	Royal Air Force
RCAF	Royal Canadian Air Force
RCN	Royal Canadian Navy
RN	Royal Navy
SIS	the Secret Intelligence Service in the UK, later commonly known as MI6
SS	*Schutzstaffel*, a major paramilitary organization under Adolf Hitler and the Nazi Party

U-boat   *Unterseeboot* (under-sea-boat), German submarines
                used during WWI and WWII

Walther PPK   a small, easily concealed semi-automatic pistol

Wehrmacht   the unified armed forces of Nazi Germany
                from 1935–45